Louisa Ab

THE DINNER DATE

This edition first published in paperback by
Michael Terence Publishing in 2025
www.mtp.agency

Copyright © 2025 Louisa Abbott

Louisa Abbott has asserted the right to be identified as
the author of this work in accordance with the
Copyright, Designs and Patents Act 1988

ISBN 9781800949911

This is a work of fiction. Unless otherwise indicated,
all the names, characters, businesses, places, events and
incidents in this book are either the product of the author's imagination
or used in a fictitious manner. Any resemblance to actual persons,
living or dead, or actual events is purely coincidental

No part of this publication may be reproduced, stored
in a retrieval system, or transmitted, in any form or
by any means, electronic, mechanical, photocopying,
recording or otherwise, without the prior
permission of the publisher

Cover design (AI)
2025 Michael Terence Publishing

In memory of Anne whose house was full of books – which encouraged me to read – which in turn led to writing...

***

As I come to from the oblivion of a deep sleep I open my eyes and look around. I have no idea where I am. I can see I am lying in a double bed. I quickly look to the side of me, my heart is racing and to my relief I see I am alone. I stretch my arm out to feel the space next to me, it is cold. Does that mean I have slept alone? As I move my arm it hurts. I look down at both my arms and see strange bruises. Where did they come from? It is daylight so I can clearly see the room but I don't recognise it. It's not my bedroom. Where am I? How did I get here? I sit up and search the room and also my mind trying to find answers. None will come. Why have I got no memory of how I got here, it frightens me. I listen for any sound that I might recognise but there is only silence. I start to shiver with fear. I am scared, I am very scared. I try to sit up but every part of me hurts. What has happened to me? I lie back, close my eyes and take a deep breath. I know when I next open my eyes I will be in my own bedroom and this has all been a nightmare. But it doesn't happen. As I open my eyes again I'm still in the same room and then I hear footsteps. I shut my eyes tightly the fear of who or what I might see engulfing me.

***

1

As Eva stood watching the crowd of happy relaxed party goers, the early evening summer heat gave a warm glow to the proceedings, two arms came from behind and wrapped around her.

'Guess who?' the voice whispered in her ear.

It could only be one person she thought. 'Nick, how are you?'

'Better for seeing you,' he said with a grin.

She turned around to face him.

'Where's my little brother?' he enquired.

'My husband is mingling with the production crew and cast members thanking them for another wonderful stage production.'

'And why isn't he thanking you, you were the leading female dancer.'

'Later, he'll do that later,' she replied with mischief in her eyes.

Nick immediately let go and put his hands in the air, 'Hold on, I don't want to know any more, you'll make me blush.'

She laughed, 'Just as if.'

'Let's go and find my kid brother, the great Theatre Director and kiss his feet in adoration.'

'Nick, sometimes you go a bit too far.' But laughing she linked arms with him as they made their way to the beer and food tent where they guessed Robert would be mixing with his colleagues. Robert's Assistant, Josie, had found this perfect small country pub where the landlord was more than happy to erect a small marquee in the adjacent field which belonged to the pub and there was ample parking. Josie had assured the landlord that it was just a gathering of the cast and crew of a small theatre production which had just ended and there would definitely be no loud music. He was fine with that and the date for the party had been arranged.

As they made their way to the beer tent she caught sight of Robert, beer in hand, in the middle of a cluster of cast members. Eva knew he would already be thinking about his next project. She too would soon be starting rehearsals for her new show which she would be doing without her husband by her side. She would miss him but it was also good to work with other directors and producers and she was looking forward to the challenge ahead. She had already met some of the other dancers that would be in the next show but once again she would be the lead dancer. That would be in a week's time and until then she would make the most of their treasured time together. She recalls Robert suggesting they go away for a few days, just the two of them with no distractions. That sounded so good to her. Thinking about it she couldn't believe it was almost one year since they had spent some quality time together and on that occasion they had been on their honeymoon after the surprise wedding Robert had arranged. The time was right for a short holiday she thought.

She could see Robert looking across as they approached and he shouted to Nick, 'Hands off my wife please.'

'I think you will find she's linking me,' Nick replied laughing as he raised their arms.

'Fair enough,' Robert said turning back to talk to Keith, his co-director and right-hand man.

'I'm going to get a beer, do you want a drink Eva,' Nick asked.

'No I'm good thanks,' she said as she joined her husband. Nick walked off in the direction of the bar.

'I'm glad Nick could come,' Robert said turning to Eva. 'His work as a doctor gets more stressful every day. He can spend some time with us just relaxing'.

She smiled at her husband, she was so lucky. Two gorgeous men in her life and a job she adored. What more could she want. A son or daughter one day, then her life would be complete but not yet she still had lots she wanted to do with her career as a dancer.

Eva noticed that Nick didn't return and she was certain he would be chatting up a pretty member of the cast. Her brother-in-law could be extremely charming when he wanted to be. She could never understand why he couldn't keep the same girlfriend for more than a few dates. He was so popular but he seemed to tire of their company. Thankfully, he didn't tire of her company and was often a visitor at their flat.

It wasn't long before Eva caught sight of Nick among an attentive audience. She gave an inward laugh as she noticed his arms gesticulating as he relayed his tale. Her lovely but complex brother-in-law. She always thought there were two sides to Nick, the extrovert confident socialiser and the troubled introvert or was that her imagination. Perhaps we are all part introvert part extrovert she thought, although thinking about it Robert was just Robert whatever company he was in.

An hour later the sun had started to set and a cool breeze picked up. People began to disperse wishing each other good luck with whatever new projects were on the horizon for them. Eva had circulated among the party goers before sitting down watching Robert talking animatedly with some of the cast. She stood up and walked over to him and he immediately put his arms around her waist and pulled her close.

'Are you ready to go home,' he asked her. 'You look tired.'

'Yes I think we should make a move. Where's Nick?'

'No idea. Probably chatting up some pretty girl. He's such a flirt,' Robert said laughing. 'Come on let's go, we'll catch up with Nick tomorrow when we go to mum and dad's for

The Dinner Date

lunch. I think mum's doing a Sunday roast for us, she knows how much we love her roast dinners.'

As they walked to the car Eva briefly glanced back at the party and caught sight of Nick watching them, he didn't wave he just watched.

2
Robert

Three Years Earlier – The Audition

Robert tall at over 6ft, walked confidently across the stage and looked down at the cast members who had already been hired and were seated ready and waiting to watch the final auditions taking place. This was the most important one, the role of lead female dancer. It would be the first show he had directed on his own and he was pleased, albeit a bit nervous, that the production company behind the show had such faith in him even though he was still only 25. He didn't want to let them down.

This whole environment that he was now part of was so different to the middle class upbringing he had enjoyed with his mother a GP and his father a nurse. He had surprised everyone when he chose to study Fine Art and Theatre at University eventually gaining a BA Hons Degree. His older brother Nick, who had followed the same path as their mother and had become a doctor, teased him about his chosen career asking him when he was going to get a 'proper' job!

As he stood on the stage he began to feel anxious, his confidence waning slightly. He knew he had to make the right decision, his lead female dancer had to be someone very special. He took a deep breath and announced, 'Quiet everyone, the auditions will start in 5 minutes,' and a stillness immediately settled in the room. When he descended the steps of the stage and walked to his seat the eyes of the female members of the cast followed him, acknowledging how handsome he was with his dark brown almost black hair, olive skin and soft brown eyes. Robert was unaware of his good looks, rarely flirting with women. His few serious relationships had ended because he was too involved and committed to his chosen career.

As he took his seat waiting for the first audition to begin he looked around the theatre. It was a small old theatre with very traditional décor. He noticed that the stage was surprisingly large for such a small theatre. He knew it would be perfect for his first professional step into the world of theatre production. He had asked for the stage to be completely bare, with no props just a wide expanse of floor space so each dancer could perform at their best. Robert sat on his own, four rows back and directly opposite the centre of the stage. Justin, the experienced Stage Manager, had organised six dancers to take part in the auditions. Robert had asked that each dancer perform two pieces. Their first dance was to be performed to their chosen piece of music but for the second part of the audition each dancer was asked to improvise to a set piece of music which was new to them.

Robert had already decided that he disliked the responsibility of choosing the best dancers for a show but accepted it was part of the job. He would enjoy watching the performances but also felt nervous because on this occasion the final decision for the role of lead female dancer would be his alone. He knew he would hate disappointing the dancers that he hadn't chosen, they would have all tried so hard. Smiling to himself he knew he was a 'softie' and realised he would have to toughen up. He knew being successful in the entertainment business wasn't an easy job and was very competitive. With that thought in mind he made himself comfortable ready to watch the six dancers hoping one would stand out.

When Robert gave the signal for the auditions to begin, one by one the dancers entered the stage. He observed the performances of four dancers noting they were all good and he ticked a couple as possible lead female dancer but, as yet no-one stood out as being exceptional. That was until it was coming to the end of the auditions and the final two dancers remained. Robert was busy looking down at his notepad and making comments alongside the name of each dancer when he looked up and saw a young very slender pretty girl confidently taking to the stage. Eva would later comment to Robert that she hadn't felt confident and had been so nervous her legs were shaking as she walked across the stage and she had found it difficult to walk let alone dance.

Robert noticed how this dancer stood in the middle of the large stage looking so small and vulnerable, appearing to be no more than 15 and childlike but he knew she had to be older. He looked down at the list of candidates noting her name, before he resumed his gaze taking in her appearance and observing her stunning sapphire blue eyes which appeared to show such control and calmness. Her lips were heart shaped and her button nose was perfect. Her blonde straight hair was pulled tightly back into a high ponytail. He asked her to introduce herself.

'My name is Eva Thomas,' she replied smiling showing no outward sign of nerves.

'And how old are you Eva?'

'I'm 20,' she replied.

'Thank you Eva, please start your performance.'

He saw she indicated that she was ready and the music for her audition piece started. Her vulnerability disappeared and every move was carefully chosen to show off her grace and elegance. It also displayed her subtle sexuality, she was not just a dancer she was part of the music. This didn't go unnoticed by Robert as he watched spellbound and could feel the serenity of the performance and the passion she had for her dancing. All eyes were fixed on the stage and when the music ended there wasn't a sound or movement in the room. It was almost as if everyone had been hypnotised by her dancing. Then slowly there was one clap, and then another, and then a ripple of applause. She smiled and showed no surprise.

The second piece of music had been selected by the musical director. When the music began Eva did not hesitate, and Robert could see she let her whole body melt into the unfamiliar rhythm. He carefully watched as every movement was done with such natural grace. Robert felt surprised at his own feelings not only did he see a superb dancer but he also felt attracted to her. Was this 'love at first sight' he thought smiling and then quickly assured himself that he didn't believe in such things. This reaction confused and unnerved him slightly and he knew this feeling couldn't dictate the choice he made. But he had to admit to himself he was enchanted by this young dancer. For her final movement she gracefully fell to the floor, her body spent and relaxed. At peace. Robert thanked her and she left the stage.

There was one more dancer to audition but could anyone top Eva's performance. It turned out nobody could. Robert went to join the Musical Director and the Choreographer and a brief discussion took place. It was a unanimous decision that one dancer stood out as far the best and Robert made the final decision that he would offer the position of lead female dancer to Eva Thomas.

Usually the Assistant Director would relay the good news to the successful candidate but on this occasion he decided to tell Eva himself. He went backstage where the dancers waited nervously for the results of the auditions and immediately spotted Eva amongst her fellow dancers. When she turned and saw Robert, he signalled for her to follow him. He took her into a small room at the side of the stage. He had been enchanted by her dancing and wanted to meet her and tell her the good news himself or was that the only reason he questioned himself. As she entered the room Robert noticed her cheeks were slightly flushed as her stunning blue eyes confidently surveyed her surroundings. When she turned to look at him he noticed she was even prettier than she appeared on stage, the perfect English Rose.

'Please, sit down Eva,' he said motioning to one of the two chairs in the room. 'Tell me a little bit about yourself, how long have you been dancing?' As their paths had never crossed before he wanted to gain an idea of what her personality was like and also to learn more about her previous experience.

She looked directly into his eyes and smiled. 'All my life, well at least since I was 5 years old. I have never wanted to do anything else. I'm at my happiest when I'm dancing.'

'Yes I could see you were completely absorbed in your dancing,' he commented never taking his eyes away from her. He couldn't, he couldn't stop looking at her until he realised he was actually staring fixedly at her. He quickly looked down at his notes and took a minute to compose himself before he continued and asked about her dancing career so far and she briefly explained. He noted that she was still young and he realised a little inexperienced but she would soon learn he had no doubt about that. After a short pause he looked at her smiling, 'Eva, I would like to offer you the role of lead female dancer, I hope you will accept.' And then he felt an idiot for adding that comment, although that was how he really felt. He wanted this dancer in the show, she would be an asset he thought but he realised it would also give him a chance to get to know her. A smile spread across his face with that thought as he waited for her reply.

Very quietly and calmly she responded, 'I would be delighted to accept,' and with that he could see her smile widened and her cheeks flushed just a little bit more.

Grinning Robert said, 'That's good, we will see you here at 8.30 on Monday morning for the start of rehearsals. Now I will take you to meet Katie who looks after all our female dancers.' And with that he escorted her out of the room.

The Dinner Date

As he left Eva in the capable hands of Katie, Robert walked passed Justin who stopped him and said, 'The auditions went well. I thought all the girls were good but especially Eva. I knew you would like her,' he said smirking with a twinkle in his eye. 'She's very pretty, isn't she?'

'Is she? I hadn't noticed but I did think her dancing was exceptional.'

Laughing Justin replied, 'Course you didn't notice.'

As Justin walked away Robert replied, 'Yes you are right I do like her, she will make a good addition to the cast,' and he could hear Justin laughing. Robert smiled to himself and knew he couldn't disguise the fact he found Eva very attractive.

After that first meeting Robert knew he was already fascinated by this young lady and was eager to learn more about her. Slowly he got to know Eva. First professionally and then one day after the show as she left the stage, he congratulated her on her performance and then, taking courage into his own rather sweaty nervous hands, his heart beating a little too fast he asked, 'Eva, if you are not in a rush to go home would you like to go for a drink?'

She turned and looked at him causing his heart to do a somersault as he waited for her reply and smiling she said 'Yes, that would be lovely.' He was pleased when she accepted his invitation and when their busy lives allowed he began to spend more and more time with her and was delighted when their friendship easily blossomed into a romance.

One Sunday morning, a few months after their first date, Robert lay in bed in his flat with Eva in his arms. He could feel her snuggling closer to him. It was a lovely feeling. He was happily sated after they had enjoyed passionate and loving sex. He thought back to the first time they had explored each other's bodies. He had been a little nervous at first realising how tiny and delicate Eva was compared to his

6ft frame. But he needn't have worried, once engaged in the sexual act their bodies blended together as one. The sex had been gentle, loving and perfect and each time they made love he explored her beautiful body further. Very soon into the relationship Robert knew that Eva was the 'one' and he hoped that in time they would marry, if she would have him!

While Eva's reputation within the world of Arts and Dance was beginning to expand Robert's skill in directing and producing excellent shows for the theatre began to be noticed and both their lives started to become very busy.

3

Six Months After the Audition

Eva was pleased when Robert suggested they kept their relationship secret not only from cast and crew members but also their own families. There would be plenty of time later on for introductions but for now they both wanted to spend quality time just with each other. This continued for several months with Robert finding it increasingly difficult to keep the secret from his family. It was so much easier for Eva because her mum had remarried after her dad died and she was now living in Scotland so she didn't feel the same pressure. Then one morning when he had a call from his mum Robert saw the opportunity to introduce Eva to his parents.

'Hi mum, everything okay?'

'Yes, Robert everything is fine. How is your latest show going?'

'It's been successful, we've had some good reviews or so I've been told. You know I don't read reviews, far too scary,' he said laughing.

'Yes I know, you still haven't got a 'thick skin' have you. Why I called is to let you know that your dad and I have got tickets for the show this Friday and Nick is going to join us. We wondered if we could go out for a meal before or after the show?'

'That sounds great mum. A meal after the show would be better. I will book somewhere. Is Nick coming on his own or with his current girlfriend?' he asked.

'On his own.' She paused and let out a sigh before continuing, 'It would be nice if you boys could find long term partners. Your dad and I would love to have two nice daughters-in-law.'

Robert laughed and said, 'I will see what I can do. Looking forward to seeing you on Friday.'

The seed was sown in Robert's mind and now he had to persuade Eva it would be the ideal opportunity to introduce her to his family.

Eva had started to spend more and more time with Robert at his small flat. Their latest show was in a theatre less than an hour away from the flat so it made sense she stayed with him. Robert had just finished talking to his mum when Eva entered the lounge carrying two mugs of coffee.

'That was mum on the phone. She and dad are coming to see the show on Friday. I know she likes to try and see, whenever possible, all my shows. They are both so supportive and always have been,' he said pausing before continuing 'Mum has suggested we go out for a meal after the show. This would be a great opportunity to introduce you to my family. Nick will also be joining us. What do you think?' he asked hopefully already noticing she looked a bit apprehensive.

'It's a terrifying thought but it has to happen sometime and after the show is as good a time as any I suppose. They might hate me!'

'Or you might hate my family, but I don't think either will happen. They will love you just as I do.'

'Okay let's go for it,' she said.

The following morning Robert phoned his mum. 'Hi mum, I've booked a table at a restaurant near to the theatre.'

'That's good but you didn't have to phone me to let me know, you could have just sent me a text,' she said a bit bemused.

'I know but there's something else I want to tell you. I want you to meet Eva, the lead female dancer in the show,' he paused before deciding what to say, 'she has become a huge part of my life and is very special to me. I've decided that it is about time you, dad and Nick met her.'

'We would be delighted to meet her. How long have you been a couple and why keep it a secret?'

'Not long. We both agreed we wanted to keep it a secret for a while giving us time to get to know each other better. Eva is really looking forward to meeting you all.'

'I'm so looking forward to meeting her. I can't wait to tell your dad. Does Nick know?'

'Definitely not. If Nick had known the whole world would know. I must go, see you on Friday,' Robert said and ended the call.

Friday came far too quickly for Eva. She tried to put all thoughts of meeting Robert's family out of her mind as she concentrated on delivering a faultless performance. But after the show, when she was getting changed, it was a different matter. She began to feel very nervous which she acknowledged was ridiculous. She needed to make a good impression for Robert's sake and she wanted them to like her it was so important to her. If she tried too hard she might make a fool of herself. That thought made her even more nervous. As she heard a noise at her dressing room door she turned around and saw it was Robert.

'Mum, dad and Nick have come backstage to congratulate you on a stunning performance. Come and meet them.'

Robert took her hand and led her outside into the corridor where Jill and Stephen were eagerly waiting. A stocky middle-aged woman with blond hair cut in a short bob and hazel eyes stepped forward to greet Eva. Eva noticed the man behind her was an older version of Robert. He had handsome features, slightly smaller in height than Robert but with the same well defined cheek bones and his eyes were more hazel than brown. His hair was short and dark brown peppered with grey. Very distinguished looking Eva thought. The likeness to Robert was striking.

'Mum, dad this is Eva. Eva this is my mum, Jill and my dad, Stephen. I have no idea where my big brother Nick is, but that's not unusual,' Robert said with a smile.

'Hello Eva,' Jill said. There was a short awkward pause where a decision on shaking hands or a kiss on both cheeks had to be made. Jill made the decision not to do either and went straight into saying how wonderful Eva's performance had been.

'We enjoyed the show so much didn't we Stephen.' Like most couples, one person usually spoke for both of them. Stephen nodded in agreement never taking his eyes away from Eva.

'It's lovely to meet you both and I'm so glad you enjoyed the show,' Eva said noticing a slight nervous tremor in her voice confirming the importance of this first meeting.

'Mum where is Nick?' Robert asked.

'Oh, somewhere,' she said flapping her hands. 'He was following us but knowing Nick he will have stopped to chat to someone, almost certainly a pretty female.'

And with that comment Nick appeared.

'There you are Nick. I want to introduce you to Eva, my girlfriend,' Robert said with a grin. It was the first time he had openly acknowledged this fact. Eva looked at him and his grin widened.

Nick didn't hesitate in making the decision his mum had avoided, he stepped forward and, surprising Eva, he kissed her on both cheeks causing her to blush slightly. 'Lovely to meet you Eva, and congratulations on a wonderful performance.'

'Nice to meet you Nick, glad you enjoyed the show,' she said carefully taking in his appearance. He looked nothing like Robert. In fact she noted he was the complete opposite. He was smaller than Robert with light brown hair and emerald eyes. She noticed he wore his hair cut very short. He was of a slim build and she could see he carried no excess fat.

The Dinner Date

But most of all she noticed he had a warm friendly smile and she couldn't help but smile back at him.

'Eva, are you ready to go to the restaurant?' Robert asked.

'Nearly, just give me a few more minutes.'

'Okay. Dad if you make your way back to your car I will wait for Eva. Shall we meet at the restaurant? It's only a 10-minute drive away. I'll text you the details.'

'That's a good idea Robert. Come on Nick we don't want to lose you again.'

Nick started to follow his mum and dad but couldn't resist turning around and taking a second look at Eva. Robert left Eva to finish changing while he went to have a quick word with one of the stage hands.

Half an hour later the family were sitting in the restaurant discussing what to have to eat. Once the food was ordered Jill engaged Eva in conversation.

'You are so talented Eva, when did you start dancing?'

'When I was five. Mum made me go to dancing classes. She had always wanted to be a dancer but had never had the opportunity to take part in dancing classes. Unlike most of the girls in the class I hated it at first. Years later my teacher said she could see from the very first lesson that I had a natural ability and it seems she was right. I've never looked back. I'm so lucky and even luckier now I've met Robert,' she replied smiling and looking at Robert.

'That was going to be my next question. When and how did you two meet?'

Robert took over answering, describing Eva's audition much to her embarrassment. 'And the rest is history,' he concluded.

'Where do you live Eva,' Nick asked.

'If that's a subtle way of asking if we are living together, no we're not. Eva's rental contract on her flat ends in two months so we will see what happens then,' Robert answered.

Eva was relieved when the food soon arrived and all talk was focused on the delicious meal and before long it was time to make their separate ways home. She wasn't ready to share details of their relationship with anyone especially Robert's brother. Robert had asked her to move in with him and she knew she would very soon but that was a detail they wanted to keep private.

4

Over time Eva had become close to Robert's parents. As her own dad had died a few years ago and her mum had moved to Scotland she hardly ever saw her so Jill had become not only a good friend but also someone to talk to when she needed advice. Eva valued her thoughts on most subjects and was looking forward to the family Sunday lunch the day after the end of show party.

Robert and Eva arrived early, before Nick. Stephen answered the door and as soon as Robert walked into the house his dad said, 'Robert come into the conservatory I want to show you my new camera.' Robert smiled, his dad was passionate about his hobby and to be fair he had become very accomplished as an amateur photographer. Robert didn't share his passion but he could see how excited his dad was with his new 'toy' and dutifully followed.

The doors to the conservatory were wide open and the camera positioned on a tripod pointing towards the garden. 'It's a video camera. I thought I would try my hand at capturing some of the wild life that we know, or rather we think, visits our garden,' Stephen explained.

The garden looked a picture on this summer morning with a selection of early flowering plants including Roses, Peonies and Cornflowers. Stephen proceeded to explain to Robert the intricacies of the camera, which were all completely lost on him but he still listened and feigned interest. He did notice the video camera looked ready to take more footage of the 'family' visit. He smiled to himself, Eva would just love that!

While Robert accompanied his dad to the conservatory Eva wandered through the now familiar house straight to the large kitchen. She could see pans on the hob bubbling away producing a steamy haze and she spotted two shelves in the eye level oven full of roasting food. The smells coming from this area were tantalising. Eva was anxious to help with lunch but of course Jill wouldn't hear of it and as she turned round said, 'No, it's all under control. I just hope Nick is on his way, you know what he's like. I sometimes wonder how that son of mine ever became a doctor, and a very good one, he's so scatty at times.'

Eva laughed and replied, 'Both your sons are a credit to you. Nick would never let you or anyone down.'

'That's kind of you to say, I am proud of both boys. Why don't you have a walk down the garden and enjoy the bird song. You've earned a rest now your show has finished.'

'Okay I will but give me a shout if you need help.'

Jill smiled at her and Eva knew she would never ask for help.

The large, detached house enjoyed the luxury of a huge garden laid mainly to lawn. It included a small fenced off wooded area which led to a small stream bordering farm land. It was idyllic and so peaceful.

Eva walked down across the garden and through the gate and sat down on the small bench to listen to the sound of the water gently babbling on its journey downstream. A variety of birds were calling to each other. She let out a sigh and closed her eyes enjoying the sounds of nature only to be disturbed by the noise of footsteps crunching on the dry leaves which carpeted the ground. She opened her eyes to find Nick standing watching her.

'Sorry to disturb you, mum says dinner is nearly ready.'

Shielding her eyes from the sun she looked up and replied, 'Okay Nick,' as she stood up and with a glint in his eye, Nick grabbed hold of her playfully threatening to throw her in the stream.

'Don't you dare Nick. How old are you Doctor Nicholas Brown,' she said laughing. He let go of her and as they walked back to the house she thought how Nick was more like a brother to her than a brother-in-law. As an only child she had missed not having a sibling and now she felt she had one.

As she re-entered the kitchen Eva immediately once again asked Jill if she needed help. 'No thanks, it's all done.' And it was. As Eva walked into the dining room she looked at the table which was beautifully set as usual with the wonderful smells of a roast dinner tickling her nostrils. She knew she was so lucky to be part of this wonderful family and she never took it for granted.

Seated around the table with plates piled high with food the conversation began. 'Have you anything planned for this week, perhaps a short break somewhere,' Stephen enquired.

'Nothing booked,' Robert answered and continued, 'it will be good to just do nothing and spend some time together.'

Stephen then asked, 'Nick, when is your next holiday. You must need a break, you have been working such long hours.'

'We are short staffed, but you are right dad, I do need a break.'

'Book yourself some time off and go away for a few days. Find a nice girl to take with you,' Stephen suggested.

'Oh dad, you know the only girl for me is Eva,' Nick said with a wink at Eva. I'm waiting for Robert to get tired of her and pass her on to me.'

'Nick, you know that will never happen. Eva and I were made for each other.'

'Okay.' Nobody was offended by Nick's comment, it was the normal harmless banter the brothers enjoyed.

'Seriously bro', you need someone special in your life,' Robert said.

'I know, but I've yet to find that someone. I'm still looking and sampling what's out there.'

Jill glanced at Eva shaking her head which caused Eva to smile.

Once they had finished eating the delicious Sunday roast and indulgent chocolate pudding they sat outside drinking coffee and enjoying the sunshine. Nick left first giving his brother a man hug and then his sister-in-law a kiss on both cheeks saying he would see them soon. Robert and Eva followed shortly after complaining to each other they felt so full they could hardly move.

5

Eva woke early the next morning to find an empty space beside her. Robert was missing. Then she heard the clatter of dishes in the kitchen and smiled wondering how anyone could make so much noise just making a cup of tea and toast. She waited for him to return but he didn't appear and she slowly stretched her limbs and then snuggled up again for a longer lie-in.

Robert was making breakfast for Eva but it was taking a bit longer than expected as he had become distracted. He had his laptop open and while he waited for a confirmation message his phone vibrated indicating a text. Looking down he saw it was from his mum saying how lovely it was to see them yesterday but they looked tired and he must book a short break.

He grinned and replied, *already done as a surprise for Eva*. At the same moment the confirmation of the booking came through – 3 days in Jersey. He checked the booking, flying early tomorrow which would mean they would have the best part of Tuesday in Jersey and returning on Friday afternoon, perfect. He went back to the bedroom to share the news that he had booked a short break in the Cotswolds, the real location would hopefully be a pleasant surprise, but he found Eva fast asleep. It could wait he thought, let her sleep.

It was almost one year since their wedding in Jersey which he had secretly arranged. It had been a perfect day but had caused some upset among family and friends particularly Nick who was annoyed he hadn't been best man. Robert couldn't have risked telling Nick, even as a child Nick could never keep a secret big or small.

Eva woke up and looked at her phone. It said 10.30, it must be wrong. If the time was correct she couldn't believe she had slept in so late and where was Robert? Her mouth felt stale and dry, she needed a cup of tea. She got up and threw on a light dressing gown and went in search of her husband. She found him sitting absorbed in something on his laptop. She joined him on the sofa. He turned to her grinning and reached over to kiss her.

'What are you looking at?' she asked.

He turned the laptop around so she could see the screen. It was a scene of a beautiful beach with a vast stretch of golden sand and the sun shining on the ocean blue sea. She recognised it. Confused she asked, 'Why are you looking at the beach we walked along on our honeymoon?'

'Oh, I was just remembering how wonderful those few days were. It's almost a year ago. It would be so nice to go back.'

'Yes it would be and I'm sure we will one day. I need breakfast I'm starving. Have you booked somewhere to stay in the Cotswolds?

'Yes, all done, tomorrow until Friday.'

He smiled. Would it work out as he had planned. He couldn't believe she hadn't guessed or had she! After breakfast they took a shopping trip into Oxford so Eva could buy a few essentials for their short break away and then the rest of the day was spent packing for their holiday and just relaxing.

The next morning Robert woke up early and turning to look at Eva his heart missed a beat. She was still asleep looking so peaceful. He very carefully pulled back the duvet, slid out of bed and as quiet as a mouse tip-toed across the bedroom and out into the hallway. Their bags were ready packed and waiting by the front door. Smiling to himself he quickly double checked that he had packed both passports. Yes, both safely hidden in his overnight bag. Moving on to the kitchen he started preparing a light breakfast of tea and toast which he put onto a tray and took into Eva. He put the tray down on the small table by the side of the bed.

Pretending to be asleep Eva waited for Robert to lean over and kiss her.

Yawning she said, 'What time is it?'

'Time you got up, I want to make an early start. There's tea and toast on the tray, we can always stop a little later and have some brunch.'

'Are you sure we haven't got time for something else, and I don't mean food,' she said reaching out and pulling him down onto the bed. Taken by surprise he wasn't quite sure what to say. He knew they had to catch a plane but she didn't. Eva thought they had all the time in the world.

Thinking quickly he replied, 'Plenty of time for that later, I want to make an early start so we have more time in the Cotswolds.'

'Okay, if you are quite sure,'

Laughing he said, 'Yes I am, now eat your breakfast and we can make a start.'

It wasn't long before they were in the car starting their journey when Eva noticed they didn't seem to be driving to the Cotswolds. 'Where are we going,' she asked although she suspected she knew. 'Are we going to the airport by any chance?'

Smiling Robert confirmed, 'Yes we are. We are going to Jersey just like we did a year ago for our wedding. We have an early flight and return on Friday. Have I done the right thing, are you pleased?'

'Oh yes, it will be a perfect way to celebrate our 1st wedding anniversary. I can't wait to be walking across one of Jersey's beautiful sandy beaches remembering my wonderful surprise wedding day. Thank you, it's a great idea you are such a romantic.'

6

One Year Ago

Robert sometimes couldn't believe they had been together for 2 years, time seemed to have flown by so quickly. During those two years their lives had become even busier, they were both in such demand. This was good but also frustrating. Robert wanted to direct Eva in another show but neither of them could find a time when they were both free to even talk about it let alone arrange and put on a new show. He sat alone one evening and thought about their lives. They both loved their work and neither of them ever wanted to turn down the opportunity of new work, but that had its drawbacks. They hardly ever saw each other. When they did have time together it was so good and very much treasured.

Robert began to wonder where their lives were going. Were they going to manage a future together or were they going to allow their blossoming careers to dissolve their personal lives? It was there and then that he made the decision. He would never let that happen. He knew what he had to do, and he would do it.

Although Eva was unaware, Robert had planned for her to take a short break from her latest rehearsals. As she walked through the door of their flat one Thursday evening, totally exhausted he took her in his arms and said, 'You look so tired, I think a few days away relaxing would be good for you.'

She laughed at the suggestion, 'That would be lovely, if only that was possible.'

To her surprise Robert replied, 'Well it is possible, we are going away for a few days.'

She was amazed and bewildered and immediately began to protest. 'I'm in the middle of rehearsals, I can't just not turn up, I would let everyone down and probably be fired.'

He laughed at that thought, that would never happen, she was far too important. 'I have sorted everything out and all you have to do is sit in the car while I drive us to the airport.'

'To the airport? Where are we going?'

'I'm not telling you, it's a surprise.'

Still shocked and confused but also delighted, Eva realised this was all out of her hands so she just had to go with the flow. 'I will go and pack. What should I take?' she asked as she began to make her way to the bedroom.

'I have already packed everything you will need and your case is in the car,' he replied with a grin and gently turned her around and escorted her to the sofa. 'I will make you a coffee to revive you and then we can start our journey,' he said smiling, he was enjoying this.

Exhausted, Eva couldn't help falling asleep during the car journey. When Robert brought the car to a stop in the Airport Car Park he gently shook Eva to wake her. When she opened her eyes and looked around Robert told her they were soon to board a flight to the beautiful island of Jersey. They had been twice before as a couple and it had become one of their favourite places. She found the excitement bubbling up inside her and she couldn't wait to set foot on one of the beautiful sandy beaches.

When everyone was settled into their seats the plane taxied the runway and then took off. Eva turned to Robert who was beaming. 'I can't believe you have arranged this secretly and I never suspected anything. What else have you done?'

He laughed when she looked a little worried. 'Be patient, all will be revealed,' he replied although he was just a tiny bit worried she might not like the surprise.

'So far this is a wonderful surprise, thank you.' She thought how lucky she was to have met Robert. Fate had been kind to them, she hoped it would last!

The flight took no time at all and on landing they were met by a chauffeur driven limousine which took them through the beautiful streets of Jersey to a luxury hotel on the cliff top. The light had faded and all they could see was the darkness broken by twinkling street and house lights. It didn't matter, Eva knew exactly where she was and that the view tomorrow would be spectacular. They were escorted into the hotel, passing reception and up to the most exquisite suite of rooms. Once the hotel porter had left, Robert drew her into his arms and they kissed.

'Do you like your surprise?'

'It's amazing,' she said as she looked around the room. 'I had no idea you were planning this. A few days just to relax in each other's company will be so good. Thank you, I love you so much.'

They clung together neither wanting to break away. Eva wanted to stay in Robert's arms forever, feeling safe and content. And Robert wanted to always be able to protect her.

That night was the most passionate she had ever known. Sensuous luxurious lovemaking. Every stroke and intimate caress was executed with such love. The slow, erotic pathway to an explosive climax reached simultaneously. They were both sated and held each other tightly until Eva fell asleep.

Robert lovingly looked at Eva as she slept. He very gently brushed a lock of hair from her cheek. She didn't move. She looked so peaceful and content. He fell asleep excited and looking forward to their wedding day, which Eva knew nothing about although he was beginning to feel a little bit anxious she may not accept his marriage proposal!

The next morning Eva was woken up by a knock on their door. Surprised she looked around and found that Robert wasn't beside her. He was already up and answering the door.

The Dinner Date

She could hear voices as someone entered the apartment. After a short pause Robert came back into the bedroom.

'Good morning, are you hungry? I have arranged for a special breakfast to be delivered from room service.'

'Yes, I'm starving, that sounds wonderful,' she replied already getting out of bed.

They savoured every bite as they looked out at the clear blue ocean. The view was even more breathtaking than Eva could have imagined. Suddenly, and much to her surprise, Robert went down on one knee and produced the most beautiful diamond engagement ring.

'Eva, will you marry me,' he asked, looking up into her beautiful blue eyes.

His heart was pounding as he waited for her answer. He needn't have worried. She flung her arms around him and, without hesitation, said 'yes please.' They kissed, a long and passionate kiss.

Robert confessed that he was so relieved she had said yes. Laughing Eva said, 'And what would you have done if I had said no?'

'I have no idea, but it would have been awkward because I have something else to tell you.' She could never have guessed what he was going to say. He realised this could go disastrously wrong but continued with some trepidation. 'I am so relieved you said yes because we are booked in to get married at a Registry Office at 2pm this afternoon.' He looked at Eva, was she pleased or horrified – he couldn't decide but she was definitely speechless.

He continued, 'We never have time to arrange anything let alone a wedding, so I decided to go ahead and arrange everything myself. No-one knows, it will be a surprise to all our family and friends. I guess there will be a few people upset but I think it's the right thing for us.'

She looked at Robert shocked and a little anxious but also agreed it was the right decision for them, although secretly she wasn't sure. What would their family and friends think – no doubt they would find out when they arrived home.

Robert continued to explain, 'I have bought the most gorgeous wedding dress for you to wear, it's already hanging in the wardrobe. No peeking.'

Eva looked at him in utter amazement. 'Are you telling me you chose a wedding dress for me?'

'Yes', he replied laughing, 'but I had help.' He explained as he saw the astonishment on her face, 'I employed the services of a company who specialise in surprise weddings to help organise everything, including a make-up artist/hairdresser and dresser. The team will be arriving just before midday and you can't see the dress until they arrive.'

She was bursting with excitement and thought she would never be able to wait until then, but she had to. 'I'm stunned. This is the best surprise ever. I am so glad I said yes,' she said laughing and embraced the thoughtfulness and kindness of Robert but especially the love they had for each other.

'So am I,' Robert said letting out a huge sigh of relief.

They spent the next couple of hours doing nothing but relaxing. Something they never usually had time to do. They sat and watched families enjoying time together on the beach. Children running around excitedly, screaming as the gentle waves rolled in and the water touched their toes. Eva began to imagine the children that she would share with Robert and excitement rose in her. They watched the small boats gently bobbing up and down on the sea, content in each other's company just relaxing. That was until Robert said, 'I think it's time we started to get ready for our wedding.'

The butterflies started in Eva's stomach as they went to separate bedrooms both with luxury en-suite bathrooms. Eva languished in a bath smelling of rose petals and Robert enjoyed a refreshing shower.

The team arrived just before midday and consisted of the dresser, Annie, and make-up artist/hairdresser, Kelly. They

The Dinner Date

introduced themselves and immediately started to organise everything, putting Eva at ease. Her hair was washed and dried and left long but fashioned into a natural style with a few very simple corkscrew curls. Small flowers were attached to the curls. Eva had beautiful flawless skin and very little make-up was needed. Kelly combined just the right subtle tone of copper and blue to enhance Eva's stunning blue eyes, but it also gave a natural look.

It was now time to reveal the dress! Much to Eva's surprise Kelly and Annie went to the wardrobe and carefully lifted out the dress. It dawned on her that during the short time they had been in the suite Robert had made sure she was never alone in this room. He had planned this so carefully she thought.

They unzipped and peeled off the protective covering to reveal the most gorgeous wedding dress. Eva's slight frame needed the simplest of designs, just enough to enhance her slim figure and draw in her tiny waist. They helped her into the dress. The bodice was made of white satin overlaid with lace. Three quarter length sleeves also made of lace completed the bodice and then the material continued down to hug her slim waist gently flaring out across her narrow hips down to her ankles. Once zipped up the dress was a perfect fit. Kelly collected a box from the shelf in the wardrobe and revealed a beautiful pair of satin shoes. Just perfect.

There was a knock at the apartment door and Eva could hear Robert accepting the flowers for the wedding. Kelly went into the lounge and took the beautiful bouquet of red, pink and white roses from Robert. She walked back into the bedroom and handed them to Eva. The simple wedding outfit was now complete.

Robert, in his charcoal wedding suit, waited nervously for Eva to appear, and when she did it took his breath away. She looked stunning. So natural and glowing with excitement. The dress hugged her petite figure showing off her elegant dancer's body. Robert sighed with relief, the dress fitted her size 8 figure perfectly. She beamed with delight when she saw how handsome Robert looked. Arm in arm they made their way to the waiting car. Every head in the foyer turned and a slow ripple of gasps and applause began. Their smiles said everything, a couple very much in love.

They were driven the short journey to the registry office in St Helier where two witnesses, supplied by the wedding organisers, waited to escort the couple inside. Once inside and much to Eva's surprise, Robert produced a pair of matching wedding rings from his pocket. These were handed to the witnesses and the wedding service began. Robert had specially prepared his vows endorsing how much he loved Eva. Eva, of course, knew nothing about the wedding, so her vows were traditional but also modern.

After the short service and signing of the register they emerged into bright sunshine on the steps of the Registry Office. There was much laughter as biodegradable confetti was thrown and photos taken. The small crowd that had gathered to watch soon joined in with the celebrations. Little children started to gather handfuls of discarded confetti throwing it for a second time at the blushing bride. There were gasps of delight from the crowd when a horse drawn carriage appeared to take the bride and groom on the short journey back to their hotel.

On arriving at the hotel they were escorted to their suite and when the door opened, they were met by flowers completely decorating the room with a wedding high tea laid out and a bottle of perfectly chilled champagne waiting. Eva was so touched by the effort Robert had made. Every detail had been thought through carefully.

'Oh Robert this is amazing. I couldn't have had a better wedding. Thank you so much.'

'I had a lot of help. All I did was provide the Wedding Service Company with a lot of information, mostly about you. I must have been able to paint them an accurate picture of your likes and dislikes because the dress they chose was perfect on you.'

'Yes, I couldn't have chosen a better dress.'

'I'm so glad you enjoyed the surprise and you were not annoyed that I had kept such a huge occasion a secret. I think this is a good omen and our marriage will be blessed and perfect like our wedding day.' Taking Eva into his arms Robert confessed, 'I know our families will be upset that they have not been part of this special day, but we will have a family 'wedding' party at a later date. This is a day just for us to share and cement our love for each other.'

They both agreed it was a day never to forget.

They spent the rest of their short stay enjoying the beautiful island of Jersey and, more importantly, enjoying uninterrupted time together. It was during a relaxing stroll along a beautiful sandy beach near to their hotel that Robert brought up the subject of children. 'How many children should we have?' he said with a mischievous twinkle in his eye. Eva stopped and turned to look at him, she knew he was teasing her. 'I want at least two children, if you could manage it,' he said with a grin, 'but if not a little girl would be just fine. I know men usually want a son but all I want is another copy of you.'

'Yes, that's okay with me, I'll see what I can do but not for a few years, I don't want to stop dancing just yet,' she replied with a grin and snuggled closer to Robert.

Sadly the three-day break was over too soon and they flew back home as Mr and Mrs Brown.

They both contacted their families and, with some guilt, told them about their wedding in Jersey. Robert explained the reasons for the secrecy surrounding the wedding, he wanted to surprise Eva, and he had! They understood but were still disappointed not to be part of their special day. The news was soon leaked to the media and congratulations flooded in.

7

Two Weeks After the Wedding

One Sunday, a couple of weeks after their wedding, Robert suggested that they visit his mum and dad with some flowers as an apology for not inviting them to their wedding. They could take with them a large piece of the beautiful wedding cake the hotel had provided. Eva agreed that would be a good idea and along with the cake she packed a bottle of champagne.

Robert texted Nick and asked if he would join them. Reading his reply Robert said, 'That's a shame, Nick can't join us he's working. Oh well we will catch up with him another time.'

On arrival at his parents' house the newlyweds stood at the door feeling just a little anxious, unsure whether they would be told off for keeping such a huge event as their wedding a secret. Jill opened the door and immediately put her arms around Eva. 'Congratulations, Mrs Brown, welcome to the family.'

Stephen stood behind her grinning from ear to ear. Eva chuckled as she heard Robert sigh with relief, all was forgiven. As Robert stepped inside he said, 'We've brought some wedding cake and champagne to toast our wedding.'

Jill hugged her son and said, 'It's just like you to do something like this. Go through to the conservatory and I will bring plates and glasses. You can tell us all about your wedding. Is Nick coming?'

'No, he's working.'

'Never mind we can all get together another time and do it all again,' she replied with a smile.'

Stephen insisted on making a short speech before the toast. Raising their glasses he said, 'Eva, we are so happy that you are officially part of our family and welcome you with open arms. Robert is very lucky to have met you. You are very special to both of us and of course Nick adores you. Just a pity you haven't got a twin for Nick,' he said laughing.

'Now tell us all about the wedding,' Jill said eagerly.

'We will tell you all about the lead up to the wedding but we have the actual service on video and we have brought a copy for you,' Robert explained.

The look of delight on both his mum and dad's faces brought a huge smile to Robert's face. It had been worth the effort of arranging a video at the very last moment. After they had exhausted the 'wedding' talk Jill unexpectedly and much to their surprise said 'I guess it will be children next. I can't wait to have grandchildren.'

Stephen, Robert and Eva looked at each other in shock. Robert could see that Eva had actually blushed.

'Mum, we have only been married 2 weeks.'

Jill laughed, 'Sorry that was a bit forward of me. I guess it all stems from the fact that your father and I took it for granted we would have children as soon as we decided we wanted them. But of course it didn't happen and that's why we eventually decided to adopt Nick. And you Robert, you were such a lovely and unexpected surprise, we had given up on having a child of our own.'

'We do hope to give you a grandchild at some stage but not just yet,' Robert assured her. 'And if there was a problem we would also consider adopting. It worked out well for you.'

Jill went quiet at this comment and Robert noticed Stephen turned to look at his wife. 'Yes, it did turn out well,' Jill agreed, 'but we made some mistakes.'

'What do you mean mum?'

'At the time of your surprise arrival Nick didn't know he had been adopted. We intended to tell him but we left it, we left it too long. He was so excited when he knew he had a brother. Nick loved you so much but as time went on he seemed to resent you. I was told that this was quite normal when a new sibling came along so I wasn't particularly worried. When Nick was 10 we were advised that he should be told he was adopted. We had left it too long thinking the age he was told wasn't important but of course it was. We should have explained to Nick much earlier that he was adopted. I always thought it may have caused some emotional problems for him, knowing this information appeared to change him and he became for a time quite withdrawn.'

'You've never told me this,' Robert said surprised.

'No,' Jill said continuing, 'it wasn't something we wanted to share with you when you were growing up.'

Do you know much about his birth parents,' Robert asked.

'Not really. All we know is that his mum had two other children by her husband but Nick was conceived when she had an affair. Her husband took her back for the sake of the two older siblings but insisted the baby was put up for adoption. How much of that was correct we were never sure,' Jill explained.

'Does Nick know all this?'

'As a small child we told him his mum was poorly and couldn't keep him but when he reached about 14 he started asking more questions, he wanted more details. Your dad and I discussed it and thought he should know as much as we did about his background. We thought he might one day want to find his half siblings.'

'We have often regretted not telling him when he was younger,' Stephen explained with sadness in his eyes.

Jill decided that they should change the subject, she hated talking about Nick behind his back even if it was only within the family and she concluded, 'Nick seems a very well adjusted, kind human being who is a brilliant doctor and we are very proud of him. We are proud of both you boys and, of course now our new daughter-in-law.'

The Dinner Date

And with that she hugged Eva and the conversation moved on.

In the car on the way home Eva asked Robert, 'Have you ever spoken to Nick about being adopted?'

'Nope, we've never mentioned it. I've known from an early age he was adopted but to me he was just my big brother who I adored and still do.'

Eva was very thoughtful for the rest of the journey and when they reached home she couldn't help but comment, 'Do you think Nick could be suppressing a lot of emotional feelings he has built up over the years about his adoption. I can't imagine what it must feel like to suddenly be told you were adopted and your brother wasn't.

Robert looked at Eva and she could see from his eyes his was annoyed she was continuing this conversation. For the first time he felt that this was none of his wife's business.

'Eva, Nick is fine. He has a good job and friends and now he is lucky to have a beautiful sister-in-law and I am lucky to have a sexy wife. Why don't we perfect the art of making babies,' and with that he pulled her towards him.

8
The Shopping Trip

The short break in Jersey to celebrate their wedding anniversary had been a great success. They had not long been back home in the flat when Robert's phone rang. He noticed it was his mum and hoped nothing was wrong.

'Hi mum, is everything okay?'

'Yes fine, just wondered how your holiday in Jersey went. Was Eva surprised.'

'I think so but have a word with her yourself and she will tell you all about it,' and he handed his phone to Eva.

They chatted for a while and then Jill asked Eva if she was busy tomorrow, Saturday and explained, 'I need help in picking a dress for an informal dinner party Stephen and I have been invited to. I would love some help in choosing something. You have got such good taste. If you are free we could go shopping or is it too short notice?'

Eva was a bit surprised but also delighted that Jill had asked her. 'That would be lovely Jill, we've nothing planned for tomorrow.' And so they agreed to meet up the next day in Oxford town centre.

On Saturday, as Jill sat waiting in the small café for Eva to arrive, she started to think how lucky she was to have two wonderful successful sons and a delightful daughter-in-law. This would be the first time she had spent a few hours shopping with Eva and she was really looking forward to it. Eva was the daughter she had never had.

She didn't have to wait long before Eva arrived and they were soon on their way around the many shops in Oxford. It gave Jill the chance to see a different side of Eva. She already knew that Eva's temperament was gentle and she was quietly spoken but she was surprised to see that when Eva found something funny, she would throw her head back and laugh heartily. It was somewhat out of character but so infectious. The first time Jill saw this was when they sat having a cup of coffee in John Lewis after a major 'trying on' session. Exciting for Eva but just a little bit depressing for Jill. Changing room mirrors and lights are never very flattering for the older generation as Jill knew only too well! She sat opposite Eva drinking her coffee when they both recalled, at the same time, the dreadful dress Jill had picked to try on. She had marched out of the changing room to show Eva. The dress was too tight, too short, the wrong material, a garish bright pink, and totally unsuitable for the slightly overweight middle-aged lady Jill was. Eva's face had started to twitch as she tried to suppress the start of a giggle until Jill beat her to it and laughed so much she nearly wet herself. Another problem for the older lady she thought.

Tears of laughter ran down Eva's face and Jill thought how good it was to laugh together. As they sat with their coffee they started to giggle again and then Eva threw her head back and once again laughed heartily causing quite a stir. Smiles soon began to multiply on the faces of the customers of the coffee shop. Laughter and seeing someone else laugh could lift everyone's spirits.

At the end of almost three hours shopping they were exhausted but agreed it had been such a good shopping trip and both came home laden with bags and there was definitely not a pink dress among them. Of course, relaying the fun and laughter is never the same as participating in it, and both men failed miserably to see anything funny when the story was told. They looked at each other in bewilderment but also delight that Jill and Eva had had such a good time.

Jill hugged Eva when Robert and Eva were leaving, promising to do another shopping trip again very soon. It had been such a good day and both Jill and Stephen were so delighted that Eva was their daughter-in-law.

Robert and Eva drove home chatting about the lovely day they had enjoyed. 'Did you have a good time with mum. I know I'm biased but she is good company,' Robert enquired.

'Yes it was a good laugh. We got on really well. I saw a different side to your mum and I'm sure she saw a different side to me. Without you boys around your mum became more relaxed. You know it took years off her, she was able to leave the role of mother and wife behind and her true personality shone through. I wonder if I will change when I have children.'

'I don't think you will ever change Eva, and I don't want you to.'

Robert had been able to spend quality time with his dad who he had always been very close to, in a lot of ways they were so similar. They were still close, but time and circumstances didn't allow them to see as much of each other as they would like. Robert hoped in the future that would change and perhaps when grandchildren came along they would see more of each other.

'I enjoyed the time I spent with dad. I know I shouldn't say it, and don't repeat it, but it was nice to have time together, just the two of us, without Nick. I adore Nick but sometimes he can be a bit much. When the three of us are together Nick seems to want all of dad's attention. As far as I can remember he's always been like that. It's as if he's jealous of me and needs to prove he is better. I'm probably totally mistaken and it is just normal sibling rivalry, but still it was nice just the two of us.'

On their return home Eva entered the flat first and when she turned around she saw Robert walking, or rather staggering, towards the door carrying the many bags she had acquired on her shopping trip. He stepped inside the flat and put them down with an exaggerated huff. Then he went over and pulled Eva into his arms.

'Do you know something,' he said, 'I am the luckiest man in the world to have you as my wife. I'm so glad you auditioned for me. That day and that decision I made changed my life.'

'Yes, that was definitely the best audition I have ever done or will ever do. I'm glad I didn't know at the time I was auditioning in front my future husband!'

They kissed passionately. Like in a movie, he shut the door with his foot and carried her to the bedroom. They carefully undressed each other and gently explored one another's body's. Their desire for each other made every time feel like it was the first time, always finding new ways to excite each other, gently caressing, leading to passionate lovemaking. Afterwards they lay back spent, exhausted and very happy. Robert hoped they would never lose this passion for each other. He couldn't imagine that would ever happen and he hoped Eva felt the same.

9
Eva

One Friday evening Eva sat waiting for Robert to return home. She knew he would be tired from a busy week and the drive back from London. She didn't know why he always insisted on taking his car when he worked in London, she thought that just caused added stress. Eva made herself a coffee and sat down picking up a magazine from the coffee table. As she flicked through the pages of the Stage Magazine she saw a picture of a theatre with an article relating to the history of the building. She recognised the theatre, it was where she had first auditioned for Robert. It triggers memories of the day which had changed her life and thinking about it still caused feelings of excitement in her stomach.

The day she auditioned for Robert she remembers starting her preparation in her normal way. Her warm-up routine was exactly the same for every audition she attended, followed by a short dance routine to relax her. Smiling to herself she recalls waiting at the side of the stage for her name to be called with increasing excitement and butterflies in her stomach. She can't remember feeling any apprehension because she knew that as soon as she started to dance she would be lost in her own world and would be unaware of the audience watching her. And this time had been no exception although as she had stepped onto the stage her legs had felt like jelly but as soon as the music started her body began to relax.

As she danced she had been oblivious to the fact that Robert had been intently watching her, he later confessed his eyes had never strayed from the exquisite movements she was performing. When she had finished dancing she had smiled

The Dinner Date

and turned to look at him. The minute their eyes met she had felt a strong attraction which at the time had taken her by surprise.

As she sat in the flat staring into space she recalls how delighted she had been but not surprised when Robert offered her the role of lead female dancer. Thinking back it was during rehearsals she had begun to realise that Robert was spending more time with her than with the other dancers. At first she had only concentrated on perfecting her performance and then slowly she began to realise that Robert's attention to her was more on a personal level than professional. She had welcomed this as she enjoyed his company. She felt herself smile thinking about how Robert still teases her about how long it took her to realise he fancied her.

She thinks back to the time one evening after the performance when he had asked her if she would like to go for a drink. She had been pleasantly surprised and had eagerly accepted. Robert suggested they went to a small country pub he knew away from the theatre, there would be less chance they would meet up with the other performers.

She let her mind wander back to that first drink they had together when she had watched him return from the bar, drinks in hand and had taken in his appearance. She had guessed he must have been over 6 foot tall with broad shoulders and she had felt so tiny when she stood next to him. She had noticed his thick dark brown hair was cut short against his olive skin, but what she had observed most of all was his soft dark brown eyes which held a twinkle in them and his laughter lines which were just starting to be visible when he smiled. Watching him walk towards her it had confirmed her first thought, he was very handsome and immediately they started talking she had felt so relaxed and at ease in his company, almost as if she had known him all her life.

After that first drink they often went out after a performance, sometimes with other cast members but more often than not, just the two of them and it wasn't long before she had realised it was more than just a friendship, she was very attracted to him. This was the romance she hadn't been looking for, but when it came she hadn't been able to and didn't want to stop the intensity of the feelings she had for Robert, and it soon became clear the feelings were mutual.

She had been in a trance remembering the audition and suddenly came to when she heard Robert's key in the door. He walked into the room and she smiled. If she hadn't decided to attend the audition at the last minute her life would have been very different.

10

Several times recently Nick's mum had asked him when they were going to meet Kate, his girlfriend! Yes, she was a girl and yes, she was a friend and they enjoyed sex but their relationship was very casual which suited them both. Nick knew his mum and dad were old fashioned and they wouldn't understand this kind of relationship. He also knew his mum was keen to become a grandmother and laughing to himself he thought he would let Robert and Eva fulfil that desire.

Nick knew Kate wasn't eager to meet his parents, she felt that implied they were a serious couple and they both knew they weren't, so he had a plan. It was Saturday morning and they both had the weekend off. He had just finished a phone call to Kate suggesting that they meet up with some friends and she was keen on that idea, but he avoided telling her that on the way home they would visit his parents. He would tell her at the last minute and if she really didn't want to meet them he would accept that and drive passed the house, but he was sure that wouldn't happen.

With a sigh Nick put his feet up on the sofa to relax for half an hour before he picked up Kate. This relationship with Kate was all he needed right now. His life so far had gone as planned and he began to look back at all he had achieved.

Nick knew he was lucky, he had absorbed everything he was taught at school and passing exams proved to be easy. When other children had got in a state about forthcoming exams he had just become excited, it was another step towards his final goal. When he left school he proudly took up his place at Oxford University much to his parents' delight. After studying medicine for six enjoyable years, he left with a degree and an additional undergraduate BSc. He was nearly always top of the class without even trying.

Nick smiled when he thought about his time at university. He had enjoyed the company of friends both male and female and he reckoned he had been popular. He had very soon realised that it was mainly because he could tell a good story which was usually very much embellished. He found he could easily capture and keep the attention of his audience, whether the tales he told were true he knew was often a topic for discussion amongst his friends, he liked to keep them guessing. He remembers the feeling of being in front of an audience, his fellow students, and how he felt like a showman constantly acting, even he sometimes began to wonder who the real Nick was!

As he relaxed into the sofa, his eyes closed and he turned his thoughts to the relationships he had with women during his university years. He wanted and at times needed female company but he was never looking for a long term relationship. He had imagined that when he went to university this could become awkward so he made the decision to look for female company away from the campus. He wanted 'Friends with Benefits' (FWB), no commitment. Some of his 'girl friends' were unaware of this until it was too late and he had walked away. The strange thing was, he had always felt guilty but he knew he had to stay in control and it was what he wanted at that time.

Moving on with his thoughts he reminded himself of how much fun the Graduation Party had been. A lot of alcohol was drunk if his memory was correct. At this stage his life had been going as planned and this continued when he was successful in securing a post as a junior doctor within a local community hospital. Reflecting on those first 3 years as a doctor he recalls the excitement of actually becoming a doctor and then the realisation of the hard work involved. Also the times of feeling utterly exhausted but now, looking back, he remembers mainly enjoying every minute of the work and play!

The Dinner Date

After 3 years he had decided it was time for the next stage of his career. To gain more varied experience he moved on to join staff at a hospital providing acute medical and surgical services. He clearly remembers that when he had joined this hospital he was looking forward to the professional challenges that lay ahead but he had also been keen to start the next stage of his personal life. He had been quietly confident that with his good looks and friendly manner he would soon have single nurses, and sometimes married nurses, interested in him and he hadn't been wrong. But for Nick the challenge had begun! As he sat in his flat he was thinking that he was definitely a 'planner'. Nothing in his life so far had just happened, he had carefully planned it and executed each plan successfully and this had been very much the case when he met Kate.

He had not been interested in any woman that would flirt with him expecting to be asked out. That wasn't for him. He wanted to find a woman who was attractive, intelligent and showed little or no interest in him other than polite friendliness. Then he could work on winning her around. He knew it had been a bit like game for him, a challenge which he had risen to. It hadn't taken him long before he realised he had found the right girl in a pretty petite nurse in her second year of nursing.

Kate had always been pleasant to him but treated him purely as a male colleague and nothing more. Slowly but surely, in his gentle persuasive way, he had set to work to win her round and smiling to himself he recalls how his tactics had worked and Kate had accepted his invitation to have a drink after work one evening. He had noticed that she soon relaxed in his company and he found her to be gentle, kind and funny. This was just what he had wanted and he knew it would work, for a time.

They had been just good friends at first but naturally had progressed to become romantically involved on a very casual basis. They both liked their own space. Nick needed Kate, she was his smokescreen. Now in his 30s he was tired of people, including his own family, asking him if he had a partner or when was he going to get married and have a family.

Bringing his mind back to the present he knew why Kate had not been keen to meet his family. She had thought it might give them the idea that marriage and children would follow and it wouldn't, well not with her anyway. Kate had explained to him that she didn't want marriage or children, she was a career girl. Nick felt the same about the relationship but for a different reason, he was scared of becoming too involved and being rejected. Kate agreed for Nick's sake that she would, at some point, meet his mum and dad. Today he felt presented a good opportunity to introduce her to his parents, mainly to stop his mum asking if he had a girlfriend, and Robert teasing him that he would end his days a lonely old bachelor.

Nick was brought out of his reminiscing when he heard a text message had come through on his phone. It was Kate asking if he was on his way. He was surprised when he looked at the time, that half hour had gone so quickly while he was emersed in his memories. He grabbed his car keys and went to pick up Kate.

It was late Saturday afternoon when the introductions took place. After spending time with their friends Nick casually drove passed his parents' house and raised the question, 'Kate do you mind if we stop by at mum and dad's. I've got a photography magazine for dad. We could then get the introductions over with and not have to stay too long. You don't mind do you?'

'I'm not dressed to meet your folks,' Kate said pausing. 'Did you plan this?'

Nick hesitated. 'Well yes, I suppose I did. Mum has been nagging me for ages to bring you around for a meal. I thought

The Dinner Date

if we dropped in on passing we could have the excuse that we are going out with friends later this evening.'

'Okay, I suppose that's a good idea,' Kate agreed.

Parking the car in the drive they made their way to the front door and as expected Jill was delighted to meet Kate although a little annoyed at Nick for not telling her they were going to visit.

'How lovely to meet you at last Kate. I was beginning to think you didn't exist. Come on in. Sorry about the state of the place and me, I'm in the middle of gardening. Stephen,' she shouted, 'We have a guest. I'll stick the kettle on, tea or coffee.'

'Coffee would be great, thank you. You have a lovely house Jill,' Kate said looking around.

'Thank you. It's been a great family home hasn't it Nick. Although I do sometimes think it's now a bit big for just the two of us. Ah, here's Stephen.'

Introductions were made and then they took their coffee into the conservatory where Jill tried to find out a bit more about Kate but as always she gave very little away, a trait she shared with Nick.

'Your garden is beautiful,' Kate enthused, 'I bet it takes a lot of work.'

'Yes it does. I enjoy gardening but I have to confess we do also have a gardener to help out.' Suddenly they heard footsteps coming round the side of the house. Jill knew immediately it would be Robert but was surprised and delighted to see Eva with him.

'Robert, Eva how lovely. What good timing, you can meet Kate.'

'Hi everyone. I did ring the bell but when there was no answer I guessed you would be in the conservatory. Hi Kate, lovely to meet you at last. This is Eva, my wife,' Robert said turning to Eva grinning.

'Hello Kate,' Eva said smiling.

49

'Robert, Eva do you want coffee,' Jill asked.

'It's okay mum I will make some coffee. Anyone want a refill?' Robert asked.

Robert made a coffee for Eva and himself and then rejoined his family and Kate in the conservatory. He took in Kate's appearance. She was small, smaller than Eva with petite features showing off her beautiful soft brown eyes. Not really the type of girl Robert envisaged Nick going out with.

Jill, always sensitive to other people's feelings, felt it was a little overwhelming to all be sitting around with a newcomer amongst them so she suggested that she and Eva show Kate the garden. 'We could walk down to the woodland and stream leaving the men to discuss football,' she suggested. With relief Kate thought this was an excellent idea and said, 'That sounds lovely I would love to see the garden and woodland.'

The three of them walked across the garden down to the bench and sat down. Kate looked around and said, 'This is so pretty, very secluded. You are very lucky to have this as part of your garden.'

'It's why we bought the house years ago. Somewhere so peaceful to come and sit after a hard day at work. Stephen and I never forget how lucky we are.'

They sat in silence for a while enjoying the peace and quiet and then Jill asked, 'So Kate, is nursing something you have always wanted to do?' And then continued, 'Sorry Kate that's something you are probably always being asked, I know I'm always asked the same question about being a doctor.'

'That's okay,' Kate replied, 'Yes I've never wanted to do anything else. I would like to work my way up to the top of my profession and eventually lead a team of highly trained expert nurses working with children with very complex needs.'

The Dinner Date

Jill was taken aback and somewhat surprised at someone so young knowing exactly the way they wanted their career to go. 'That's a very definite answer. What's your reason behind choosing that path?'

'It's a personal reason. I only had one sibling, Becky. She was amazing but not strong and was very often ill. She had very complex medical needs. Becky was younger than me and I saw in her such determination which inspired me and nurtured the desire in me to follow the career path I have chosen. Sadly she died far too young.'

There was a brief spell of silence and then Kate said, 'Very different to your career, Eva. I have watched clips of you dancing and you are amazing.'

'Thank you Kate, but I think you are more amazing taking on the role you have chosen,' and laughing she continued, 'And brave taking on Nick, good luck with that one.' Jill looked at Eva and smiled knowing she was right. 'Kate, next time I'm in a show perhaps you could persuade Nick to bring you along. We could go out for a meal afterwards,' Eva said.

'I think that's an excellent idea,' Jill added, 'we could make it a family occasion.'

They changed the subject and Jill and Eva tried to get to know Kate a little bit more but without much success. A short time later they heard Nick calling to Kate and saying it was time they left. They made their way slowly back through the garden, Jill having sensed that Kate's relationship with Nick was not in any way serious.

As they were leaving, Robert suggested that the four of them go out for a meal sometime. Nick agreed it would be a good idea but deep down he didn't really think so and nothing was ever arranged. Nick's decision.

11

Eva sat alone in the studio adjacent to the theatre where she was performing in a show. She had been looking forward to a short break from dancing to recharge her batteries when a friend of Robert's had tentatively enquired if Eva was in a show at the moment. He explained that one of his dancers in his current show had been rushed to hospital with an appendicitis. The part she was playing was only a small part but still important in the show and he wondered if Eva was available would she be interested in helping out. He seemed to remember that Eva had been in the same show a couple of years ago. He also explained there were only three more shows left. Robert asked Eva and slightly reluctantly she said yes. She couldn't refuse someone who needed help.

That was how she came to be in the studio near to the theatre where she had pre-booked a time slot so she could do a short warm up session. She stared at her image in the mirror willing all thoughts to leave her mind, ready to absorb the music which was about to play. When the music began, she gracefully stood up to begin her warming up session. She moved her elegant long limbs and noticed how much taller she felt than her 5' 5" which was considered small in stature for a dancer. Effortlessly she danced around the studio watching and correcting any wrong movements and postures. When the music stopped playing, she sank to the floor, warmed up and relaxed. She sat cross legged again and as she stared at her reflection in the mirror she noticed she looked different. Her whole body had come alive.

As she sat relaxing she thought of the evening ahead of her. Once she had agreed to do this show an idea had come to her. Robert was working away so there was no reason to rush home and she wondered if Kate would like to come to the

The Dinner Date

show as her guest and then they could go out for a meal, just the two of them. Eva remembered that Kate had said that she would love to see her in a show and it was something that Nick was supposed to arrange but he never had. This would be the ideal opportunity for Eva to get to know Kate without Nick around. She didn't have a contact number for Kate and neither did Robert and she didn't want to ask Nick. She thought he wouldn't be keen to share this information, he was very secretive about Kate and didn't talk about her or their relationship. In fact when she thought about it he seldom mentioned Kate unless someone asked about her. The only way she could get Kate's number was to ring the hospital and leave a message asking Kate to contact her which was exactly what happened.

Kate had seemed pleased with the invitation and luckily was not working this evening so Eva left a complementary ticket at the ticket office and had arranged to meet Kate in the foyer after the performance. She was looking forward to spending some time with Kate.

Eva collected her belongings and left the Studio making her way to the theatre. She walked up the shallow steps to the front door. It didn't matter how big or small the theatre was, she just loved walking into the foyer. The expectation of what was to come always produced butterflies in her stomach, and she loved the tantalising unique smell of each theatre. She walked through the foyer to the door leading backstage and pulled it open and as she walked through her excitement, as always, increased.

She made her way to her small dressing room hoping to relax before her performance. This would not be easy she knew once her fellow cast members started to arrive they would seek her out. She didn't mind, their company was always welcome.

'Your performance last night was outstanding Eva,' Jilly commented popping her head into Eva's dressing room. 'I think you're getting the hang of this dancing,' she continued grinning.

Eva laughed. 'I only look good because I have amazing dancers around me,' and then Eva could hear the banter starting in the larger dressing room next door. 'Katie, you were just amazing,' Jeannie quipped. 'Sandy your performance was the best yet,' Lilly commented. And then it got silly. Everyone outdoing each other with praise until they all started to giggle, slightly out of control. Eva laughing sensed they were all in good form this evening, it would be a good show.

The time for the start of the performance drew near and there was an excited buzz in the dressing rooms. Eva's hair was swept up into a neat bun and she carefully applied her make-up. Finally, she stepped into her costume and she was ready to begin her performance. As she waited in the wings she began to get incredibly nervous. She knew the build-up of nerves was all part of the performance and had learnt to welcome it.

'Are you ready Eva,' Jack the Stage Manager asked as he stood arm raised.

'Yes Jack,' she replied and he gave her the cue to enter the stage. When she stepped onto the stage and started to dance the nerves flew away and the enchanting performance took place.

After the show she quickly changed and made her way to meet Kate. A little bit of Eva did wonder if Kate would turn up, but she did and was sitting in the foyer waiting for her. Kate smiled when she saw Eva and immediately stood up. Eva noticed that Kate seemed a little nervous but then again she felt nervous, after all she hadn't told Nick she had invited Kate.

'Well, did you enjoy the show?' Eva asked.

'It was brilliant and this is a real treat, thank you for asking me. I can't believe I'm going for a meal with a 'celeb,'' she said laughing.

'I'm only a 'celeb' in the theatre world. People of a certain age wouldn't even know me, I've not been on Love Island and I don't do Tik Tok,' she replied laughing. 'Come on let's go, I've booked a table in a restaurant just around the corner. It's not a very posh restaurant but I've heard they serve good food.'

Over the meal they chatted about all sorts of things and Eva soon warmed to Kate and saw what a lovely natural person she was. It was now that Eva had to be really honest with herself, she wanted, through Kate, to try and know and possibly understand a little bit more about Nick. She had always thought he was such a complex person. He gave the impression of being easy going and full of fun but sometimes she would catch his face darken when he thought no one was watching him as if he held a secret or perhaps a desire. She had no idea what that could be and concluded she was probably imagining it. By spending some time with Kate she had wondered if she could gleam a better insight into Nick as a person but it turned out she couldn't. Kate enthused about the show but when Eva steered the conversation towards Nick, Kate carefully changed the subject and talked about her work which to be fair Eva found very interesting. So, by the end of the evening Eva had not learned anything new about Nick or if their relationship was serious. He was still a bit of a mystery to her. Oh well she thought, she had tried. It had been a nice evening and she found Kate very easy to get on with and she hoped that Nick and Kate would stay together but she very much doubted it.

12

Eva constantly surprised Robert. She would be so confident when rehearsing, making decisions about the choreography and the actual performance, but away from her comfort zone she could be quite anxious and unsure of herself. One weekend when they were having a well-deserved lie in after a hectic week for both of them that proved to be the case. They had just engaged in gentle lovemaking and Eva was snuggled up to Robert, feeling warm and safe in his arms. These were the best times, she thought. She sighed wishing she could capture this feeling and take it with her tomorrow. Robert commented on her sigh.

'What's the sigh for? Is it a good sigh, one of contentment or is there something wrong,' he asked slightly concerned.

She looked up and smiled at him. Robert was so sensitive to her feelings. He could always tell when something was bothering her. She hesitated for a brief moment and then confessed.

'I've got a photo shoot tomorrow and I hate doing them. I am so self-conscious. I hate having my photo taken.'

Robert sat up and looked at her in disbelief.

'But you are so beautiful, why would you hate having your photo taken? Your whole career is about being on stage with everyone's eyes on you.'

He lay back down and she snuggled into his arms.

'That's different,' she said, 'I don't see the audience when I'm dancing, there is just me and the music. I'm lost in a world of my own and completely unaware of anyone watching me. But a photo shoot is so static – everyone staring at me. I feel so self-conscious and strangely exposed.'

They lay for a while in silence, both with their own thoughts.

The Dinner Date

Eva's mind went back to when she had begun to mature into an extremely pretty young woman. She remembered walking into social gatherings causing all the men present to stop and stare in admiration, the women with envy. She was aware at the time of the impact she had on men and she hated it. Her personality didn't match her looks. She felt shy, nervous and self-conscious as she walked by the admiring males. Eva recalled she would fix her gaze on her destination looking neither left or right as she walked passed the appreciating glances. With time and experience she accepted the attention and would find herself shyly smiling, but she never enjoyed the effect she had on men. She also remembered it was different when she was whistled at from a moving vehicle, the attention passed quickly and she found it amusing. That thought made her smile!

Robert's thought took him back to the first time he saw Eva at the audition, dancing with such confidence. It wasn't long before he realised that away from performing Eva could sometimes be vulnerable and almost child-like. He brushed away a stray strand of soft blond hair and kissed her forehead.

'You must never feel self-conscious, you are who you are and always remember you are beautiful static or dancing and inside and out. Tomorrow, when the camera is pointing at you, imagine you are dancing across the stage. Hear your favourite music in your ears and let the power of imagination takeover and give you confidence. Every challenge you have in life you will overcome, I promise you.'

The following day arrived much too quickly for Eva. A car had been arranged to pick her up and take her to the studio. As Robert left for work, he gave her a huge hug. 'Good luck with your photo shoot, you will be fine, and I think, if you let yourself you will enjoy it,' he encouraged her.

She smiled but wasn't convinced that would happen. It was so quiet with Robert gone and Eva felt lost as she waited anxiously all alone in the flat. The car arrived and before long she was at the studio. With her hair and make-up completed, an outfit was selected for the photo shoot. She waited self-consciously while the lighting was arranged. Her thoughts went back to yesterday, snuggled up warm and safe in Robert's arms, and she remembered his wise words and did just what he had suggested. She could hear the music playing in her mind and she imagined herself dancing. Immediately she relaxed and the shoot began. This was the first time she had enjoyed having her photo taken. She couldn't bear to think what life would be like without Robert, he was her rock.

13

Robert and Eva were enjoying a few days together before Eva started rehearsals and Robert would be helping to co-ordinate a very unique production which he was very excited about. Robert left Eva in bed and made his way to the kitchen to make some tea after a slow very enjoyable sexual start to the day. His mobile rang and he saw it was Nick.

'Hi Nick, what can I do for you, everything okay?'

'Yep, I'm outside your flat, thought I would come and say hello.'

'Okay mate I'll let you in.'

'Hi Bro,' Nick said as he entered the flat, slapping his brother on the back.

'This is a nice surprise, not on duty today,' Robert asked.

'Later,' Nick replied.

'Sit down Nick, oh you already have,' Robert said, and continued, 'Get your feet off the coffee table,' he instructed laughing.

'Where's Eva?' Nick asked.

'She's just getting up, we had a lie in this morning.'

'Ooh nice,' he commented with a knowing wink.

And right on cue Eva walked in. 'Hi Nick, thought I heard your voice. It's lovely to see you but what have you come for, you usually want something,' she asked grinning.

'I just came to see my little brother but if you really want to invite me to lunch I wouldn't say no.'

'See, I knew you would want something.'

Robert and Eva looked at each other, they would have liked some time on their own but of course wouldn't say that to Nick. Eva was the first to speak. 'Of course Nick you are always welcome but isn't it about time you cooked for me and Robert instead of me cooking for you.'

'I will cook for you anytime,' he replied smiling at Eva, 'not so sure about Robert.'

'Nick, I love my wife,' and Robert turned to Eva, 'Don't you dare let him cook for you, we all know he can't cook and is likely to poison you.'

Laughing Eva said, 'I'll go and see what I can rustle up.'

And with that Nick went across and playfully hugged Eva, 'You are the best sister-in-law I have.'

The impromptu lunch ended up more of a brunch but satisfied their hunger needs. After they had eaten Robert enquired, 'What time are you on duty Nick?'

'Are you trying to get rid of me.'

'Yes, but also I didn't want you to be rushing to get to the hospital. You always seem to be rushing everywhere.'

'I know I do, you are quite right. I'm on-call from 6 pm onwards. It's a shift I particularly hate. It's too quiet for me, boring.'

'I'm sure you will find some pretty nurse to flirt with.' And with that a cushion was flung at Robert.

Nick didn't stay much longer but as he was leaving he turned to Eva and said, 'Don't forget we need to arrange when I can cook for you, it will probably end up being a take-away,' Nick said laughing.

Robert and Eva had enjoyed Nick's visit but were glad when he left. They wanted time on their own before their busy work schedules took over.

'I'm glad you and Nick get on so well, it means a lot to me and I know it does to mum and dad.'

She smiled, 'He's a tease but it's all so innocent. Why don't we go for a walk, I need some fresh air.'

'Great idea.' And that's what they did.

14

A couple of weeks later at his mum and dad's, Nick sat watching Robert and Eva throwing the ball to each other. Nigel, the Golden Retriever, was running frantically, desperate to catch the ball. His mum and dad were looking after Nigel for a friend and Robert had been instructed to 'tire him out' which at this moment looked like an almost impossible task.

'Come and help us Nick,' Robert pleaded.

Nick wouldn't join in. 'No thanks, I'm happy watching two adults behaving as kids.'

It was rare for him these days to feel like this but today he felt in a bad mood. Everything was annoying him and he felt angry but he didn't know why. Nick watched his mum and dad walk hand in hand down to the small stream at the bottom of the garden. They always seemed so content. It wasn't the same for him. As he watched his family once again he felt like the 'Cuckoo in the Nest.' He had been adopted and these people weren't really his family. He didn't know where he had come from or who his mother and father had been. Jill had told him he had been borne as a result of his biological mother having an affair. Her husband would only take her back if she had the new baby adopted, so for the sake of her other children she gave him away. He couldn't imagine how anyone could give their child away. Somewhere he had siblings, did they know about him? He would often wonder if he had sisters, brothers or both.

Jill had been watching Nick and was concerned he didn't seem his usual self. As they walked down to the stream she asked Stephen, 'Do you think Nick is okay? He looks very down and serious. I hope he isn't going to go into one of those awful black moods he used to have as an adolescent.'

'I wouldn't worry he's probably just had a bad few days at the hospital. He wouldn't be human if he didn't sometimes bring home with him some of the awful sights he's seen at work. Just let him relax watching his brother making a fool of himself. Robert has no ball skills whatsoever,' Stephen commented laughing.

It wasn't long before Nick decided he wanted to go home. He needed some time to himself to recharge his batteries for the coming week.

'Rob, I'm going to make a move and go home,' Nick shouted to Robert.

Robert stopped chasing Nigel and went over to Nick. 'Are you okay?

'Yes, I'm fine. It's just been a difficult week at the hospital and I need some time on my own.' Smiling he continued, 'Don't take it personally, it was fun watching you act like a kid again. Tell mum I will speak to her later.'

Laughing Robert said, 'Okay Nick, look after yourself,' and he rejoined Eva still throwing a ball to a dog with never ending energy.

Arriving home Nick opened the door and stepped inside. He threw his keys on the table and sat down looking around his flat. It was a nice flat, comfortable but sparsely furnished, very much a bachelor flat meeting his basic needs. He only had one framed photo on display which was of Robert and Eva on their wedding day. Eva looked amazing, a radiant bride. He had been so upset, and yes angry, that Robert had organised a surprise wedding for Eva. He had been looking forward to playing the role of best man at their wedding sometime in the future but it was not to be and he felt a bit cheated and deprived of that honour. But now that Eva was part of the family he felt lucky and privileged to be her brother-in-law.

He had been living in this flat for almost two years and it still didn't feel like home. He remembers his mum telling him

The Dinner Date

he needed to put some pictures up and buy some house plants. He had laughed at that suggestion. House plants! He was no horticulturists and although he was a doctor and used to trying to save patients he was more than capable of killing house plants. Kate had bought him several plants but after the death of the last one she had given up. Perhaps he should decorate, replacing the white walls with vibrant colours he thought, then again perhaps not!

Seeing Robert and Eva together always made him jealous. Like his mum and dad, Robert had found his soul mate. The difficult week at the hospital had taken its toll and the death of one particular patient was praying on his mind. He needed a distraction and immediately turned on the television. He sat down and stared at the screen not seeing or hearing anything at first, his thoughts elsewhere and then he heard the word adoption. He had no idea what programme or channel it was so he turned up the sound and then saw that a discussion was taking place on the correct age to tell a child they were adopted. According to the experts as soon as a child is old enough to understand, they should be told they were adopted. He wondered if he had been told at an earlier age would he have felt different. He listened to all the experts and then his mind began to revisit the time when his parents had shared with him the news that he was adopted.

He remembers the first five years of his life had been good. He had been happy and content. They did everything together as a family, his family. A smile broadened his face as he recalled how very spoilt he had been, the much-loved only child adored by his parents. The surprise arrival of his baby brother, Robert, changed all that in subtle ways. His mother, understandably with a tiny baby to care for, had less time for him. At just five years old Nick didn't understand why she had to spend so much time with this noisy, crying, red faced creature. He had felt rejected. Things improved as Robert grew up. Nick found he had someone to play with and to boss around but all the time he couldn't help but watch the way his mother looked at Robert. He was jealous of the strong bond she had with her youngest son but it wasn't until he was 10 years old that he knew why.

On this particular day he clearly remembers Robert was at his friend Thomas' house enjoying a 'play date' when his mum and dad informed him that they had something to tell him. With trepidation he had sat down and his mum had taken his hands in hers. Nick will always remember his mum seemed anxious but looked him straight in the eyes and told him how much they both loved him and then explained that they were not his birth parents and that they had adopted him as a tiny baby. He recalls at first not really understanding what she had told him and then realising that these two people he had always thought were his mum and dad weren't. He recollects looking from his mum to his dad not believing what his mum had just told him. He loved these two people it couldn't be true. Fear had gripped him, he didn't want another mum and dad he only wanted this mum and dad. Looking back he remembers crying and then he had started to become angry, shouting that his mum was lying. Etched in his memory is the face of his distressed mum as she went to him and wrapped her arms around him but he had pushed her away running out of the room passed his dad who had been watching uncertain what to do.

He had fled to his bedroom slamming the door behind him. After a few minutes his mum joined him and taking him into her arms had held him close. She told him how much they loved him and that they would always be his mum and dad. After a short while he had relaxed and then he had asked the most important question, was Robert also adopted. She had carefully tried to explain to him that Robert wasn't adopted but came as a lovely and unexpected surprise. She had turned his face towards her and looking straight into his eyes told him that he was very special because they had

The Dinner Date

chosen him. He knew that after that huge 'secret' had been revealed he never felt the same. He looked at himself differently often questioning did he take after his mother or his father.

He realised he had to shake himself out of this black mood, his experience had shown him that he could feel overwhelmed at times and he knew his jealousy towards his brother had recently been growing. Was it because Robert had everything, a successful career and a beautiful wife who Nick knew he adored. Nick struggled with his feelings, he wasn't content. He wasn't sure if it was the feeling of rejection or jealousy which hurt the most.

Nick had never told his mum and dad how he really felt, they thought he had accepted the news. He kept his true feelings and emotions well-hidden and had decided as a young adult, to develop a persona he could show to the world, one which was very different to how he really felt. That moment when he had been told he was adopted had had such a profound effect on his life that he believed he could never really trust anyone however much he wanted and needed to. It was then that he made the decision he would always be the one in control and he would never depend on anyone, financially or emotionally.

Returning to the discussion taking place he agreed with the experts, he should have been told sooner that he was adopted.

15

After finishing a short run of a show, Eva sat alone in the flat enjoying some free time when Robert texted her. He said he was in a meeting but had some good news for her and would phone shortly.

They seemed to have spent a lot of time apart recently which she knew was all part of their chosen careers but a part she disliked. Some mornings she would wake up on her own in their king-sized bed when Robert would be away directing or producing a show. She would reach over and feel the coldness of the empty space next to her. She missed the warmth and the comfort of his body. The bed had been one of the first pieces of furniture they had bought together for the flat, and to them at the time, the most important.

There were other times when she would wake up in a B & B or small hotel. These were the times when she was working too far away from home to commute. She hated being alone and away from Robert but the exhilaration and joy of performing made it bearable.

She waited eagerly for his call wondering what the good news could be. She didn't have to wait long and as soon as her phone sprang into life she answered it.

'Hi Rob, what's your good news? she asked excitedly.

'I've been approached by a new production company who are looking for an experienced director to stage a new show. I have accepted the job and have put your name down to audition along with the other dancers, if you are happy with that? I know you haven't anything else lined up at the moment. The audition is just a formality because I know you will be perfect for the lead female role.'

'Sounds good, tell me more.'

The Dinner Date

He explained, 'Initially it is to be trialled at a theatre in Cambridge which means we can commute from the flat in Oxford. Towards the end of rehearsals we could decide if we want to find accommodation nearer to the theatre for the 4 weeks of the performance. It won't matter what the accommodation is like as long as we are together.'

'That sounds great,' Eva said excitedly.

'Listen I've got to go. I'll see you later,' Robert said.

Eva's smile grew. She was now looking forward to the next few weeks, it would be fun working with Robert again. They were lucky not only were they a team in their personal life but also their professional life.

They both loved their chosen careers but hated the way it kept them apart. This new show was unexpected but welcomed. Any time together was so special, and they often spent the first few hours just being together and enjoying each other, both physically and emotionally. If their time apart had been an extended period, Eva always felt their renewed acquaintance felt like a first date, which made it all the more exciting. She was delighted that once again they would have the opportunity to work together allowing them to spend more quality time in each other's company.

It was during the second week of the run that Nick surprised them by going to see the show. He arrived just before the start and as he walked through the busy foyer he kept his eyes peeled. He didn't want to bump into Robert until after the performance, he wanted to keep it a surprise, a nice one he hoped. He quickly found his seat which was ten rows back from the stage and waited with bated breath for Eva to appear, anticipation and excitement rising in him. As she entered the stage he watched her intently. Nick was mesmerized by her and couldn't take his eyes away from her body moving across the stage as she confidently danced. Although it wasn't the first time he had seen her performing each time he was captivated by her. He smiled to himself realising that he didn't even see the other dancers. This was the reason he had come, Eva was so beautiful. It was at times like this that he felt so proud she was his sister-in-law.

After the performance he decided to go backstage to surprise them both. He walked with confidence and no-one questioned his motives. He could see Eva's dressing room which was clearly marked <u>Eva Brown.</u> As he approached the door to her room he could see it was very slightly ajar and he stood motionless, transfixed by what he saw. She was sitting in front of a mirror taking her stage make-up off. He watched her, almost holding his breath as he saw she had undressed and was in a flimsy dressing gown which let him see the shape of her naked body. He knew he should move, look away but he couldn't, he felt rooted to the spot. He just wanted to stand and watch her, feast on the sight before his eyes.

The sound of footsteps broke the spell and he quickly moved away from the door. He looked towards the sound and saw Robert approaching from the opposite corridor. He composed himself and moved forward to greet his brother.

'Hi Rob,' Nick said grinning at the surprise on Robert's face.

'I didn't expect to see you here Nick,' Robert said.

'I know, I thought I would surprise you and Eva,' Nick replied smiling.

'Well you did that. It's great you could come,' Robert said as he walked over and gave his brother a hug. 'What did you think of the show?'

'The show was great, I loved it. I came backstage to congratulate my sister-in-law, she was amazing,' Nick said smiling.

'Eva is always amazing. She will be delighted you came to watch the show. I'll just see if she is receiving visitors,' Robert said with a grin.

The Dinner Date

Robert knocked on his wife's dressing room door and stepped inside to make sure she was decent and said, 'Eva, you have a visitor, is it okay to let them in?'

'Yes, of course,' she answered carefully fastening her dressing gown.

'Nick, what a lovely surprise,' Eva said beaming.

Nick greeted her with a delicate kiss on each cheek.

'You were wonderful, you owned the stage.'

Nick saw a soft blush creep across her face and, embarrassed, she looked away. Robert noticed and stepped in and hugged his wife. He knew she always struggled with compliments, even if they were from her brother-in-law.

Nick continued to rave about the show, just about managing to keep his composure with the vision of the outline of Eva's naked body still vivid in his mind.

'Is Kate with you,' Eva asked.

'No, she couldn't get the time off work, as usual there was a shortage of nurses,' Nick replied. The truth was he had never asked her. He didn't want to watch Eva dancing when he was sitting next to Kate. It had been a good decision.

'Nick are you able to stay for something to eat, we could go to the Italian restaurant just round the corner. We know it's good we've used it a lot lately,' Robert said raising his eyebrows.

'Sounds good to me, I'll wait for you in the foyer.'

As Nick made his way to the foyer, Eva changed into a pair of jeans and a pale blue v-necked jumper, while Robert went off to find the executive producer to discuss a few minor changes which he thought were needed to enhance the show.

Standing in the foyer, Nick stood and watched with interest people coming and going, enjoying themselves at the theatre. He thought how different this was to his work environment where very distressed people needed support and care. They would reach out with hope, expecting the doctors and nurses to work magic and cure all ills, making them or their relatives well again. But of course they couldn't, not every time. The theatre and the hospital were two very different places; the theatre could lift spirits while the hospital often sadly shattered them he thought.

He wondered if he had made the right choice. Did he make this choice to please his parents, to make them proud, especially his mother. He sometimes had many doubts about his decision although he knew it wasn't all bad. The thanks and appreciation when a patient walked away cured and optimistic for the future was always exhilarating. On the other hand it could be devastating and hard to deal with when a cure was not possible. He had come to understand that all doctors had to deal with the successes and failures which sometimes seemed an impossible task.

He watched Robert and Eva as they emerged from backstage, hand in hand still looking like newlyweds and he appreciated how stunning Eva looked in her simple outfit. They walked to the Italian restaurant where the staff greeted Robert and Eva like old friends. They were quickly shown to a table in a small alcove and the waiter asked if they would like to order drinks. Before Nick could say anything, Robert had ordered a beer for himself and a small glass of red wine for Eva.

'Nick, what would you like to drink?'

'I will have a beer as well, thanks.'

As the waiter left to get their drinks Robert said as he picked up the menu, 'Now for the food. We could all be boring and just order pizza or, as it's a rare occasion that we are all together at a show, we could have their wonderful Spaghetti alla Carbonara. We can recommend it,' he said looking at his wife. 'What would you like, Nick?'

'That sounds great, I will go with your recommendation.'

With their choice of food decided Robert continued, 'It's great you could come and watch the show. I know finding the time is always a challenge for you.'

The Dinner Date

'I'm glad I could come but I wasn't keen on the star of the show. I thought her dancing was rubbish,' Nick said with a straight face.

'Yes, I agree,' Robert said, 'I think I will have to replace her.'

'Thanks for your support guys,' Eva said laughing.

'Now I'm going to be boring and ask how's work Nick?' Robert enquired.

'Busy as always,' Nick responded, 'the hospital is short staffed and the staff overworked. I don't think that will ever change.'

'Oh dear, let's change the subject. How's Fulham doing?' he asked with a grin.

'You know only too well that Fulham are struggling and your team, Chelsea FC are doing extremely well,' Nick laughed.

Robert turned to his wife and said, 'Okay Eva your turn to suggest a topic.'

Which she did, she asked about Kate. As nobody in the family knew much about Kate she tried to encourage Nick to talk about her, but it didn't work and instead Robert ended up talking about his passion, the theatre and different projects he had in mind. The evening was over far too quickly and soon they parted company and went their separate ways.

Later that evening in their digs Robert and Eva discussed how good it was to see Nick. Snuggled up to Robert, Eva commented on how each time they met up with Nick she felt she was able to get to know him a little better and she was even beginning to realise when he was teasing her. 'He has a good sense of humour and seems to be able to see the funny side of most situations. No wonder he is popular with patients and staff alike,' she commented.

'Yes,' Robert said laughing, 'he's a good raconteur, but I'm not always sure his stories are completely accurate. Not lies exactly but embellished tales.'

'I will bear that in mind when he next tells a story,' Eva said laughing as her eyes slowly started to close and she fell into a deep contented sleep.

Nick travelled back to his flat in Oxford. He got ready for bed, glad that he had made the journey to see Eva dancing. As he lay in bed his thoughts focused on her. He revisited in every detail the outline of her body in the flimsy dressing gown. He could feel himself becoming aroused and then his phone rang. He looked across at his phone on the bedside table and he saw it was Kate but he couldn't answer it, not the way he was feeling. He let it ring and then as soon as it stopped, he switched the phone to silent and then resumed his thoughts about the evening before he fell into slightly erotic dreams.

16

One morning Nick sat in his flat considering an idea that had started to develop in his mind. He would love a weekend away to relax and have some fun and he knew just the two people he would like to share this weekend with, Robert and Eva. He wondered if, and when, the three of them would be available at the same time. He looked at his work schedule and decided that he would call Robert, the sooner they had some dates the better. The call went to voicemail. He left a message asking Robert to call him and added 'No Urgency' then he deleted the message. There was an urgency he needed some dates. He left a second message asking Robert to call as soon as possible. He knew it would be a miracle if they all had a weekend free at the same time but it was worth a try.

It was later that evening when Robert was sitting with Eva that he suddenly remembered Nick's voicemail. 'I completely forgot Nick called, I had better give him a call back. I hope nothing is wrong,' he said to Eva. Picking up his mobile he phoned Nick's number. He was just beginning to think it would go to voicemail when Nick answered.

'Hi Rob.'

'Hi Nick, sorry I forgot you called, are you okay?'

'Yes I'm fine. I just had a thought, I fancy a weekend away somewhere. I really need a break from the hospital, it has been very intense lately. I was wondering if you and Eva have any free weekends coming up. It would be great for the three of us,' he paused before proceeding, 'or possibly four if Kate is available, to get away somewhere and have a bit of fun. What do you think, are you interested?

Robert was a bit surprised but as soon as the seed was planted he thought it would be an excellent idea. 'That sounds good to me. I will get together with Eva and as soon as I have some dates I will get back to you, is that okay?'

'Yes, that's okay, but if you could let me know as soon as possible and I can see what I can arrange. I have an idea.'

'Would you care to share that with me,' Robert asked, his curiosity fuelled.

'No', Nick said laughing, 'You always were impatient as a child. If we can organise some dates I promise you, you will like what I have in mind. Get back to me as soon as you can.'

'Will do,' Robert replied and hung up.

'What did Nick want,' Eva asked.

'He was suggesting that we join him and possibly Kate on a weekend away. He said he needs a break and would love to spend some time with us. What do you think?'

'Yes sounds great. Where was he thinking of?'

'He wouldn't say but assured me we would enjoy it!' Robert said with a smile and continued, 'Let's look at our schedules and see what weekends we both have available. Nick wants to know as soon as possible.'

The next day Robert texted Nick and asked him to call as soon as he had time. Once Nick had a break between seeing patients he called Robert.

'Hi Rob, have you got some dates for me?'

'Yes. Eva has got rehearsals for a new show in just over two weeks' time so the following two weekends are free. I'm in the early stages of a proposed new play so I also have the next two weekends free. Is that any good for you and Kate or is it too soon? After that it could be quite difficult for both of us to find the time.'

'Next weekend I'm working but not the following weekend. Let me see what I can book and I will get back to you. Really looking forward to it.'

'So are we, but very curious to see what you have in mind. Speak to you later.'

The Dinner Date

Nick knew he could swap shifts the weekend after next, his colleague Tom owed him a favour. He sat back in his chair pleased his idea was coming together and he settled down to book the accommodation. He soon found there was one problem, everywhere seemed to be booked and then he remembered that one of his colleagues, Dr John Graham, owned a small cottage on the edge of the Forest of Dean. Nick recalled John had invited him to stay there anytime he felt in need of a break. He had explained that during the busy summer months the cottage was a holiday let but out of season it was nearly always left empty. That would be ideal Nick thought and contacted John. Fate was being kind to Nick as John explained that he had had a cancellation for that same weekend they all had free and the cottage was now available. Nick quickly booked it and then looked up to see what sort of things were available nearby. There was a Nature Reserve and also Puzzlewood, an enchanted woodland where Star Wars had been filmed. He remembered John saying there was a small craft centre in the forest run by volunteers. If none of these events inspired them they could just enjoy the peace and quiet of the forest.

Nick texted Robert confirming the weekend was booked.

Hi Rob, all booked for the weekend after next. I will pick you up Friday evening if that's okay. We will travel back late Sunday evening. Pack some outdoor clothes as well as something smart.

That evening Robert showed Eva the text.

'I wonder where we are going,' she said.

'We'll soon see. I hope it's not rock climbing or bungee jumping.'

'So do I,' Eva replied feeling a little bit anxious.

On Friday evening at 7pm Robert and Eva, as instructed by Nick, were sitting waiting for him.

'Nick's late as usual. I don't think my brother has ever been on time with the exception of work. No text so I guess he's on his way.'

'Yes, you two brothers are very different, you are a stickler for time and Nick is the opposite. Do you want a coffee while we wait?'

They sat drinking coffee and waiting. An hour later Nick arrived.

'Sorry I'm late. Come on let's go,' he said as he grabbed Eva's bag.

'Is Kate waiting in the car,' Eva asked.

'No, she couldn't make it, she had a family occasion she had to attend.'

'Oh that's a shame. Perhaps another time,' Eva suggested.'

Nick just smiled but didn't comment.

As they got in the car Robert asked, 'Nick, where are we going?'

'You will see, just trust me.'

'It will be the first time if I do,' Robert said with a laugh.

It took them longer than Nick had expected to arrive at their destination. The SAT NAV had directed them to all sorts of places, mostly dead ends but eventually they arrived at the cottage which was situated down a very narrow lane. At the end of the lane there was a small parking area with a narrow pathway leading to the front door of the cottage. The pretty cottage was very secluded with no neighbours nearby. They sat in the car looking out at almost complete darkness. 'Where have you brought us Nick?' Robert asked in a slightly worried tone.

Nick was also a bit concerned but he wasn't going to let his brother and Eva know. 'Don't worry it will look great in the day light, you will be impressed, but in the meantime I have brought a couple of torches to light the way, come on let's go and view the accommodation,' Nick said trying hard

The Dinner Date

to include a touch of excitement in his voice. 'I will leave the headlights of the car on full beam that should help while we walk down the path to the front door,' Nick explained.

John had warned Nick to take some torches but of course he had completely forgotten to mention it to Robert and the sum total of torches he had brought with him to share was two but of course they did have their phones.

'It's very isolated,' Robert commented looking round.

'Yes, it is. It will be great just for the weekend, peace and quiet and good company and then we can return back to civilisation,' Nick said trying very hard to be enthusiastic but a bit worried it might be just a bit too isolated.

They walked up the winding path to the front door of the cottage. Nick had been given the passcode and directions for the key safe which he found at the side of the cottage and soon they were entering their weekend accommodation. Robert quickly went round and switched on every light including the outside lights. They stood back and surveyed their accommodation. It was surprisingly spacious. The living area was large with an expanse of wooden floor leading to a large patio window. The patio was lit up and they could see a hot tub and table and chairs. There were two bedrooms next to each other with the bathroom opposite and down a small hallway they found the kitchen. Out of one of the bags Nick was carrying he produced a bottle of wine.

'Eva can you find some glasses. We can go outside and sit on the patio and listen to the silence,' Nick said grinning.

Eva searched through the cupboards in the kitchen and found some wine glasses which she carried on a tray to the patio where she joined the boys. Nick had already opened the bottle of wine and as soon as Eva brought the glasses he filled them and gave a toast, 'Here's to a fun and relaxing weekend with good company.'

Sitting back relaxing in the very comfortable patio chairs they agreed it was pleasant just sitting listening to the sounds of the forest, although Eva confessed she was a little scared of some of the noises.

'I think the hot tub can wait until tomorrow,' Robert said. Nick does this cottage come with food provided?'

'No, but don't worry I have brought essentials with me. We have breakfast catered for and tomorrow I have booked a table at a local restaurant that John recommended.'

'All sounds good to me,' Robert said looking at Eva who didn't seem quite so sure.

After chatting and finishing the bottle of wine Robert and Eva made their way to the larger of the bedrooms. Nick remained outside for a while longer enjoying the silence and looking forward to the next day.

Nick woke up early the next morning and, a bit like a child, he was eager and excited to get the day started. He very quietly, so as not to wake Robert and Eva, explored the cottage and came to the conclusion it was perfect for the weekend. He made himself a coffee and sat outside enjoying the peace and quiet while he read through the leaflets he had found in the cottage. It wasn't long before Robert and Eva joined him and together they enjoyed a simple breakfast outside.

'There are directions showing how to get to a small craft fair where they have workshops. It's run by volunteers and opens at 10 am until 5 pm depending on the weather. There are all sorts of crafts we can try,' Nick said.

'Nick, this is so not like you,' Robert said laughing.

'I know but sometimes it's good to try something new and you were always artistic at school. I don't know about Eva.'

'I'm just happy to be in this gorgeous peaceful location with my two favourite men,' Eva replied.

Smiling Robert said, 'It sounds like a good idea. I'm sure they will have some food there for lunch. If we come back mid-afternoon we can spend some time in the hot tub before we go out for our meal.'

The Dinner Date

'That's sorted then. What we mustn't do is forget or lose the map. I would imagine it could be easy to get lost in these woods,' Nick said.

Stepping outside they saw there was a large field opposite the front of the property but the rest of the cottage was surrounded by thick woodland. They found the pathway marked Forest of Dean and set off at a slow pace following the map down narrow tracks leading deeper into the forest. After 10 mins walking they reached a small clearing with a few tents and craft stalls. Eva was happy to browse the stalls while the boys went off in search of crafts they might want to try.

At lunch time Robert went to find Eva. He found her sitting with a 'teacher' absorbed in lace making. 'That looks good,' he said encouraging her. 'Nick and I have noticed the enticing smell of bacon cooking. It's making us very hungry. I'm going to queue for a bacon and egg sandwich which is made with homemade artisan bread. It looks and smells wonderful. Do you want one?'

'Yes please that sounds great. I will just finish this bit of lace making and I will come and join you outside.'

It wasn't long before they were sitting on the benches provided enjoying their sandwiches with the egg yolk slightly oozing out of the sides of the delicious homemade bread, and in Nick's case dribbling down the side of his face.

Robert teasing Nick said, 'Nick, you don't have to eat so quickly no one is going to steal your food.'

Nick replied laughing, 'I don't want to risk it, this is so nice.'

After finishing their coffees they went their separate ways to complete their chosen craft pursuits. By the end of the afternoon they had enjoyed trying pottery, albeit very messy, archery after creating an arrow and lastly Robert and Nick tried woodwork while Eva attempted basket weaving.

Eva, carrying the small basket she had made, went to find Robert. She was ready to go back to the cottage but he wasn't. 'I just want to finish what I'm doing. It's going to be a surprise for you,' he said grinning and added, 'it will be a surprise to me if it looks like anything recognisable.'

Nick joined them and said he was ready to walk back.

'That's good, Eva wants to go back so you can see her safely back to the cottage. As soon as I finish this *thing* I'm making I will follow you. If that's okay with you Nick?'

'Of course I would be delighted to escort Eva. I will leave a torch with you in case you need it on the way back. Come on Eva let's go and be the first in the hot tub.'

Slowly Nick and Eva made their way through the trees chatting, comfortable in each other's company. Nick teasing her as usual. It surprised them how quickly it started to get dark, the huge trees making it feel even darker. Eva suddenly heard a rustle in the undergrowth and focusing on where the sound had come from she saw a squirrel emerge seemingly at ease with these strangers sharing it's habitat. She kept perfectly still and quiet until it decided to scale a tree and then she turned round to Nick ready to complete the journey back to the cottage. She turned full circle. He wasn't there.

'Nick, where have you gone? She called his name, thinking he must have carried on down the path. There was no answer. She shouted again as loud as she could. No answer. She hoped he had realised she wasn't following him and would have turned back. She stayed still and waited, listening. No footsteps. Where the hell was he? She took out her phone and used the torch, shining it all around the area. No sign of Nick. Quickly she thought of her options – to turn around and try to find her way back to Robert although she realised she hadn't taken much notice of the route they had taken – to take the path which she guessed Nick had taken back to the cottage or to stay where she was and hope Nick came back for her which she was sure he would. After just a few minutes alone in the forest she began to get frightened. Rain clouds were forming and the darkness was drawing in. If she waited here surely Robert would take the same route back to the cottage, wouldn't he?

She started shouting for Nick. Still no answer. If Nick was playing a joke on her it wasn't funny. The sounds of the forest started to become exaggerated in her mind. She was scared, she was very scared. She had to get back to the cottage, it can't be far away. They had been walking for a while so she knew the cottage must be nearby but which direction. The panic rising in her was making her confused. She had lost sight of which direction she should go if she started walking. She noticed there were three paths and she had no idea which one to choose. Her heart was racing and her hands were beginning to shake. She gripped her phone tightly. Still no signal and she noticed that she had very little battery life left, which made her even more anxious knowing that if her phone died she would be left in complete darkness. She began to tremble. Small spots of rain started to fall, she could hear them gently tapping on the dried leaves on the floor of the forest. Then she heard a noise, was it footsteps? She had a terrifying feeling that she was being watched. Using the torch on her phone she kept turning around to light the forest making sure no one was behind her. A couple of times she dared to speak, 'Nick is that you. Are you playing a game with me? It's not funny Nick, I'm scared.' No answer. The minutes ticked away. She wanted to curl up in a ball and hide – hide from whatever was watching her. The panic was rising and her breath became laboured. She heard a twig snap and she turned quickly to where the sound was coming from terrified at what she might see.

'Eva, I thought you were behind me. I was talking to you and it wasn't until I asked you a question and there was no answer that I turned around and there was no sign of you. I retraced my footsteps as quickly as I could.'

'Nick,' she said running to him, the tears flowing. 'I was so scared, didn't you hear me shouting.'

'No I didn't hear a thing. Why didn't you follow me?'

'I stopped briefly to watch a squirrel and when I turned around you had disappeared. I was terrified. This forest is so scary in the dark. I was sure someone was watching me.'

Nick laughed. 'That would be your imagination playing tricks on you. I didn't see anyone. The cottage is only 5 minutes away down this small path but I know it all looks so different when the light is fading. I'm sorry you were so frightened but you are safe now with me. We can go and sit in the hot tub with a glass of wine. That will relax you.'

As she walked back down the path with Nick she realised how near she had been to the cottage and she began to feel such a fool. No doubt Nick would tell Robert and they would both laugh at her. She had been so scared and couldn't shake off the thought that someone had been watching her, had she imagined it? By the time Robert returned the rain had stopped and she was in the hot tub drinking a glass of red wine feeling relaxed but a little ashamed of being so scared.

'Hi Rob, are you coming to join me in the hot tub?' Eva asked.

'Of course but first I want to show you why I needed to stay a bit longer to finish the *thing* I was making for you.' As he walked over to Eva he took out of his pocket a small wooden carving. He held it up for her to see.

'Wow did you make that, it's lovely,' she said as he handed her a small wooden plaque with EVA carved into it.

'It's got a chain attached so you can hang it outside on your dressing room door. I confess I did need a bit of help with the letter 'A' but the 'E' and 'V' were easier. Do you like it?'

Laughing she replied, 'It's lovely, I will treasure it.'

It was at this moment that Nick emerged from his room dressed in his swimming trunks with a towel round his shoulders. 'I'm so looking forward to this hot tub, are you joining us Rob?'

'Can't wait, I will be back in a sec. Eva show Nick the wooden carving I made for you.'

And she did but Nick made very little comment as he stepped into the hot tub and lay back with his eyes closed. It wasn't until they were all sharing the hot tub that Nick mentioned to Robert what had happened.

'You know Rob, I would never let anything happen to Eva, she was safe with me.'

'I know you wouldn't Nick and so does Eva, don't you Eva?'

'Yes,' she whispered feeling embarrassed at being so scared. The minutes she had waited alone for Nick had seemed like hours.

Robert could see Eva's embarrassment and changed the subject. 'Is everyone looking forward to the meal this evening?' he asked and they all agreed they were.

Later on when Robert and Eva were getting dressed to go out Robert turned to Eva and said, 'How are you feeling now, are you okay?'

She looked across at him, 'No, I'm not. Please hold me Robert, I still feel so shaky inside. I need your big strong arms around me so I can feel safe again.'

As he held her in his arms he reminded her, 'Nick was only a short distance away from you and you know he would never let anything happen to you, you were safe,' he once again re-assured her. 'Standing there shining the torch you probably terrified all the woodland creatures that were watching. They were probably more frightened than you were,' he said laughing. 'Just put it out of your mind, tomorrow you will have forgotten how scared you were. We have a lovely evening to look forward to.'

'I feel calmer already just with you holding me. I love you so much.'

The table Nick had booked was in a quaint local pub a couple of miles away from the cottage. 'Is everyone hungry,' Nick asked as they walked through the door and the delicious smell of food hit their nostrils.

'Yes, I am,' Robert replied. How about you Eva?'

'Me too,' she replied. But it wasn't said with conviction and Robert was very aware that the episode in the forest that afternoon had really shaken her.

They were shown to their table and as the evening wore on Eva began to relax and enjoy the meal and the friendly atmosphere in the delightful pub. But she couldn't altogether shake off the feeling that someone had been watching her in the forest.

The meal was a success and the next morning they went for a short walk and Eva could see in daylight how near she had been to the cottage. She did wonder why Nick hadn't come back to her sooner but she realised the terror she felt alone in the forest had made the minutes feel like hours and Nick had 'rescued' her very quickly. The afternoon was spent in the hot tub and then they journeyed home. Robert thanked Nick for organising the short break and said how much he had enjoyed it. Eva agreed with him but with some reservations.

17

Eva sat in the flat she shared with Robert and looked around. It was so neat and tidy but quite small. She had never been particularly tidy, unlike Robert who was extremely tidy and house proud and had taught her well. It now came second nature to her to keep a tidy home. The flat consisted of a small hallway leading to the kitchen/diner on the left with the large lounge opposite. The largest bedroom was next to the kitchen/diner with a smaller bedroom alongside. On the opposite side of the hallway there was the bathroom/shower room which was next to the lounge where Eva was now sitting with her foot strapped and elevated. Once the rental of her own flat had ended she had moved in with Robert and with the permission of the landlord they had given the mustard-coloured walls several coatings of a shade of paint called warm white which gave the feeling of light and space.

She liked the flat and for the moment it was all they needed, a base where they could meet and be husband and wife! Once again she thought about the time spent apart, it was a challenge and something they both disliked about their lives but accepted it as an inevitable result of the careers they had chosen. She smiled when she remembered how they had discussed plans to make a change in the future but for now this was where they called home. She hadn't expected to spend so much time in the flat especially not on her own, but that all changed when she had the accident.

Eva's accident and subsequent injury was a nasty shock. It was her first accident as a dancer and what was so annoying to her was that it could so easily have been avoided. She had been asked by Andrew Packs, a director and good friend, if she would join the company for a short tour of a show that she had performed in previously. It meant she would be working with one of her favourite directors and she knew she couldn't refuse.

The show had already been running for 3 weeks when she started her warming up session on stage before the evening performance. As she turned, her foot slipped on some liquid which had been spilt causing her foot to bend over at a strange angle and pulling the muscle in her ankle. Eva realised immediately she had done some damage and cried out in pain. Everyone had rushed to her aid and one of the strong male cast members carried her to the first aid room. When the trained first aider saw that the ankle was swelling rapidly, ice was packed around it and Eva was carried to a waiting car to be taken to a nearby private hospital.

On arrival she was immediately attended to and taken for an X-ray. As she waited for the results she was resigned to the fact that it could be bad news. After only a few minutes the young male doctor returned and confirmed, 'I've had a look at the X-ray and you have sustained a bad sprain but not a break.' Eva was shocked when he continued, 'It will take at least 3 weeks to mend, but another 3 weeks minimum before you will be able to very slowly start dancing again.'

Kim, the Stage Manager, who had accompanied Eva to the hospital said, 'I am so sorry Eva, I don't know how the spillage had not been noticed. I can only think it happened a few seconds before you took to the stage. I will try and find out how it happened and most importantly who is responsible and didn't clear it up.'

'Kim, we can't undo what's happened. It's not the end of the world, and the injury will heal in time. It's just an annoying minor accident and certainly not your fault. I am sure no one will own up!'

Eva was taken back to the theatre and arrangements were made for her belongings to be collected and then she would be driven home to her flat for an unspecified period of rest.

The Dinner Date

The production finished in 3 weeks so she knew she would not be returning to the show.

When Robert had got a text to say that Eva had been injured while on stage, he thought the worst. He contacted Kim who was able to re-assure him that she was not badly hurt but had injured one of her two main assets as a dancer – her foot. Kim continued to explain, 'Eva has had an X-ray and it confirmed that she hasn't sustained a break but unfortunately has a bad sprain. She will need to rest at home for, at the very least, 3 weeks and then another 3-4 weeks before she can resume dancing, by then the show will have ended so Eva will be unable to return to her role. This enforced rest will give her time to slowly work at regaining the strength in her injured ankle, ready for her next role. We are all so sorry this has happened. We will try to find out who is responsible but of course it won't change anything.'

'Poor Eva, how is she taking it,' Robert asked?

'You know Eva, she is taking it all in her stride. No fuss, just resigned to what has happened but disappointed she will be letting people down.'

'Yes, that sounds like Eva, always thinking of other people and not herself. Is she on her way home now?'

'As soon as we can arrange a driver she will be on her way home. I'm so sorry Robert unfortunately accidents do sometimes happen.'

'Yes, I know. I will text her to call me. Thanks for letting me know.' He couldn't wait to hear Eva's voice and was so relieved when she did phone.

'Hi Robert, please don't worry, I'm okay and on my way home.'

'What bad luck, have you found out who spilt the liquid and didn't clear it up?'

'No, and I don't want to know, knowing will not change what has happened. Whoever did it will know and feel bad enough. I'm just so disappointed I'm letting the cast down.'

'Eva you are not letting anyone down. I'm more worried about how you will cope without dancing for at least 6 weeks.'

'I'll be okay, I have no choice. We can't undo what has happened.'

'No we can't,' he agreed and said he loved her and missed her and would see her at the weekend.

Eva had reassured Robert that she would be able to manage just fine on her own and said she couldn't wait to see him at the weekend which was only two days' away.

Robert made a quick call to his mum explaining what had happened and asking her if she could call Eva and as soon as she could she did just that. By then Eva had returned home and was surprised but delighted to hear from Jill.

'Eva, Robert's just told me about your accident. How's the ankle, very painful I'm sure.'

'Hi, Jill. Yes it is painful but I'm on very strong pain killers and they are helping although they are making me feel very tired.'

'Well that's a good thing, it will make you sit and rest your foot. Have you mastered the crutches yet?' she said laughing.'

'Still practicing but it's early days, I will get there,' Eva replied.

'Can Stephen and I do anything to help? What about cooking and shopping?'

'I should be fine until Robert comes home. I've not much appetite at the moment. I think the shock of the accident is just kicking in. I'm sure I will be fine. Don't worry about me.'

'Well if you do need anything just let us know even if it's just company you need. If I'm around I can always come over to see you.'

'That's kind Jill, thank you for the offer but I think I will be okay. I will enjoy some time on my own with my feet up, indulging in eating chocolates and watching soppy films. But it's lovely to know I have support if I need it. I'm very lucky to be part of your family.'

'We are lucky to have you have as our daughter-in-law. Take care and don't forget to call if you need us.' And with that she hung up and Eva was left alone feeling sorry for herself.

When Jill had ended the phone call she decided that she would call or at least text Eva every day. She knew Eva would hate to be confined to sitting around on her own. Robert always said Eva was like a butterfly, never still, flitting from one task to another. Jill also knew that Eva would hate to be a nuisance to anyone.

Late Friday night Robert let himself into the flat. He put his bag down and crept silently down the corridor. The bedroom door was ajar, and he peered in. Eva was sleeping peacefully. She looked more beautiful than ever. He never took her for granted and always realised how lucky he was to have her in his life!

He didn't want to wake her, so he grabbed a blanket from the chair in the bedroom and went into the lounge. He was so tired after the long drive home and soon fell asleep on the large very comfortable sofa. He had every intention of waking up early and taking his gorgeous wife breakfast in bed, but that didn't happen. He woke up to see Eva sitting in the armchair opposite, crutches by her side, just watching him. As his eyes and mind adapted to where he was, he saw she smiled and he got up and went to her, kissing her passionately.

He stepped back and she noticed the look of concern on his face. Reassuringly she said, 'I'm fine, I will master these crutches, probably just before I don't need them anymore,' she laughed.

Robert knew his wife and that the worst part for her was not the pain of the ankle but the fact that she would not be able to dance. She had very rarely had any time when she wasn't dancing, and the thought of several weeks sitting in a chair was not something she would be looking forward to. He knew he couldn't even take time off work to be with her. He would ask Nick, who lived a short distance away, to pop in occasionally to make sure she was okay. He was a good brother and Robert knew he would be delighted to help.

Their weekend consisted of watching several films they had always meant to watch. Robert went shopping and bought enough easy to cook supplies of food to last the week and then it was time for him to leave. He had decided to spend Sunday evening with Eva, meaning it would be a very early start on Monday morning. Eva put on a brave face when Robert was about to leave, but she really didn't want him to go.

'Don't worry about me, I will be fine.'

'I know you will, but I will still worry,' he said with a grin, 'I'm your husband and lover, it's my job to worry.'

She laughed and sent him on his way with a final hug. As soon as the door shut she realised how much she didn't want to be alone, she wasn't used to it. She was used to being part of a cast at work, constantly surrounded by people. She didn't know how she was going to cope with the loneliness. She realised how lucky she was to love and be loved, and to have Robert care about her so much. Lots of people weren't so lucky.

Robert hated to leave her on her own but he knew Nick would make sure she was okay. He hadn't told Eva that he was going to ask Nick to go and visit her. He thought it would be a nice surprise!

18

Eva had put on a brave face in front of Robert but after he had left and she sat alone in the flat she found it too quiet. Since moving in with Robert she had not had the chance to get to know her neighbours or to make friends, she had just been too busy and she guessed they had as well. She knew no-one close by and she felt very alone. Feeling sorry for herself she indulgently let tears stream down her face. After a while no more tears came and she slowly made her way to the bathroom where she splashed cold water on her face and pulled herself together. No good crying she thought, she couldn't change the situation so she would just have to learn to live with it for now!

With Robert's help and much practice over the weekend she had just about been able to hobble around with the aid of the crutches. She couldn't believe how difficult it was to use them. She had given Robert a quick basic cookery lesson and it turned out he was very good and enjoyed cooking. Robert learning to cook meant at least something good had come out of the accident, she thought smiling. Meals during the week were going to be ready meals which she would microwave, or something on toast. By the end of her enforced isolation she knew she would be longing for something more exciting to eat during the week.

Weekends would be different. Robert had said that he should be able to come home most weekends and spend some time helping Eva. The cast and crew of the show were very experienced and unless a 'crisis' developed the show should run smoothly without him. He felt confident he could let his Assistant Director take charge. So nothing for him to worry about he hoped.

No-one at the theatre had owned up to the spillage, but then again she knew they wouldn't! She was upset that she was forced to rest but philosophical, she would have to be patient and wait for the healing process to be completed. Robert would soon be back and then he could spoil her again. She was looking forward to that, but in the meantime she was getting steadily lonelier and very bored with her own company.

Later that day Jill called her. 'How are you? Did you have a good weekend with Robert. I hope he spoiled you.'

'I'm fine,' Eva lied. 'I've got everything I need except for two good feet,' she said laughing. 'Yes Robert did spoil me. He wouldn't let me lift a finger. I sat and supervised him cooking a meal and he told me he quite enjoyed learning how to cook.'

'Oh well done. I only ever managed to teach the boys a few very simple things just to get them by when they went to university. Neither boys were interested in the art of cooking. I think I spoiled them. How is your ankle?'

'Painful once the painkillers have worn off but I'm not complaining. I know with time it will get better.'

'Yes, it's early days yet. Do you need anything?'

'No thanks I've got everything I need. I'm going to spend most of the day reading a book that I bought ages ago and haven't had time to read.'

'That sounds like a good idea, with plenty of rest you will soon be back on two feet I'm sure. Don't forget I'm here if you need me, even if it's only someone to talk to.'

'Thanks Jill,' and with that she ended the call. She knew that with the help of her family she would get through this temporary period of loneliness and delight in her normal wonderful life when it returned. She couldn't wait and knew she was very lucky.

It was almost one week after the accident and Eva was starting to dislike her own company even more, when she heard a knock at the door. She gathered up her crutches and quite expertly made her way to answer the door. She looked through the peep hole and saw it was Nick. She guessed a neighbour must have let him through the main door. What a lovely surprise she thought. She opened the door grinning from ear to ear. It was so nice to see another person, especially Nick, her lovely brother-in-law.

Nick's first words were, 'Wow, you got to the door quickly, I expected to be waiting ages.'

Eva smiled with pleasure and did think about hugging Nick, but decided it was a bit difficult with crutches.

Eva's beauty always took Nick's breath away. To him she was perfect, and he knew that he was insanely jealous of Robert. But at least now she was family, and he could see her as often as he wanted – his beautiful sister-in-law.

'How lovely to have company,' she said with delight and turned very carefully to hobble back to the lounge.

Nick followed slowly behind and then offered to make them both some coffee. After a quick search he found everything he needed in the very tidy kitchen, which he knew was influenced by his almost obsessively tidy brother. He took the mugs of steaming coffee into the lounge where Eva was waiting with her injured ankle raised resting on a stool.

'Glad to see you are following doctor's orders,' Nick said as he placed her coffee on the small table near her chair before sitting opposite her.

The slightly tense atmosphere showed that they both felt a little awkward. This was the first time they had been alone together without Robert and it felt strange, there was something missing, but that feeling soon passed and they started to easily engage in conversation. Nick's charm soon kicked in and he started asking all the right questions to encourage Eva to talk about herself, which as he expected was all about dancing. That was fine with him, it had been her life so far. There were a few questions he wanted to ask her and he started by saying, 'Eva, do you get nervous when you are on stage?'

'Not so much when I'm on stage but just before I go on I'm so nervous, but it's nervous excitement and I know it will pass once I'm on stage and starting my dance routine.'

'There's something else I've always wanted to ask a dancer, do you ever forget the dance routine,' Nick enquired staring intently at Eva.

'Of course, we all do occasionally but I think every dancer has learnt to cover up and improvise if this does happen.' By the way Nick was staring at her Eva wasn't sure if he was really interested or even listening to the answer. She changed the subject and asked him a question.

'And here's something I've always wanted to ask you,' Eva said. 'Do you enjoy being a doctor? Was it something you always wanted to do?' Eva noticed there seemed to be quite a long pause and Nick had looked away breaking eye contact with her.

He looked back at her and said, 'Becoming a doctor was something I knew I had to do from an early age and,' he paused before continuing 'I don't regret it.'

Eva realised that Nick hadn't really answered the question but she decided not to ask him to explain although she was curious as to why he had said it was something he had to do instead of what he wanted to do.

Nick quickly changed the subject mentioning Robert's new show which as nearly always was a big success. After a while he reluctantly said he would have to leave, he was on duty at the hospital in a couple of hours. He stood up and walked over to Eva and kissed her on the cheek gently caressing her neck as he did so.

'Don't get up,' he said laughing, 'I will see myself out,' and, after returning the empty coffee cups to the kitchen, he called goodbye as he made his way to the front door and then

The Dinner Date

he was gone. Eva sat and thought what a kind gesture it was for Nick to visit her and couldn't wait to tell Robert.

As usual Robert phoned later that evening and asked, 'How was your day?'

'It was okay. Nick came to see me this afternoon, it was so lovely to see and talk to someone. I'm getting tired of talking to myself,' she said laughing. Did you know he was going to come round?'

'Yes, I asked him to keep an eye on you. I am so glad he managed to find the time, he's a good brother. Was he good company and didn't tease you too much?'

'Yes, he was good company and no he didn't tease me. We seemed to talk for ages, well thinking about it, I talked, he didn't say much. I guess that's what happens when you spend hours on your own and then you have someone to talk to, it becomes hard to stop. It made me think about how important interacting with other people is for mental health and wellbeing. We are so lucky to have each other and the jobs we do.'

Robert agreed, and after talking for a while Eva said, 'I'm going to have to move, my leg is aching. I need to take some more pain killers.'

'Oh poor you. I wish I was there to help but I soon will be. Love you,' Robert said feeling very guilty.

It was passed midnight and Eva lay in bed attempting to get to sleep. She had enjoyed Nick's company but something was bothering her, the way he had been looking at her. It had made her feel uncomfortable and she had noticed the way he had very slightly caressed her neck. She brushed these ridiculous thoughts from her mind; she was tired, her ankle was hurting and she couldn't sleep. She was making something out of nothing, and as she closed her eyes she thought of Robert.

19

After his visit to see Eva, Nick had decided he wanted to spend more time alone with his sister-in-law. He wanted to get to know Eva a little bit better and he felt that would be easier without Robert present. Well that was what he was convincing himself. He hadn't figured out yet when and how he would do this, that was until fate was kind to him. Things began to fall nicely into place and he could see a way he could make this happen. With Eva injured and resting at home and Robert working away all week and only returning home at weekends, he could call around to see Eva whenever he had time during the week. After all, he was just being the very helpful brother-in-law, checking that his sister-in-law was okay.

On his second visit he surprised Eva by texting her saying he was outside the door. She made her way very slowly to the door and pressed the button to let him in the main door while opening the door to her flat. Much to her surprise he was standing at the door beaming and holding a small bunch of roses.

'Hope these cheer you up,' he said. 'How are you, is the ankle any better?'

'These are lovely, thank you Nick. I'm struggling a bit. The ankle is still very painful.'

'Just as well you have a doctor in the house,' he said smiling. 'I can take a look at it. I will take the flowers into the kitchen while you make your way to the lounge.' With the roses in a large milk jug Nick made his way back to join Eva in the lounge. Seeing the look on her face he explained, 'I couldn't find anything else to put them in.'

'You didn't look Nick, there is a vase in the cupboard.'

The Dinner Date

'Okay I'm guilty, I didn't look properly,' he replied placing the flowers on the coffee table. 'Now let's take a look at your ankle.' With that he carefully put her leg on a small stool and undid the bandage. He started to gently caress her foot and then slowly started to move up towards her ankle. Although he was very gentle she flinched with the pain. He didn't stop but continued to stroke further up her leg almost to her thigh.

'Nick it's only the ankle that hurts,' Eva said feeling a little uncomfortable and confused.

He looked up at her and smiled. 'That's good but I was just checking that the pain hadn't extended further up the leg. If it had it could have indicated complications had started. If it's only the ankle that hurts then I suspect the bandage could have been too tight. I will re-bandage and then you can see if it feels any better.'

Nick very gently and expertly re-bandaged her ankle and then suggested, 'Why don't you walk around a bit and see how that feels while I make us some coffee.'

Eva cautiously walked around tentatively placing her foot on the floor. 'It feels much better thanks Nick,' she called to him, but was still wondering why he had slowly moved his hands nearly up to her thigh and then thinking about it his explanation made sense, after all he was a doctor.

Nick walked back into the room with two mugs of steaming coffee. Handing her the coffee he said, 'be careful it's very hot,' and smiling she took the mug thinking how kind and caring Nick was. Nick continued, 'See how your ankle feels over the next 24 hours. I'm happy to come back if you are still having problems. You might as well make use of having a doctor as a brother-in-law,' he said grinning.

As they sat drinking their coffees Eva decided to ask Nick a question that had been on her mind since their weekend away. 'Nick, why did it take you so long to realise I wasn't behind you when we were in the Forest of Dean. The Forest was so quiet surely you must have noticed that the sound of my footsteps had stopped?'

'I was talking away to you and it was only when I asked you a question and you didn't answer that I looked around and immediately retraced my footsteps to find you. I think I have already told you that, don't you believe me. Why would I leave you in the 'scary' forest on your own?' he said half laughing.

'I don't know why but you seemed to take ages to come back for me,' Eva commented and then remembered how scared she had felt and that memory still made her shiver.

'Well I'm sorry you were frightened but you should have had more faith in me, I wouldn't let any harm come to you. Let's just forget about it.'

'Okay,' she answered but knew that wouldn't be easy, she didn't believe his answer but didn't know why he would lie.

After drinking their coffees and remembering the rest of their weekend away the tension between them eased and Nick asked, 'Is there anything else I can do for you before I go?'

'I don't think so. Thanks again for the roses, they are lovely.'

'You are very welcome and don't forget if the ankle becomes more painful let me know. Don't get up, I will see myself out.' And with that he walked over and hugged Eva. 'Look after yourself.'

Eva heard the door close and as she sat thinking she pushed aside her irrational thoughts about Nick's behaviour and concentrated on how lucky she was to have Nick as her brother-in-law and good friend.

After a couple more brief visits giving his 'professional' opinion of her injury, Eva started to make good progress. It was on his fifth visit he suggested that the next evening he had off he could come and pick her up and take her out for a meal. Eva was delighted with his offer and gratefully accepted. To be away from the flat enjoying a meal with Nick

The Dinner Date

was a treat she was really looking forward to. Nick would let Robert know what he was doing and phoned him that evening. 'Hi, bruv, I just thought I better let you know I have asked your wife out on a date and she's accepted!'

'That's fine Nick, hope you both have a lovely time,' he replied laughing and continued, 'I'm sure she is delighted. She's so lonely and bored at home all alone. I feel so guilty I can't be with her. To know she is in your safe hands is great news.'

'I promise I will take good care of her,' Nick confirmed and after catching up on other family news they ended the call. Robert was pleased that Nick was looking after Eva, he could now relax knowing that she was in good hands. Nick had said the date would be on Wednesday, that was as long as Eva didn't have anything else planned – they had both laughed.

On Monday evening he phoned Eva and suggested that he pick her up on Wednesday, around 7 pm. She was excited and couldn't wait for Wednesday to arrive. He booked the table at a restaurant in a pub near to where he lived.

20

As Eva woke up on Wednesday morning she stretched her limbs briefly forgetting her injury until the pain of her ankle made her cry out. She lay back catching her breath and letting the pain subside while she searched her mind to remember what day it was. With her enforced break from working every day seemed the same. And then she smiled when she remembered it was Wednesday and she had a date! She was looking forward to stepping back into the outside world away from these four walls but she also felt a little nervous and she wasn't sure why. Perhaps it was because she hadn't spent much time alone with Nick and it would feel strange going out with him without Robert. It would be fine and an enjoyable evening she assured herself.

She sat up in bed and cautiously swung her legs over the side putting her good leg down first followed very carefully by her injured foot. She winced with the pain and quickly realised that she would have to rest with her leg up for most of the day just doing sporadic gentle exercises to keep the ankle flexible. She didn't want to take painkillers today. Nick had advised her that taking painkillers and alcohol was not a good idea and she did want to have a glass of wine this evening. She smiled to herself, she wasn't a great drinker but tonight a glass of wine with the meal would help to relax her. She didn't know why she felt anxious or was it just excitement?

After breakfast she placed the waterproof cover that Nick had brought her over her ankle and carefully took a refreshing shower, then she had the rest of the day to fill. Since she had been confined to the house she had become an avid reader, something that had never really interested her before. Jill had kindly given her several books, all psychological thrillers

The Dinner Date

which, at first she thought wouldn't interest her but now she was hooked. She sat and read until her phone interrupted her at an exciting stage in the book. She looked at the caller, it was Jill. She quickly answered it.

'Hi Eva, how are you today? Is your ankle any better?'

'Hi Jill, it's a bit sore today so I'm resting it and reading the latest novel you gave me. It's a bit scary but I'm hooked.'

Jill laughed. 'I'm glad you're enjoying the books.'

'Did you know I have a date tonight,' Eva said.

There was silence at the other end of the phone and then Jill asked, 'Oh is Robert home tonight?'

'No, it's not with Robert,' Eva said and laughing continued to explain, 'it's with Nick!'

'That's lovely, good old Nick looking after you. Where are you going?'

'Nick is taking me out for a meal, he thinks I need feeding with some proper food instead of a microwave meal. I don't know where we are going.'

'Nick will have chosen somewhere nice I'm sure. What are you going to wear? Have you decided?'

'I've no idea. I will have to rummage through my wardrobe to find something suitable to wear with my strapped up ankle.'

'Would you like help. I can come round after lunch.'

'Yes please that would be lovely, but only if you have time.'

'Yes I have, I will see you later, about 2 pm.'

'That's great, thank you,' and Eva ended the call. She noticed the time on her phone was 1pm and decided that she would make a sandwich before Jill came although she wasn't hungry. Sitting around all the time seemed to have made her appetite vanish, she hoped it would return this evening. Hobbling into the kitchen she huffed and puffed at the frustration of not being able to walk properly and then she chastised herself, she hadn't lost a limb, her injury would heal and she proceeded to make a cheese and pickle sandwich.

Jill arrived on time as always at 2pm.

'You look tired Eva.'

'It's all this hobbling around, it's exhausting. Using these crutches isn't easy.'

Jill smiled, as a doctor she knew only too well how difficult an injury, albeit minor, to a foot could be and how frustrating it could be trying to the use the crutches.

'I will have a rest before I go on my date. Follow me to the bedroom and you can search through my wardrobe.'

With Jill's help Eva tried on several outfits realising that long skirts were a trip hazard when worn with trainers and trousers were too long without wearing heels. Tops were fine, bottoms were the problem until Jill found a pair of black wide short length culottes pushed to the back of the wardrobe.

'How about these trousers matched with this white blouse. I can see you have some patterned black and white trainers which would be safe for you to walk in. Try it all on and see what it looks like.' And she did.

'Perfect,' Eva said. 'Well,' shrugging her shoulders, 'it's not the best outfit I have ever worn but it will be fine. Thank you so much for your help. Shall we have a coffee now?' Eva changed out of her perfect outfit and when they sat in the lounge drinking coffee she confessed, 'It will seem strange going out with Nick instead of Robert.'

'Nick's a good lad, he'll look after you. I'm so pleased he suggested taking you out and I bet Robert is. I'm sure you will have a lovely evening. Can I do anything else for you while I'm here?'

'No thanks, I'm fine.'

'Okay then I will leave you to have a rest. Just be careful this evening, we don't anything else to happen to you. I will see myself out. Enjoy your evening.'

The Dinner Date

And then once again Eva was alone wondering what sort of evening she would have with Nick. She was looking forward to it but with a small amount of niggling nervous apprehension which she didn't understand.

21

On Wednesday morning Nick woke up feeling a kind of childish excitement for the date with Eva. As the evening approached he tidied the flat, stepping back to view his work. He was pleased with what he saw.

He had carefully picked his clothes to look casual but slick, applying his favourite Hugo Boss aftershave and, viewing himself in the full-length mirror, he was satisfied with the way he looked. He then laughed at himself, was he trying to impress his sister-in-law, he already knew the answer to that question. He wanted Eva to enjoy a change of scenery and more importantly his company this evening.

He double checked he had placed the expensive bottle of red wine on the kitchen table with two glasses and then he was ready to collect his date. He hesitated for a few minutes wondering whether he should call Eva, just in case she had forgotten. But no she wouldn't forget it was an important occasion or perhaps it was more important to him than to her. He decided to send a text saying he was on his way and then closed the front door smiling to himself, he was going to enjoy this evening.

He picked the easier but longer route to Eva's flat and arrived at exactly 7pm. This was a first for him, he had never before arrived for a date on time and smiling to himself he knew how important this date with Eva was to him. By the time he arrived at her front door he realised his hands were sweating and he felt ridiculously nervous. Eva, still hobbling but now using only a stick, arrived at the door beaming with delight at seeing Nick.

'Are you ready to go Eva?' Nick asked looking her up and down which he couldn't help doing. She looked stunning in a simple white blouse and black trousers which he noticed she had sensibly teamed with a pair of patterned trainers. He also noticed she had slightly curled her long blonde hair which she was wearing loose. He could see she had made such an effort and it pleased him.

'Yes I'm ready to go. I hope I look okay. I have to wear these trainers, they are the only shoes that would fit over the support bandage around my foot.'

'You look lovely and smell delightful.'

'It's the perfume Rob gave me last Christmas, Paco Rabanne Fame, if you're interested,' she replied.

'I'm always interested in you Eva,' he replied with a grin. Which Eva thought was a strange thing to say and she noticed how nervous he looked which wasn't like Nick. So she wasn't the only one feeling nervous which pleased her.

They arrived at the pub in high spirits looking forward to a relaxing evening. During the short car journey they had soon become at ease in each other's company albeit a bit strange at first without Robert. Nick parked the car as near to the pub as he could, although Eva still had a short walk to the front door.

'Here is your number one outfit accessory,' he said laughing and handed her the walking stick. Nick knew it wasn't just any walking stick; it had been commissioned and bought by the cast and crew of the production company Eva had been part of when she had encountered her accident.

Eva took the walking stick from Nick recalling the day Andrew Packs, her friend and Director, had visited her one afternoon a couple of weeks ago. She had been delighted to see him and touched by, not only the walking stick, but the great thought that had been put into making the stick so personal. The beautiful walking stick had been specially hand carved with images of a dancer in various stages of dancing encircling the length of the stick. The dancer, of course, was Eva. If she had to have a walking stick for a short time, then she was proud to use this one.

As she took the stick Nick walked to her left side and, to steady Eva, he linked his arm in her arm. It felt so good, he thought. 'Take your time Eva, there's no hurry. Feel free to lean on me. Isn't that a song?'

'Don't you dare start singing,' Eva laughed, 'You are tone deaf.'

'Okay seeing as you asked nicely I won't sing. But I do mean it, please lean on me, I'm here to support you.'

When Nick had phoned to book the table in the restaurant, he had explained that his companion had an injured foot and would be using a walking stick. He suggested it might be a good idea if they were given a table away from other tables so she could have ample room to stretch her injured leg and, if necessary, raise the leg on a stool. This was a good excuse to have a table a bit more private away from other diners.

As soon as they arrived at the restaurant they were taken to a table in a bay window which looked out onto a garden with a small pond and water feature. Tables and chairs were arranged around the garden and looking at the view Eva thought how enjoyable it would be to sit out on a lovely summer evening. She made a note it was something she must do with Robert when they got the chance.

The inside of the restaurant was modern and bright and the walls were adorned with watercolour paintings of local scenes. All the paintings were by different local artists and had tickets on with the sale price. Eva would have enjoyed browsing through the artwork, but she knew that would be impossible with an injured foot. Another reason to come back with Robert when she was more mobile she thought.

Once they were settled in their seats the waiter brought the menus. Nick was pleased to notice that no-one seemed to pay them much attention although he guessed some people would have recognised Eva. Of course, Oxford was home to quite a few celebrities so it wasn't unusual to see a familiar face dining out.

The Dinner Date

They both ordered scallops for starters. Eva chose Confit Chicken for her main course while Nick went for the traditional Sirloin Steak. As they sat waiting for their first course Eva once again asked Nick if he enjoyed being a doctor. She was curious to see if his answer changed now they were more relaxed with each other.

'Most of the time,' he replied, 'but there are times when I wonder if I made the right career choice.'

Eva was so surprised by Nick's reply. She had always thought Nick was the perfect doctor, kind, caring and compassionate. 'I didn't expect that answer, Nick. You always appear to be so dedicated to your career and your patients. Would you consider changing careers,' she asked.

'It's a thought,' he replied, 'but not just yet, I have things I want to do first,' he replied.

Eva noticed he didn't seem to want to talk about his future plans and how he had quickly changed the subject. How mysterious she thought and wondered what he had in mind?

'This is lovely having the chance to take you out for dinner. I hope you are enjoying it as much as I am. I'm almost glad you injured your ankle,' Nick said grinning.

'Yes it's great to get out of the flat and have someone to talk to, even if that person is you!' she said laughing and continued, 'You know I don't mean that. You are like a brother to me and this is a real treat, thank you.'

'It's my pleasure and you are very welcome,' he replied.

It wasn't long before the waiter returned with their first course. They ate the delicious scallops with relish. As they waited for the main course Eva tried to steer the conversation towards when Nick and Robert were children, but Nick appeared reluctant to share much information about their childhood. The waiter brought the main course, and the conversation temporarily stopped while they enjoyed their chosen meals and finished off with desserts of Blackberry and Lemon baked Alaska. Both agreed it was one of the best meals they had enjoyed, and Nick finished off with, 'and excellent company.' When he made the comment he looked straight into her eyes. Was he coming on to her? Eva quickly looked away. For the first time that evening she felt a little uncomfortable with Nick. He noticed her reaction and immediately tried to lighten the moment. 'How lucky am I to have the privilege to be in the company of a *famous* dancer,' he said grinning. His comment made Eva smile and she once again relaxed.

She asked, 'What is Kate doing this evening?

Nick was able to say, very truthfully, that she was working.

'It would have been nice if she could have joined us. I like Kate, I think you are well matched,' but she saw he didn't comment.

Eva had noticed that during the meal Nick had drunk very little wine but of course he was doing the driving so it was understandable. Not being a great drinker she was conscious that as soon as her glass became nearly empty Nick tried to refill it and on several occasions was successful. He had got it down to a fine art. When she realised what he was doing she became careful and sipped the wine slowly, she didn't want to get drunk or even slightly tipsy, she never liked that feeling of being out of control. While they waited for their coffee to arrive, they turned their attention to the two watercolour paintings that were nearest to them.

'Which of these two paintings is your favourite,' Nick asked.

'It's hard to choose, they are both lovely.' After a short pause she continued, 'I think the painting depicting the pub's small pond and garden is exquisite, it is so lifelike, it makes me want to jump into the painting and sit relaxing in the garden.'

'Yes, I agree that's my favourite and for the same reason although the painting of the outside of the pub is equally as

The Dinner Date

good.' Nick made a mental note to return and buy Eva's favourite painting for her, and Robert.

After they had enjoyed an excellent cup of coffee after the meal Nick suggested they made their way home. As soon as they walked outside, or in Eva's case hobbled, she realised, as the air hit her, she did feel just a little tipsy so she held on to Nick's arm to steady herself.

Nick noticed and laughing he questioned her, 'You aren't a little bit drunk are you Mrs Brown?'

'No, of course not,' Eva answered, 'My ankle just feels a bit stiff after sitting in the chair for so long. Once I get moving I will be fine.'

'Oh of course that must be the reason why you are clinging on to me,' he replied grinning as they reached the car.

As the journey continued Eva noticed that they didn't appear to be driving to her flat. At first she thought she was mistaken, she was after all just slightly tipsy, but then she was sure they were going an alternative route and as the journey continued she began to feel a little confused by the detour and mentioned it to Nick.

'Nick, why are we going this way, it's not the way to my flat?'

He laughed and teased her, 'So you are not that drunk then. I need to pick up something from my flat.'

'What do you want to pick up?' Eva asked.

'Wait and see,' he replied.

She felt the effect of the alcohol was now making her even more relaxed and she closed her eyes. Suddenly she heard a noise and startled she opened her eyes. She was immediately confused but was aware that the car had stopped and the door was opening. Nick laughed at her confusion and explained she had fallen asleep. She smiled sleepily as Nick helped her out of the car. At first she didn't know where she was and then remembered Nick wanted to go to his flat. But why was he getting her out of the car?

When questioned Nick replied, 'I just want to show you something in the flat.' He knew it seemed a lame answer but she appeared to accept it and leaning on his arm she walked with him to the flat. They entered the flat and she sat down on the sofa while Nick went into the kitchen.

Eva had only been in Nick's flat once before and that was on the day he moved in. He had been happy to show both her and Robert around. She knew Robert had only been to the flat a couple more times since that day. Nick seemed to like to keep this space very private. She wondered if Kate ever stayed over but she didn't like to ask, it wasn't really any of her business although that didn't mean she wasn't curious. When she looked around the room there was nothing much to see, no feminine touches. It looked so empty with no pictures on the walls and only one photo of her and Robert's wedding day on a small bookcase. No photos of Jill and Stephen. That seemed strange to her. Perhaps he didn't like clutter or was the tidiness for her benefit? Was his intention always to bring her back here? She had so many questions and once again began to feel a little uncomfortable. She wanted to go home but she was too scared to tell Nick. Why was she scared? She didn't know. She knew she would be fine, she was with Nick, her lovely kind brother-in-law. She began to have the strange feeling that something was not quite right or perhaps she was imagining it and wondered if it was the effect of the wine she had drunk. She told herself to relax and she would be just fine.

In the kitchen Nick poured red wine into two small glasses, a full glass for Eva and half a glass for himself. He placed the glasses on a tray with a tiny wooden box and returned to where Eva was sitting. She looked up and was surprised to see he was carrying a tray.

'More wine?' she asked a bit confused.

The Dinner Date

He laughed, 'Just a small glass to finish off a lovely evening and a present for my favourite and only sister-in-law.'

He handed her the box. Surprised she opened it and inside there was a small pendant.

'It's a lucky crystal and now everything you wish for will come true,' Nick said smiling.

She laughed as she felt the beautiful softness of the pendant between her fingers. She had never believed in anything like this and when she looked up at Nick she realised that he was teasing her.

'You need something to give you good luck so you don't slip and hurt your foot again,' he said, 'we don't any more accidents.

Very silly but a sweet gesture she thought. 'Thank you, it's lovely.'

He carefully handed her the full glass of wine and picked up the half glass for himself. She made no comment and didn't seem to notice the difference.

'Here's to many more enjoyable evenings together,' and quickly added, 'with Robert and Kate,' and clinked glasses with Eva.

The full bodied deep rich red wine was the most beautiful wine she had ever tasted and Nick explained, 'A friend of mine has just bought a small vineyard and has started producing his own wine of which this bottle was out of one of the first batches.'

Eva watched him hold up the glass to the light as if he was a professional wine taster, it made her smile.

He continued, 'This was the real reason I have brought you back to the flat. My friend gave me a bottle to taste and asked me to give him my unbiased opinion. I couldn't take a bottle of wine into the pub so I thought I would bring you back here and we could taste it together. I knew that if I had suggested we came back here you would have said no, so I kidnapped you,' he said laughing. 'So, what do you think,' he asked. 'The more you taste it, the more the flavour develops in your mouth,' he said encouraging her to drink more.

After several more mouthfuls she confirmed, 'This is the most divine wine I have ever tasted.' She paused, her head spinning, 'Nick can you take me home, I'm so tired and I'm beginning to feel very sleepy.'

She didn't look sleepy to him or sound it but easily gave in when he picked her up and carefully carried her into the bedroom. 'Just rest here for a little while and then when you feel better I can take you home,' Nick said.

He gave her 5 minutes on her own and then went back in. She was still lying on the bed, eyes wide open, appearing to be conscious. He went over and carefully stroked her face and she smiled and looked into his eyes, but he knew she wasn't really seeing him. He kissed her gently on the lips and she didn't resist.

Sometime later as Nick made his way to the spare bedroom he looked in on Eva. She hadn't moved, she was still sleeping peacefully. As he curled up on the bed in the spare room he smiled, he had enjoyed his evening with Eva, very much!!

22

The next morning when Eva opened her eyes she saw it was daylight. She looked around. She didn't recognise the room. It wasn't her bedroom. She was in a strange double bed, alone. She slid her hand across the bed touching the empty space next to her. It was cold. Had there been anyone next to her? Where was she? She had no idea. She lay completely still and let her eyes search the room for any clues. There wasn't much in the room. Plain white fitted wardrobes adorned one wall and she noticed there was a single bedside table next to the bed. On the wall directly opposite the bed there was a painting of a sunset over a beautiful beach. She could see some clothes crumpled in the corner of the room but she couldn't make out what they were. She wondered if the clothes she saw on the floor belonged to her. But who had removed them. In panic she lifted the duvet and saw to her relief she wasn't naked. She had on her bra and pants but no outer clothing. She couldn't remember anything. How did she get here and where was she? As she tried to sit up she felt so weak and her arms felt sore. When she examined each arm she could see signs of bruising.

Looking across the room she caught sight of a very ornate walking stick, she knew it belonged to her and as she glanced back to the bedside table she noticed a crystal pendant lay discarded on the surface. The pendant triggered her memory. Nick gave it to her when he brought her back to his flat after their dinner date. Was this his flat, his bedroom. Panic started to rise in her. Was this his bed? What happened last night, what had she done? She doesn't remember anything after sitting with Nick when he gave her some more wine. Her mouth was dry, she could taste the stale effect of last night's alcohol. She felt scared. Where was Nick? She heard a noise and quickly shut her eyes and listened as footsteps approached her heart beginning to beat rapidly and echoing in her ears.

***

The next morning Nick got up early and made his way to the bathroom to have a shower, looking in on Eva as he passed the bedroom. She was still fast asleep. He would let her sleep while he took a shower. As he stood in the shower he let the water cascade over his body enjoying the sensation of the water cleansing and refreshing him. He finished showering and slowly dried himself smiling as he remembered the previous evening. He had really enjoyed his date with Eva. He dressed and then made coffee which he took into her. As he stood by the side of the bed he called her name and gently stroked her cheek. She looked so peaceful, so childlike.

'Eva, wake up sleepy head I've brought you some coffee.'

Her eyes slowly opened and she stared at him looking frightened and bewildered.

She asked, 'Nick, where am I.'

'You are in my flat. Don't you remember we came back here after our date,' Nick replied laughing.

'I'm so confused, I don't remember what happened last night. Did you put me in this bed and why didn't you take me home?'

Nick sat down on the side of the bed. Laughing he said, 'Eva you were so drunk last night. One minute you seemed sober and the next you were saying things you shouldn't have said.' He stared intently at her as he continued, 'I managed to resist you but it wasn't easy.' He grinned that annoyingly charming way he had perfected but this time his eyes weren't laughing and full of fun, they were cold and secretive. 'I decided you needed a strong coffee to sober you up so I went into the kitchen to make the coffee. That's when I heard you singing loudly and then there was silence. When I walked

The Dinner Date

back into the lounge with the coffee you were curled up on the sofa fast asleep. I can't believe you don't remember any of that. I carried you into my bedroom and put you to bed. Don't worry,' he said laughing and raising his hand 'I slept in the spare bedroom. Don't you remember any of that? Before you fell asleep you insisted singing, several times "Padam Padam". A very drunken version of it.'

'I don't remember any of that,' she said struggling to sit up.

'Here, let me help you,' Nick offered putting the coffee cup on the bedside table. He gently pulled her forward placing several pillows behind her back. As he touched her she could feel he shivered slightly.

Very gently he started to question her, asking, 'Do you remember going for a meal?'

Slowly the memory of the pub restaurant started to come back to her. 'Yes, I think I do.'

'It was a very enjoyable meal with excellent company,' he said and continued, 'Do you remember why I brought you back to my flat?'

'Not really, but I did notice this pendant on the bedside table. I think you gave it to me but I don't know why.'

'Yes I did, it's a lucky pendant to keep you safe. I thought you needed it to stop any further accidents happening to you.'

'Thank you, that was kind of you. Nick why don't I remember you putting me into this bed. It's scary not remembering all of last night.'

'As I said Eva, you were *very* drunk. Do you remember I asked you if you had stopped taking the prescribed painkillers you had been taking for your injury? They could have reacted with the alcohol and made you even more sleepy.'

'I don't remember you asking me but yes, I had stopped taking the painkillers as you suggested. As you know Nick, I hate taking any sort of drugs.'

'Don't worry about the memory loss Eva, you were safe here with me although I didn't always feel safe with you last night,' he said laughing and raising his eyebrows. 'The drunken Eva is very different from the sober Eva. You had no inhibitions. I'll say no more,' he said as he raised his hand.

'What do you mean Nick? What did I do?'

'I'm far too much of a gentleman to say. If I told you, you would blush the colour of beetroot.'

She sipped her coffee very conscious that Nick was watching her every move. She couldn't understand why it made her feel so uncomfortable. Looking down at her arms she asked, 'Nick, why have I got bruising on my arms.' She noticed he paused not replying immediately as if searching for an answer.

'Let me see,' he said as he gently examined her left arm. 'That must have happened when I grabbed hold of you just in time to stop you falling. You tried to walk without your stick and, as you were very light headed with the effect of the alcohol, you began to fall. It could have been worse. If I hadn't stopped you falling you could have broken an arm or both arms. Don't worry the bruises will soon fade.' Nick laughed and said, 'Yes you liked the wine and drank a little too much.'

Suddenly Eva felt very embarrassed. Try as hard as she could, she couldn't remember anything after she had tasted the wine. It felt like there was an abyss of emptiness where there should have been memory. She began to wonder if Nick was telling the truth, but why would he lie?

'Eva you don't know how much wine you had at the restaurant, it was a lot more than you think and you were more than a little drunk when we drove here, although neither of us realised it. You are a good actress and appeared sober when you were quite drunk,' he continued.

By now Eva was feeling even more embarrassed and said, 'Nothing like this has ever happened before. I have been tipsy

The Dinner Date

but never so drunk that I have no memory of what has happened. Usually if I start to feel light headed I will always change to drinking soft drinks but I don't remember feeling light headed. The last thing I can recall is tasting the delicious wine you gave me but after that there is nothing. I hate the feeling that I don't know what I did, it scares me.'

'Don't worry about it, just forget it, Eva. I'm just glad it happened when you were in the safe hands of your brother-in-law.' She wanted to agree but she couldn't. She couldn't shake off the feeling that she hadn't been safe.

Nick smiled at her and asked if she could manage to get to the shower on her own. She immediately said that she could but really had no idea if she could stand, let alone walk to the bathroom, wherever it was! She felt so fragile and weak, but she wasn't going to tell Nick.

'Let me take the bandage off your ankle before you take a shower. I can re-bandage when you get out.' Before she could agree, Nick had carefully pulled the duvet up away from her feet and was carefully unwrapping the bandage from around her ankle. She shivered when he touched her. Why? She couldn't understand her reaction. She felt something wasn't right.

'The ankle is looking good, no swelling,' he said gently caressing her foot. He looked up at her and kept his gaze on her a bit too long. She shivered again.

'I can help you to the bathroom.'

'No, it's okay, I can manage.' She couldn't understand why but she didn't want Nick touching her, it didn't feel right. How strange she thought.

Nick explained that the bathroom was opposite the bedroom and if she needed help to call him. He left the room and she lay in this strange bed in this strange room wondering why she felt different about Nick, something must have happened last night. Did she make a fool of herself in front of Nick she wondered or did she just feel embarrassed that Nick saw her drunk. And then another thought came into her mind, perhaps she had done something really stupid. In her drunken stupor had she come on to him and Nick was being a gentleman and saving her from embarrassment by not telling her. She shook her head she couldn't imagine she had done that.

Eva felt so shaky getting out of bed. She hurt everywhere. Very slowly, with the aid of her stick, she made her way to the bathroom. She felt pain as she walked but it was not just her ankle that hurt. She was sore between her legs and that soreness extended up into her pelvis. She couldn't understand why. She undressed and stepped into the shower steadying herself against the side of the cubicle. She felt dizzy and confused and vowed never to drink alcohol again but especially wine! She switched on the shower and let the water gently soothe her body but her mind was still racing struggling to understand what had happened to her.

Her body felt bruised inside and outside, almost as if something heavy had been on top of her or that she had fallen heavily onto the floor. Perhaps that is what did happen, she had fallen when she had been drunk, but Nick said he stopped her from falling and that's why she had bruises on her arms. Was he lying? He didn't seem surprised to see the bruises. Did he already know they were there and how they got there? She was so sure she hadn't been drunk, yes a bit tipsy perhaps but not drunk. So why couldn't she remember, none of it made any sense to her.

As she showered she thought about the one time when she had been very drunk. She had been 17 years old and not used to alcohol. She hadn't realised she was getting drunk but her friends had taken control of the situation, safely escorting her home. She remembers waking up the next morning feeling terribly nauseous and with an awful headache. It was then she promised herself never to get very drunk again and she had kept that promise that was until now. But this time she didn't

The Dinner Date

have a headache and she didn't feel sick, instead she felt confused and scared about what had happened during the missing hours. Nick had tried to convince her that nothing did happen and that she had been safe with him, she wanted to believe him but somehow she didn't.

She switched off the water and carefully stepped out of the shower. When she came back to the bedroom she sat on the edge of the bed continuing to try to remember the events of the previous evening but still without much success. Her head felt like it was full of cottonwool. She started to slowly go through each part of the evening dragging back any tiny bit of memory she could. She could now remember going for the meal with Nick and he was so lovely. He made her laugh which was just what she needed. She had started to recall coming back to Nick's flat but she struggled to remember much after that! Nick said she had drunk a lot during and after the meal, but she doesn't recall drinking that much. She thinks she remembers Nick giving her a present and she turns to look at the crystal pendant by the bed but she's not sure she does remember. Is she mixing up memory with what Nick has just told her, she doesn't know. In despair with her head in her hands she realises the harder she tries to make sense of the evening the more confused she is becoming.

She feels something isn't right. Her body feels as if it has been abused, why does it feel like that? She wants to ask Nick but then again she is afraid at what he might say. She doesn't want to stay any longer, she just wants to go home where she can feel safe. Not remembering the events of last night is disturbing her, she wants to believe that Nick has taken care of her, but did he? Did he get her drunk on purpose she began to ask herself? No of course he didn't, why would he? She starts to have a feeling of dread in the pit of her stomach which she tries to shake off. A terrible thought enters her mind but she quickly brushes it away. By the time she gets home she is sure more of her memory of last night will start to come back. She will tell Nick she wants to go home now. She doesn't feel safe here but why?

***

Nick sat trying to read but he couldn't concentrate and when he looked up Eva was standing in front of him. She was dressed. Her long hair towel dried and cascading around her shoulders, her cheeks were blushed pink. It took Nick's breath away how beautiful and sensual she looked.

'How are you feeling now, better after a shower?' Nick asked.

'Yes a little, but still very confused.'

'That will pass. Now sit down and I will re-bandage your ankle.'

Very reluctantly she sat down. Nick returned with a fresh bandage and a small stool. He carefully placed her ankle on the stool and expertly replaced the bandage. 'There is an advantage to having a doctor as your brother-in-law,' he said with a grin.

Any other time she would have agreed but not this time she had begun to feel so uncomfortable in his company. She had to ask the question, 'Nick, as a doctor can you explain why the alcohol affected me in the way it did. I'm sure I didn't drink a huge amount, you wouldn't have let me, would you? If you knew I was a little drunk when we came back to your flat why did you give me more alcohol? And why does my body feel so sore? It's scaring me that I can't remember what happened.'

Nick smiled, 'Eva, I explained I didn't realise you were so drunk, you didn't appear to be. If I had thought you were drunk I wouldn't have offered you more wine but anyway you didn't refuse it! As I have told you, you were *very* drunk and you fell asleep. Eva noticed he emphasised the word *very*. He continued, 'That's all that happened. Your memory should slowly come back but some of it may stay hidden.

The Dinner Date

Please trust me Eva nothing happened other than you fell asleep in my flat.'

She wanted to trust him but she didn't. Why did he seem to find it so amusing that she had been drunk? Had she done something she would regret? She wished she could remember.

'Eva everything is fine, don't be embarrassed. Everyone gets drunk at least once in their lives when they don't remember what they did and your turn was last night so stop worrying about it. Forget about it. I won't tell anyone and neither should you. We won't even tell Robert that you were so drunk you had to spend the night at my flat. It will be our secret. Just forget it and stop trying to work out what happened. You can tell Robert we had a lovely meal which we did and then I took you home.'

She wished she could believe what Nick told her but she couldn't. She needed to remember the details of last night so she would know the truth but she was also scared that when and if her memory returned what it might reveal.

'Sit down and I will make some breakfast.'

'No Nick, I just want to go home, please take me home.'

'Okay, just give me a few minutes. I need to have some toast. Are you sure you don't want any, it will soak up any residue alcohol,' he said raising his eyebrows.

'I'm sure Nick. I just want to go home.' Eva sat and watched Nick in the kitchen as he prepared his toast, carefully spreading a thick amount of butter and jam on the bread. He sat down at the table to eat and looked so relaxed. His body language showed no signs of guilt or regret. Perhaps she was mistaken. As she watched she saw a smug smile spread across his face almost as if he knew she was watching him. Did this confirm what she suspected?

Eva stood up and suggested she took a taxi home, but Nick wouldn't hear of it. He explained he wasn't working that day so had plenty of time and he wanted to make sure she got home safely. She sat back down nervously waiting, eager to be away from his flat, this room and the memories or lack of them she felt. She was beginning to feel the 'dinner date' had been a mistake, one which she would always regret.

When Nick had finished his toast and was ready to go she picked up her small black handbag which she found she had left by the sofa, although she didn't remember leaving it there, checking to make sure her phone was inside. She toyed with the idea of leaving the crystal, she didn't want it, it would always remind her of this tainted evening but Nick had other ideas. He walked towards her and said, 'Don't forget the crystal,' holding it out to her. She noticed he looked so smug and self-satisfied. Had he won whatever game he was playing with her? Reluctantly she took the crystal. When their eyes met she knew their lives had changed forever.

Nick handed her the walking stick and they slowly walked to the door. It was still early and everywhere was quiet. As she stepped outside she shivered although it wasn't cold and Nick noticed. He put his arm around her to steady her as she hobbled to the car. She didn't like the feel of his arm around her, today somehow it felt wrong.

Nick opened the car door for her and she gingerly eased herself into the passenger seat, every movement causing pain. Nick climbed into the driver's seat and turning to look at her he asked, 'Are you okay?'

'Why do I hurt all over Nick?' she asked. She noticed he frowned and his eyes narrowed. He looked angry.

'I don't know Eva. Perhaps when I stopped you falling I grabbed you a little too tightly. I have told you what happened, can we stop talking about it.'

She didn't answer she just looked straight ahead. Nick started the car and they fell silent as he concentrated on the road ahead. She felt exhausted as if she had run a marathon, her thoughts saturating her mind. Nothing would convince her that she had been that drunk and she struggled to find any

The Dinner Date

sense of what had happened. She felt uneasy in Nick's company, alone in the car with him and she hoped all these feelings would pass. He was her brother-in-law, her family. She wished she could turn the clock back and last night had never happened but she couldn't she had to live with it.

Eva realised that she hadn't even looked at her phone to see if Robert had called, she had been so preoccupied with trying to remember the events of yesterday evening. She was sure he would have called or left a message to ask how the dinner date had gone. She took her phone out of her bag and when she looked at it she realised it was switched off. She never switched her phone off when she was away from the theatre, she always wanted to make sure that Robert could contact her. She was certain she hadn't switched it off.

'Nick, did you switch my phone off,' she asked.

'What, no, of course not. Why would I?

'I don't know. But it has been switched off and I never switch it off.'

'Well I had no reason to switch your phone off. Eva, please calm down. You have to believe me that nothing happened last night.'

But she didn't. She was beginning not to believe anything Nick was telling her. She just wanted to go home, to feel safe in her own home and away from Nick. She hated the feeling of being scared of someone she had once trusted.

As Nick parked his car in the small car park alongside the flat Eva's heart began to beat rapidly. She didn't know how she was going to deal with what she knew would happen next. Nick jumped out of the car and quickly walked round to Eva's side and opened the car door. He went to help her out of the car.

'It's okay Nick I can manage.' She didn't want him touching her again, his hands on her body, the thought made her shudder.'

Nick stepped aside and watched as she struggled to get out of the car. Her foot hurt but so did every other part of her body. He walked alongside her as she slowly made her way towards the flat. As they stood at the door Nick said, 'Eva I don't know what you imagine happened last night but I promise you all I did was put you safely alone in my bed to sleep off the excess alcohol you had consumed. You have to believe me. And don't forget it will remain our secret.'

She didn't comment, she was tired and just wanted to be in her own home where she hoped she would feel safe. As he went to kiss her cheek she turned away and heard him mutter, 'Maybe in future you shouldn't drink so much.' And with that he walked away.

Eva put the key into the lock and noticed her hand was shaking. She felt this was a nightmare she couldn't wake up from. Once the door was open she hobbled into the lounge and with a huge sigh sat down on the sofa. She was glad to be home and to feel safe. She tried again to remember everything that had happened last night but there was still a huge gap in her memory, it still wasn't returning if anything she was remembering less and less. Perhaps she was just so tired. She began to doubt herself. Was she wrong about Nick? Was he innocent, maybe nothing did happen. But why wouldn't she remember Nick carrying her to his bedroom and undressing her. Why did he undress her, she had never asked him. There was no going back, everything had changed the way she felt about Nick. How would she face Robert with these thoughts in her mind.

She had a horrible stale taste in her mouth and she needed a coffee. As she hobbled through the lounge to the kitchen she paused at her wedding photo. She looked at Robert. What was she going to tell him? He was sure to ask how her date with Nick had gone. She can't tell him what she thinks has happened. Firstly he would never believe her, secondly she has no proof that anything did happen. If Nick speaks to

The Dinner Date

Robert first she is convinced he will say that she had been so drunk she has little memory of the evening. She didn't know what to do, she couldn't think of that now. This was all too difficult, all too much to bear.

She made the coffee and sat down at the kitchen table. As she put the cup to her lips the tears began to flow down her cheeks splashing into the hot drink. How and why has this happened to her. She felt so angry. Angry with Nick. The dreadful thought she had had earlier sprang back into her mind. Had Nick drugged and raped her? She had heard that the date rape drug caused memory loss. That would answer a lot of her questions. Why would he do this to her? They had been such good friends. She had always felt he was like the brother she had never had. Was it something he had been planning for a while? She couldn't think straight. She put the coffee cup down and put her head in her hands and sobbed in despair. The fear rising in her, not knowing what the future held. How could she live with her suspicions trapped deep inside her. No one would believe her. Once again she had doubts perhaps she had got it all wrong. Too much to think about. She put the coffee down and took herself to the bedroom where she lay down on the bed curled up like a baby, gently rocking herself. She can't accuse Nick in case he is innocent. If she thinks he is guilty how can she face him at family gatherings suspecting what he might have done. Either way she can't win! She fell into a tormented sleep.

23

Eva was woken by her phone ringing. She looked across at the phone which lay beside her on the bed and noticed the time 11.30 am, she had been asleep for a couple of hours. She froze when she saw who was calling, it was Robert, she knew she couldn't answer it. She wasn't ready, she wasn't prepared. Would she ever be she wondered? She had to calm down, she needed more time so she ignored his call. She lay dozing until the third time Robert rang when she knew she had to answer, by now he would be getting quite concerned that she hadn't seen his missed calls and called him back. She took a deep breath and tapped the answer call button.

'Hi Eva, where have you been? I've been trying to contact you. I was worried you didn't call back. Are you okay?'

'Hi Robert, yes I'm fine. Sorry, I put my phone on silent when we were in the pub last night and I forgot to cancel it,' Eva said with as steady a voice as she could manage.

'I was getting so worried about you I rang Nick. Thankfully he answered and told me you were fine and that he had spent a lovely evening with you and what good company you were. I told him I already knew that. Did you enjoy the evening?'

She stifled a tremor in her voice as she replied, 'Yes, it was a nice pub and the meal was good.'

'Did you go straight home afterwards?'

Eva hesitated she didn't know how to answer. Nick can't have mentioned that they had gone back to his flat. 'Yes, Nick dropped me off here before making his way home.'

'Eva, are you okay, you sound a bit strange.'

'Sorry Robert, I'm fine, just tired and I feel a bit groggy. My ankle has been hurting. I guess I walked too much yesterday.'

The Dinner Date

'Go and take some painkillers and have an early night and take it easy tomorrow. I will spoil you when I come home. You won't have to lift a finger all weekend.'

She managed a laugh and then said, 'I can't wait to see you, I wish you were here with me, love you.'

'Love you too, see you tomorrow.' And then the call ended and she sat in the silent room, her mind racing. What will she feel like when she sees Robert. She will want to tell him, share with him what she thinks has happened but she knows she can't do that. She can't say Nick didn't bring her home but took her to his flat, Robert would ask too many questions and she wouldn't know how to answer them. She had no idea how she was going to get through this weekend.

Slowly she made her way to the bathroom and as she did so she could feel the start of a panic attack as the enormity of her situation took hold. She reached the bathroom just in time and with her head over the toilet she threw up. She could feel her face was flushed and her hands were sweaty but by taking slow deep breaths she began to feel her inner strength return. Carefully on very shaky legs and leaning on her stick she walked to the kitchen knowing she would have to eat something before she took the painkillers. She managed half a slice of bread washed down with water and painkillers.

She couldn't sort out her damaged body but she would sort out her mind. She knew she was strong and would survive this nightmare. She did very little the rest of the day except constantly revisiting the past events. Finally, exhausted she went to bed but was unable to sleep. She tossed and turned and eventually got up and sat in the lounge with a cup of warm milk with a splash of honey in – her mum's antidote for almost anything but perhaps it wouldn't work, not this time. She wondered if Nick was tossing and turning and she suspected not. He was probably sleeping like a baby, with no regrets. Had she been raped, had Nick her brother-in-law raped her? The question kept turning over and over in her mind. More and more she was beginning to believe he had but she had no memory of him doing so, drink wouldn't do that to her she was sure it wouldn't. Had he done something else to her before he raped her? Again she revisited the thought that he could have drugged her so she would have no memory of what happened? Was that the real reason why he gave her the glass of wine when they came back to the flat. Had she been awake throughout and did she take any part in the sexual act or did she fight him and try to stop him, is that how she got the bruises? So many questions and Nick was the only one who knew the answers and he would never tell.

Eva needed to sleep, she needed to get it clear in her head what she should do. She searched in the kitchen drawer and found some sleeping tablets she had been given after the accident. She took one and finally fell asleep.

The next morning she woke up very groggy from the sleeping tablet induced deep sleep. Her head was throbbing. She picked up her phone and looked at the time, it was 10.30 am. There was a text from Robert sent at 7.30 am. He hoped she had slept well and he was counting the minutes until he was home with her. She read it through tear filled eyes. It was Friday and Robert would be home for the weekend later today. She couldn't wait to see him but equally she dreaded seeing him. How could she act normal? He would know something was wrong as soon as he looked into her eyes. She knew her eyes wouldn't lie and would show the fear and distress she felt. She struggled to get out of bed, her legs felt like jelly. Reaching for her stick she steadied herself before moving forward. She didn't want Robert to see her struggling to walk, it would look as though she had gone backwards in her recovery. She had the day to work on improving her walking and her emotions but first she wanted and needed a shower. She very slowly made her way to the bathroom. As she stepped into the shower she turned the dial to the highest shower pressure, the water pummelled her body as she

The Dinner Date

scrubbed and scrubbed, her skin turning red and angry as she tried to wash away the feeling of disgust she now felt about her body. And then the sobbing tears came once again mingling with the stream of water from the shower.

Once finished she carefully stepped out of the shower, her skin was stinging and the bandage Nick had put onto her ankle was now sopping wet. She violently pulled it off causing a searing pain but she didn't care, the pain she felt was worth it to get rid of one thing Nick had done to her. She wished it was that easy to get rid of everything else he may have done to her but it wasn't.

She dried herself and using her stick she made her way slowly and carefully back to the bedroom where she checked the time. Emma, the Physio had been booked to visit her twice a week and was due at 1pm. It was now 11.50 am. The loungewear she had taken off yesterday evening before she went on her date was hanging in the wardrobe. She took it down and held it in her hands. She had been so excited about going out with Nick for a meal but now all she felt was devastation. It was hard to believe that her whole world could change in just 24 hours. She slipped the loungewear on and made her way to the kitchen. She didn't feel hungry but knew she would have to eat before Emma arrived.

After she had eaten a couple of slices of toast and drank a strong cup of coffee she slowly began to feel more in control. Her head was clearer even though emotionally she was still shattered. She kept checking her phone and thankfully Nick had not tried to contact her. She wasn't sure what his next move was going to be or even if he had a next move. Would he continue to persuade her that nothing happened or would he just carry on as normal and ignore the events of the previous evening. She began to wonder had he done this sort of thing before. Had he raped other women or just her. But why did he want to do it, to force himself onto her and she wondered had he always felt this way about her. The thought made her shiver.

She checked the time. It was 12.50 pm and Emma would be here soon. She took deep breaths like she did just before she went on stage. She was acting then and she would be acting now when Emma came. She had to appear as if nothing had happened. This would be her rehearsal for when Robert came home. The bell rang. She took a deep breath before she made her way to the door. The acting started now!

Emma smiling stood at the door. She had a bubbly personality and talked a lot, which was just what Eva needed, she would let Emma do all the talking.

'How is your ankle?' Emma asked.

'Sore,' Eva replied.

Emma assessed the progress and watched Eva walking.

'It's not only your ankle that looks sore but your whole body seems stiff and painful.'

'Well I have to admit I did have a slight fall. I didn't think I had hurt myself but I do feel a bit stiff,' Eva lied.

'Okay. What if I give you a full gentle massage including your ankle. I will then show you some further exercises that should assist with the healing process of the ankle. The Theatre Company are paying for all this so you may as well take advantage of it.'

'That sounds good. I want to get back to some form of dancing as soon as I can. I would like you to come back every other day for a couple of weeks if you can. I can't sit around any longer, it's driving me crazy.' Eva had decided that she had to get back to dancing or at least help to advise and choregraph a show. After what had happened she couldn't spend time alone in the flat day after day, she had to be around people who didn't know Nick.

'That's fine, I will arrange to come 3 times a week for the next 2 weeks and we will see how you improve.'

The Dinner Date

Emma, as always, had brought the portable massage couch with her which she placed in the middle of the lounge. She helped Eva on to the couch and began the massage. 'Eva, what are these bruises on both your arms?'

'My brother-in-law kindly took me out for a meal yesterday evening. Apparently I stumbled and he caught me and stopped me from falling.'

'What do you mean apparently, don't you remember?'

'I vaguely remember,' she lied. It was at the end of the evening and I was feeling very tired and light headed.'

Emma paused taking in the information while looking at Eva's arms. 'These are deep bruises, made with some force and on both arms. He doesn't know his own strength. I can see the imprint of his fingers.'

'He said it was his quick reaction that stopped me from falling.'

Emma carried on with the massage without commenting. At the end of the session when she had left, Eva curled up on the sofa and fell into a deep sleep.

Normally as the day progressed towards Robert coming home she would get steadily excited but today all she could feel was a mixture of desire to see and be with him and almost guilt that she had done something wrong. Maybe Nick wanted her to feel that guilt. Had she somehow led him on – no she would never do that not even if she had been as drunk as Nick was making out. No there had been a reason why she had no memory, Nick had carefully planned it.

Later that day when Robert texted to say he would be arriving home in about an hour it turned out to be the longest hour Eva had ever known. She couldn't rest, she lay on the sofa listening and watching the door, her heart pounding with a combination of desire to see him and terrified of seeing him.

She had her eyes closed when she heard his key in the door and kept them closed pretending to be asleep. Normally she would have butterflies in her stomach but not this time. When she opened her eyes she saw him walking towards her. She wanted and needed him so much. He got down on his knees and asked, 'Are you okay Eva, you look very pale. What's Nick done to you, has he worn you out on the date,' he asked smiling, 'I will have to have words with him when I see him.'

She couldn't look Robert in the eyes instead she focused on the beautiful painting of the beach in Jersey. The beach they walked on after their wedding, she wished with all her heart they were on that beach right now.

'Do you want a coffee,' Robert asked, 'I'm gasping for one.'

'Let me make it,' Eva said quickly, 'I need to try and keep moving my ankle to stop it getting stiff.'

'Is that one of Dr Nick's instructions?' Robert asked grinning.

Eva felt her heart drop as she realised what a huge part of their lives Nick was and how much Robert adored his older brother. He would never believe what she suspected Nick may have done. She didn't know how she was going to cope with the next few minutes, days, months and years if she had to keep this terrible secret locked inside. She couldn't share it with anyone.

'Yes, it was his suggestion,' she replied as she started tentatively to walk to the kitchen.

They sat at the kitchen table drinking their coffee, Robert explaining the difficulties and some of the funny moments he was experiencing trying to put on this new show. 'I really need you in the show Eva, you would soon have all the dancers sorted out.'

She managed a smile and realised that now Robert was here she was beginning to relax. Her mind was focusing on Robert and not on the events of last night. Perhaps she would be able to cope, at least with masking her distress in front of

The Dinner Date

Robert. Just the very normal familiar way he was behaving made it easier. They snuggled up on the sofa that evening and watched an old James Bond film, Diamonds Are Forever. When it finished Robert looked at her and said, 'Shall we have an early night?' This is what they would usually do on their first night together after being apart. She knew she couldn't bear to be touched in an intimate way. What could she say? All she wanted was to be in Robert's arms, and for him to be telling her that everything would be alright, but of course that wouldn't happen because he didn't know anything was wrong.

'Robert, I'm sorry my foot is hurting so much I'm going to take a sleeping pill. I was tossing and turning last night and I'm sure it made my foot worse.'

'Oh poor you. Obviously the excitement of spending time with my brother was just too much for you,' he said laughing. She looked at her husband, her kind caring husband whose philosophy in life was that every problem could be solved. Not this time, not this problem.

24

The next morning when Eva eventually woke up she found Robert standing by the bed holding a mug of tea. 'I have been standing here for at least half an hour, I couldn't wake you,' he said laughing. 'Okay, really about 5 minutes. You have been in such a deep sleep. Having a meal with Nick really has exhausted you.'

She looked at him and then closed her eyes again in anguish. She didn't want to wake up, she didn't want to think about the date with Nick. She wanted it to have been just a bad dream but she knew it hadn't, it had really happened. She couldn't stop thinking about it, trying to grasp at any slight indication that her memory was returning. But it wasn't, there was just total blankness, as if for those missing hours she had been in a dreamless sleep.

'Are you okay Eva,' Robert asked becoming a little concerned.

She opened her eyes again, she had to appear normal. 'Yes,' she said trying to smile, 'I'm just a bit groggy from taking the sleeping tablet last night. A cup of tea will help. I will be fine in a minute.'

He handed her the mug and said, 'I will start making some brunch, it's nearly 11. Will that be okay, could you eat something?'

'I will try,' she said but wasn't sure she could. 'I want to take a shower, can you take the bandage off my ankle please Robert,' she asked. Emma had expertly re-bandaged Eva's ankle after the physio session.

'Of course,' he said pulling the duvet back and kneeling down by her foot. As he did so she had a flash back of Nick putting a bandage on her foot. She trembled. Robert concerned asked, 'Sorry did I hurt your foot.'

The Dinner Date

'No I'm fine,' she replied smiling at her husband.

'I'll go and start our brunch. Be careful in the shower we don't want any more accidents.'

Very slowly and carefully she managed to get up and very cautiously she took a shower letting the warm water gently refresh her. Even after the shower her body still felt so stiff and sore. She remembered Robert had helped her get undressed and into bed last night and he had commented on the bruises. She had repeated what Nick had told her and noticed that Robert looked a bit concerned although he seemed to accept the explanation. The sleeping tablets she had taken had worked and she had slept but this morning she was still so tired and so frightened. How was she going to face Nick? She pushed it to the back of her mind, she couldn't deal with that now. Hopefully it would be a while before she saw him again.

Once dressed she slowly walked towards the kitchen and heard the sound of the radio, not music but voices talking. She stopped at the door when she realised it wasn't the radio, both men turned round and looked at her.

'Nick's turned up again just in time for brunch. I don't how he does it,' Robert said laughing. 'This time he deserves it as a thank you for taking my wife out to dinner and looking after you so well. He's told me it was a great evening and you both enjoyed it. Eva you need to sit down, you still look very pale.'

She couldn't believe Nick was standing in front of her. For Robert's sake she would have to act normally, or as normal as she could. She questioned herself, could she do that when all she could think about was did Nick rape her or did they simply have an evening of too much alcohol. Nick looked at her, his usual kind warm eyes were displaying a steely gaze. Was he warning her not to say anything she wondered. Robert didn't appear to notice the tension between them, he was busy trying to rescue burnt sausages.

'Nick, how nice to see you. Have you just come to be fed or is there another reason?' Eva asked.

'You've guessed it Eva, there is something else,' Nick said pausing. 'You will see after we have eaten. Is the food ready, Rob, it smells wonderful and I'm starving.'

'You are always hungry, with the amount of food you eat you should be the size of a house. Eva, sit next to Nick,' Robert said placing two large plates of food in front of Nick and Eva. Sitting down with his plate of food Robert started eating 'Now you two, tell me all about your date. Did Eva behave herself Nick?'

Eva wanted to throw up, she started to feel hot and panicky. She felt her face blush. Her heart was pounding so hard she could hardly breathe. As she picked up her knife and fork her hands started to shake. She took a deep breath to calm herself. Nick immediately started talking to Robert, telling him all about the pub and the meal. He was acting as if nothing unusual had happened. She knew she must try to do the same, she didn't want Robert to sense there was anything wrong. As she was picking at her food and barely listening to what Nick was saying she suddenly heard the words, 'And of course Eva did get drunk, did she tell you Robert?'

'No she didn't,' Robert replied looking at Eva.

Both men looked at her. She didn't want to be here, in her kitchen where she usually felt safe. She wanted to run away but she was trapped and knew she couldn't. She realised what Nick had just done, he had planted the seed in Robert's mind that she had been drunk and she began to think he would do the same with his mum and dad. Anything she said now no-one would believe her because they thought she had been drunk, but she knew she hadn't. How could she convince anyone she had not been drunk, it was her word against Nick's.

'Well Eva, were you drunk last night,' Robert asked grinning. 'Perhaps just a little bit,' he questioned her.

The Dinner Date

Laughing he said, 'It's okay to get drunk as long as you are in safe hands and you were last night. Thanks for looking after my drunken wife, Nick.'

She sat watching them, glancing between Nick and Robert and suddenly she felt angry. She didn't want Nick to get away with what he had done to her but did she have a choice. Would anyone believe her if she told them what she suspected and there was also the possibility she may be wrong. She didn't have the answer.

'No Rob, I wasn't drunk. I do remember everything about the evening,' she said looking directly at Nick. She had to convince Nick that she remembered more than she actually did and to make him think that her memory was returning. She wanted to make him feel uncomfortable, to see his reaction. Is he worried she will tell Robert what she thinks happened? But she can see there is no reaction, he just grins. He is so cocksure of himself. She was becoming more and more convinced that the memory loss was not due to excess alcohol consumption, it was due to something Nick had done, but what that was she could only guess.

Robert laughed and said, 'It's okay Eva, it doesn't matter. You enjoyed good company and a lovely meal with Nick and the most important thing was I knew you were safe.'

She turned her head and looked at Nick. He had narrowed his eyes and she could see a smirk had spread across his face. Robert had just said what Nick wanted to hear. Eva could see that Nick had apparently devoured his food without a care in the world. She had barely touched hers. 'If you've finished I want to show you why I really came,' Nick explained.

Nick went to help her stand up but she shrugged him off. Something Eva could see Robert noticed and looked surprised but he didn't comment. They moved into the lounge and Eva could see something wrapped up in the corner of the room. Nick walked over and picked it up. She could see it was a picture and it dawned on her what he had done.

'They had some lovely paintings displayed in the pub didn't they Eva. They were all for sale. I went back this morning and bought this one for you and Rob, it was your favourite,' he said as he ripped the brown paper away from the painting of the pub garden.

'It's a beautiful painting. The garden looks lovely,' Robert said. 'Eva isn't it thoughtful of Nick. We'll have to revisit the pub, all three of us. What do you think Eva?'

She didn't know how to answer. She knew she would never go there again. She couldn't, that pub had been the start of this awful journey. 'Yes it's a lovely painting Nick, thank you. Robert I'm going to have a lie down, I don't think sleeping tablets agree with me. I will leave you two boys together and Nick can reveal more about the evening,' Eva said looking straight at Nick.

'Hope you feel better after a lie down,' Nick said staring intently at her.

She immediately felt once again he was warning her. He held all the cards and whatever she said he would clearly refute continuing to claim she had been very drunk that evening. Eva walked slowly to the bedroom listening to the two brothers talking in the background and carefully climbed onto the bed. She lay and looked up at the ceiling her mind racing. She knew she hadn't been drunk. Had he done this sort of thing before to other women. The thought scared her. Nick was not the person they all thought he was. She was physically and mentally exhausted. She thought she had only been asleep for a few minutes when she heard Robert gently calling her name.

'Eva, wake up. I've brought you a mug of tea.'

As she opened her eyes Robert's smiling face greeted her. 'You have been asleep for a couple of hours. Are you okay Eva? You don't seem yourself, even Nick commented.'

'I'm just tired. Once I start sleeping better at night I will be fine. Tea is lovely, thank you. Has Nick gone?'

The Dinner Date

Robert sat on the bed next to her. 'Yes, he didn't stay much longer. Wasn't it kind of him to buy that painting. He's such a thoughtful brother and taking you out for a meal was so kind of him, I owe him one.'

Eva didn't know how to respond to that statement so she didn't comment and changed the subject. 'I've got Emma, the physiotherapist coming three times a week for the next couple of weeks. I need to concentrate on healing this ankle and strengthening the foot. The sooner I can start dancing again the better, albeit very cautiously. I don't want to be on my own in this flat day after day, I need to be around people,' she explained to Robert with a touch of panic in her voice.

'I know you do. I think it's a good idea to work hard with Emma's guidance and to get back to dancing as soon as possible. I can see that being on your own is causing you stress. Perhaps I will ask Nick if he has time to come round more often in the week.'

'No, don't do that,' she replied a bit too quickly and then paused before continuing, 'I don't want to depend on Nick for company. I will have Emma more often the next couple of weeks and after that I will revisit my options.'

'Okay, but I know Nick would be only too happy to help, but if you don't want me to ask him that's fine.' After pausing Robert cautiously enquired, 'Is everything okay with you and Nick. You seemed a bit curt with him. I know what Nick can be like, he hasn't upset you in anyway has he?'

Eva knew she could act, she did it every time she was on stage and now she had to do it in front of Robert. She had to lie to him. 'No, Nick hasn't upset me. I'm just tired and impatient with the length of time it is taking for my ankle to heal.' Robert went over to her and put his arms around her, holding her tightly. She melted in his embrace wanting to feel safe and secure but instead she was beginning to fear for what the future held.

The rest of the weekend went far too quickly for Eva and soon it was time for Robert to leave. The precious time she had spent with him had strengthened her mentally and she now felt stronger and to some extent able to cope.

25

Eva worked hard over the next two weeks and with the guidance of Emma and the extra sessions her ankle improved and she could practice some very simple dance steps. But it was still too early to even think about resuming full time dancing and the thought of being stuck in the flat on her own for much longer with the events of the dinner date ever present in her mind was daunting.

That was when Robert came to her rescue. The last couple of times he had come home he could see how being isolated was affecting her mentally. She was agitated, nervous and depressed, not like his normal wife. So he made a decision which he put to her on Friday evening when he had just returned home. They were sitting on the sofa after eating a take-away when he came up with a suggestion. 'Eva, I think it would be a good idea if you joined me at the theatre.' She turned and looked at him a smile appearing on her face waiting eagerly for him to explain. 'We start rehearsals on Monday and I think the help and advice you could give to the dancers would be welcomed. We could stay in digs during the week and come home at the weekend. You would be surrounded by people and have company and a purpose in life which I think is what you need because you have seemed so withdrawn since the accident. I can understand how you must feel, I would find endless time on my own with nothing to do depressing. What do you think, is it a good idea?'

She didn't need much time to think about the suggestion. 'Yes please, that sounds a great idea. I don't think I could spend another week on my own. Emma has given me exercises which I can continue without seeing her for a while.'

Once Eva had started helping at the theatre she soon began to improve mentally. The buzz of the cast around her allowed her brief moments of peace when she didn't think about Nick and that night. Those brief moments became longer and very soon she was so busy the anguish she had felt lessened. Not seeing Nick helped. But what would happen when the family got together and she did see him she wondered. She knew she wouldn't be able to avoid that situation forever. It was something she kept pushing to the back of her mind until one Saturday morning when Robert came into the lounge and said, 'That was mum on the phone. She was saying that she hasn't seen us for a while and wondered if we were free tomorrow would we like to come for Sunday lunch. I said I would check it was okay with you but I didn't think it would be a problem. What do you think?'

Eva's heart sank and she could feel panic rising. So far she had managed to avoid Jill and Stephen but she knew the time would come when she would have to sit at the dining table and share a meal with them acting as if nothing had happened. She didn't know if she could do it. Did she have the strength to do it she questioned herself but she couldn't think of an excuse not to go. It was something she would have to face at some time, she couldn't avoid them forever.

'Yes, that would be okay,' she answered.

Robert looked at her and was concerned that she didn't seem keen. 'It will be lovely to get together. I hope Nick is free and can join us,' he added. When he looked at Eva he noticed she flinched when he mentioned Nick. He couldn't understand why but he was sure it was probably nothing to worry about. He still wondered if Nick had said something to upset her, he had been known to say some flippant comment that could be misunderstood. Perhaps it did happen on their date. He knew Eva would not have mentioned it to him. Something and nothing he decided.

The Dinner Date

'Great, I will let mum know. Can't wait, with Nick there it's usually good fun isn't it?'

Eva smiled but didn't answer.

The next morning Eva woke up early and lay listening to the gentle breathing of Robert next to her. She loved him so much and she knew how much he adored and looked up to his big brother. She didn't know how to deal with the situation she found herself in and felt a dread in the pit of her stomach at the thought of seeing Nick. She hoped he wasn't going to join them at the meal today.

She slowly slid out of bed so as not to wake Robert and put her feet on the floor. No pain in her ankle, all her hard work had paid off. She walked carefully into the kitchen to make a drink. She would let Robert sleep, he had been working tirelessly the past few weeks and she had noticed he seemed exhausted. Nursing her hot drink she began to wonder how she was going to cope when she was face to face with Nick across a dinner table surrounded by his family. She closed her eyes the anxiety growing inside her. If Nick does join them for the meal she will try to avoid him as much as possible, she didn't want to be alone with him.

When she opened her eyes Robert was standing in front of her.

'Couldn't you sleep last night, was your foot hurting?'

She smiled at him, 'I slept well. I was just thinking how much better my foot is and I hope I will soon be dancing again. I have decided to book several sessions with a physical therapist who specialises in dancing injuries and I've found someone who has a practice in a studio near to the theatre. The sooner I can be signed off as fit to perform the better. Dancing is my way of relaxing.'

'Yes, I've noticed what the absence of dancing has done to you. I've never known you so stressed,' Robert said shaking his head. 'The accident seems to have affected you not only physically but also emotionally and since your date with Nick you seem to have been so agitated,' he continued his eyebrows knitting together.

Eva wasn't sure how to respond to this comment. The accident wasn't the cause of her agitation but she couldn't tell Robert. As Eva sighed she said, 'I'm sorry Rob, I know I haven't been easy to live with over the last few weeks. This is the longest period of time I've had without dancing. It feels odd. I have been so restless and very impatient to regain my physical strength and return to work. Once I'm in a show again I'm sure I will be back to normal – whatever that is,' she said with a laugh but of course knew she would never be the same person she once was. She stood up and made her way to the bathroom to take a shower hoping that her explanation would satisfy Robert.

Feeling refreshed she sat in front of the mirror and stared at her face. She looked intently at her reflection and into her eyes, the eyes of a traumatised person. She began to carefully apply her make-up and wondered was she trying to paint on a mask to hide the real distress she felt. She was no longer that carefree young woman, that person was gone forever. She held a secret, a dark secret. Would this change her life, her future with Robert? Something inside her pulled at her heart but strengthened her mind – she couldn't and wouldn't let that happen.

A short time later Robert shouted, 'Are you nearly ready Eva, we need to get going to mum and dad's?'

'Okay, I will be with you in a minute.' She could feel the tension already rising in her. She sat on the bed thinking about what she could do to make herself feel more in control and then a thought came to her. If Nick was going to be there she wouldn't let him see how distressed she was, she would be confident and turn the tables making him feel fearful and unsure exactly what she was going to do and more importantly what she might say. She was sure Jill and Stephen would want to know all about their dinner date. She had to take control but without actually accusing Nick. Perhaps she could sow the seed of doubt that she was drunk and instead talk about the evening almost as if she remembered everything even if she made up bits she couldn't remember. She would watch Nick's reaction, would he be worried that she did remember what happened and would tell. She could do this, she tried to convince herself but she was still not sure.

Eva found herself babbling like an idiot on the car journey to the house. She didn't want a pregnant pause, any silence would fuel the nerves she was already feeling. As they entered the driveway Robert commented, 'Nick's car isn't here, that's a shame he must be working.' Eva felt a wave of relief wash over her and immediately her body relaxed.

When they arrived at the front door and stood outside waiting for Jill or Stephen to answer Eva thought back to other times when she had been very nervous. Those times seemed so petty compared to the seriousness of this occasion. Oh my god, if she did accuse Nick of raping her and she was wrong it could end her marriage. Robert would never forgive her. That thought didn't bear thinking about. She was so thankful she wouldn't encounter Nick today. She knew it would happen one day but not today and she felt she had been handed a reprieve, she could breathe again.

Stephen came to the door beaming and immediately hugged Eva. 'How are you Eva, you've had a rough time lately.'

Smiling she accepted his warm embrace thinking how devasted he would be if he found out what his son might have done. 'I'm much better thanks Stephen, my ankle is healing nicely. I will soon be back dancing. I can't wait.'

'Come in both of you. Jill', he shouted, 'Robert and Eva are here.'

'Hi Eva, Robert,' she shouted back. 'Dinner will be another half hour.'

'Does she need some help?' Eva asked Stephen.

'No she's got everything under control as usual, you need to rest your ankle. We'll go into the conservatory.'

Eva followed Stephen and Robert, still using her walking stick. She had always felt so welcome in this house, this home, because it was very much a home and today was no exception. The tension she had felt eased because Nick wasn't here. She could sit at the table and try to push away the invasive thoughts and images that were ever present in her mind. She suddenly realised her mind had wandered and Stephen was talking to her.

'So Eva, you will be surprised at what I've captured on the video camera,' Stephen said grinning. 'We'll watch it after dinner.'

'I'll look forward to that,' Eva replied but was unsure whether she had missed something else he had said.

Half an hour after they had arrived Jill popped her head round the conservatory door and said, 'Dinner is ready, sorry I didn't come to greet you but there was just too much going on in the kitchen, I didn't want to leave anything,' and then she stepped aside. 'And look who's here.'

To Eva's horror Nick stood smiling at them. 'I didn't know if I would make it on time, I've only just finished my shift but I didn't want to miss one of mum's excellent Sunday roasts. How are you Robert, busy as usual? And Eva, how's your ankle? All mended?'

She could feel her face slowly start to redden and her heart began pounding as Nick fixed his gaze on her. 'Yes, I'm okay Nick,' she said hurriedly looking away.

'That's good to hear,' he said smiling smugly.

'Shall we go and sit down, we don't want the food to spoil,' Jill suggested.

'Good idea,' Nick said as to Eva's horror he went to help her stand up.

The Dinner Date

'It's okay Nick I don't need any help,' Eva said as she abruptly shrugged him off. She caught the look of surprise on Robert's face at her reaction to Nick. She would have to be careful and try to act normal towards Nick but she knew that was going to be difficult.

Stephen followed Jill who led the way with Nick close behind and with Robert holding back to wait for Eva. 'You know Nick was only trying to help,' Robert said.

'I know he was, but I'm fine now and I don't want or need help. I want my independence back.' She hoped this explanation would be enough to end his questioning.

This was the moment she had been dreading, the family all gathered together seated round the table and she was facing Nick. Five plates full of food had been carried in and Jill distributed them around the table. Eva looked at her plate, it was piled high with food. Usually it was no problem to eat every scrap of Jill's delicious cooking but today was different. Before she had seen Nick she had been hungry but now she felt nauseous, bile was rising into her throat. She looked at the plateful in despair.

Robert noticed and quickly said, 'Mum, that's a huge plate of food you've given Eva. Her appetite has waned somewhat since the accident and her enforced resting. She's not using enough energy at the moment to make her feel hungry.'

'I understand Eva, just eat as much as you can,' Jill responded.

Eva looked up and saw Nick glancing at her as he wolfed down his food as if he hadn't eaten for days. Was he doing this to show her that he was relaxed and free of guilt? She began to feel hot and sweaty as she picked at her food conscious that she was being watched. And then surprisingly something inside her snapped. She wasn't going to let Nick dictate how she dealt with this situation. Seeing Nick here among his family had been her biggest fear but once again her inner strength took over and she decided she would engage him in conversation about the date or should she wait and see if someone else brought up the subject. She didn't have to answer that question, Jill answered it for her.

'So Nick I hope you behaved yourself with Eva on your date,' Jill said grinning.

All eyes turned to Nick. Eva couldn't believe what Jill had innocently asked Nick. Her heart was pounding, the noise echoing in her ears. She hoped she looked calm although she didn't feel it.

Nick slowly finished his mouthful of food, which Eva could see gave him time to consider his answer. 'Of course I did. I was the perfect gentleman, wasn't I Eva?' and continued without stopping to let her answer. 'We had a lovely evening and Eva was the perfect companion although by the end of the evening she was a little bit drunk,' he said fleetingly looking at her.

All eyes now turned to Eva. What was she to say? She wanted to stand up and shout 'no I wasn't drunk you drugged and then raped me' but she couldn't she had no real proof. There was still that very slight doubt in her mind that she may be wrong. She looked in turn at Jill, Stephen and then Robert. She couldn't hurt these people especially Robert by voicing what she thought Nick had done to her. Would anyone believe her against Nick? If she accused Nick and was wrong she could never take back the accusation she had made in front of his family.

Taking a deep breath she ignored his claim that she was 'a little drunk' and focused instead on the pub. 'I was really impressed with the restaurant. The food was excellent and it's in a lovely location, so pretty. Yes, we were both a bit giggly weren't we Nick but not drunk. I can remember everything about the evening,' she said turning to look at him and smiling. 'Perhaps we can all go there together some time,'

The Dinner Date

Eva continued hoping that the tremor in her voice couldn't be heard.

Nick looked at her with a forced smile on his face but didn't comment and quickly changed the subject. 'Dad, I believe you have some video footage of wildlife in the garden which you want to share with us.'

Stephen laughed and sitting back contented after eating every scrap said, 'Oh yes I do, but before that is there any pudding, Jill?'

Jill raised her eyebrows knowing what a sweet tooth her husband had. 'Yes there is apple pie and ice cream for anyone that wants it. Has everyone finished their meal,' she said looking around noticing how little Eva had eaten. Continuing she suggested, 'Why don't we watch the video and have coffee and pudding afterwards.'

'Good idea,' Stephen agreed as he stood up to lead the way to the conservatory where he had already set up the video to play on a large screen.

'This is fun dad,' Robert said positioning himself in between Eva and Nick.

Stephen pressed the button and the video began. The camera had been positioned to capture wildlife down the garden reaching as far as the stream. 'Just to let you know the first bit of footage was when I was testing the camera. It was taken one Sunday when we all had lunch together,' Stephen explained.

'Oh good,' Nick said, 'I wonder what you've captured.'

The first thing they saw was that the camera had filmed Nick walking down the garden towards the stream. He stopped before he got to the bench and appeared to be watching something. He knew why he had stopped, he had been watching Eva. 'I remember that Sunday,' Nick said. 'Eva was sitting on the bench and I paused before I got too near. I was considering jumping out and scaring her, but she looked so peaceful, sitting with her eyes closed so I decided not to.'

'Nick you were watching Eva for ages, I'll fast forward,' Stephen said.

'I was just enjoying the peace and quiet and the sound of the stream.'

The video was restarted at the point where Nick had moved closer to the bench and was standing in front of Eva again just watching her.

He had to comment. Laughing he said, 'I was blocking out the sun so Eva would open her eyes.'

They watched as Nick attempted to throw Eva into the stream. It had all seemed so innocent at the time but was it Eva wondered. She watched the video looking at the girl she once was just a short time ago, happy and carefree. She had not seen a hint of Nick's future intentions. The viewers saw Nick linking Eva, both smiling as they walked back up the garden to the house.

Stephen and Jill laughed at Nick's behaviour only seeing innocent fun and then Stephen said, 'This is what I wanted to show you.' They sat watching the wildlife Stephen had been proud to capture. A healthy selection of garden birds being unsuccessfully stalked by next door's cat, squirrels effortlessly running from branch to branch and lastly early in the morning the badgers annoyingly digging up Stephen's expertly mown lawn. 'For a first attempt I think that worked out very well,' Stephen commented and then continued, 'Jill, shall we have our pudding now?'

Jill went back to the kitchen to dish out the apple pie and Nick followed her. Nick took her by surprise when he said, 'None for me mum, I need to get back, I've got things I need to do.'

'That's not like you to miss out on pudding,' Jill said, 'but if you're sure.'

The Dinner Date

'Yes I'm sure. Thanks for a lovely meal.' And before she knew it he was gone.

She took the tray loaded with dessert back into the conservatory. 'Nick's gone without having pudding, very strange,' she said as she handed round bowls of homemade apple pie and ice cream.

At the end of the visit, when Robert and Eva were leaving, Jill made Eva promise she wouldn't do too much. As Eva walked ahead back to the car Jill turned to Robert and said, 'Eva doesn't look well. She didn't seem relaxed like she usually does when she's here. Is there anything wrong, she doesn't seem herself. She's very quiet and reserved, is she okay?'

'She seems fine at home and at work but I agree she seemed on edge today sitting around the table. It's not like her. She hasn't been the same since the accident or perhaps it was since the dinner with Nick, I'm not sure. I know she's frustrated at the time it's taking her ankle to heal, once she starts dancing and is back in a show I'm sure she will be fine. I'd better go I don't want Eva thinking we are talking about her. Thanks for a lovely meal mum,' he said giving her a hug.

26

It was Monday morning one week after the family Sunday dinner and Eva sat alone in the flat. Robert was working and Emma had just left. Emma had arranged a final session so she could sign off Eva and report back to the Theatre Company who were paying her. Eva felt relaxed and pleased that her body and her ankle felt so good. As she sat she lifted her leg circling her foot, she felt no pain. Her ankle was so much better and felt completely healed. Both the sessions with Emma and the specialist dance physiotherapist, Alex, at the centre near the theatre had helped to accelerate the healing, and Eva congratulated herself on the effort she had put in to complete all the exercises Emma had given her to do between visits.

When the doorbell rang she immediately thought it was Emma returning because she had forgotten something. Eva had a quick look around to see if Emma had left a bag but when she couldn't see anything she smiled wondering what Emma had forgotten to tell her. Emma was a brilliant physio but very forgetful. Without looking through the spy hole Eva opened the door and said smiling, 'What have you forgotten?' The smile vanished as she saw it was Nick standing in front of her. If she had known it was Nick she wouldn't have gone to the door. He must have waited for someone, and probably it had been Emma, to leave the building so he could walk into the entrance hall and make his way to her flat.

'Hello Eva. How are you?' Nick said, pleased at the look of surprise on her face.

She wanted to slam the door in his face but she couldn't, he had already stepped his foot inside. 'What do you want Nick, Robert isn't here.'

The Dinner Date

'I know he isn't. I just wanted to come and see how my lovely sister-in-law is getting on. How is your ankle, all healed?'

'Nick, it's not a good time I have a visitor due in 10 minutes,' she lied.

'Don't worry I will go as soon as they arrive,' he said as he walked passed her into the flat.

Eva's heart was beating fast and her legs felt like jelly but she was not going to be intimidated by Nick in her own home, her sanctuary. He walked confidently into the lounge and sat down opposite the sofa. Eva followed him but stayed standing.

'Please sit down Eva.'

She continued to stand looking down at him. 'What do you want Nick?'

'I want to talk to you Eva. I don't know what you think happened that night but apart from you getting drunk and falling asleep, nothing else happened. I keep telling you this. I didn't touch you other than to put you safely and carefully into my bed. Why don't you believe me?'

'Why did you undress me? she asked.'

'I didn't want the lovely outfit you were wearing to get creased. If you think about it you had to wear that outfit to go home. If it was creased you would have looked a mess and if anyone saw you questions might have been asked?'

'Nick, we both know I didn't drink so much alcohol that it would have caused memory loss,' Eva said pausing before she continued, 'but I did suffer memory loss didn't I Nick. Why would that be, you're the doctor, you must know the answer.'

He didn't answer, he just stared at her with a fixed smile on his face. She thought it felt like a game of tennis waiting for him to serve the next ball. And then he served.

'Do you realise what damage you could cause if you falsely accuse me of...'

Quickly, before he could finish Eva interrupted, 'Of what Nick, drugging and then raping me?'

'Eva, how can you even think I would do that,' he asked narrowing his eyes. 'You will ruin Robert's life if you accuse me and, of course, he may not believe you because as we both know it's not true. Or he may think you led me on, I could encourage that thought. Your marriage will be over. Think about that. Think about what you have to lose. If you accept that nothing happened, which it didn't, you could live your life as planned, playing happy families.'

Eva could see he was becoming anxious and clutching at straws. She wasn't going to be bullied. 'Robert would never believe you rather than me,' Eva replied.

'I know I could convince him that nothing happened, because nothing did happen. It's all in your drunken imagination,' Nick said his eyes fixed on her.

'Just go Nick, please leave. As I've said I have a visitor coming soon.'

'I'll go when you promise you will forget that evening, it's in your best interest to do so.'

'Nick, are you threatening me?'

'No Eva, I'm suggesting what the best thing is for you to do.'

'Just get out, Nick,' she shouted.

'I'll go Eva but just remember what you will lose if you falsely accuse me,' he threatened and with that comment he walked out of the flat.

Eva heard the door slam shut and she went to the window and watched as he walked to his car, he didn't look back. She turned and walked back to the sofa and sat down heavily placing her head in her hands. What the hell was she going to do now, she had no idea. Nick was right she would have so much to lose if she accused him of something he didn't do or if he had raped her, as she was sure he had, and no one believed her. It was her word against his! When she thought

The Dinner Date

about it there were so many reasons why she should keep silent but she didn't know if she could. She felt so angry, angry that this had happened to her and confused as to why Nick would do this to her. She wouldn't tell Robert that Nick had visited her.

Eva couldn't wait for the doctor's assessment which had been booked for next week and all being well she would be able to start auditioning for parts. She was hoping that life would then get back to some sort or normality, perhaps she would be able to move on!

27

Eva's first audition she had after the doctor had given her the 'all clear' was successful and she soon began to feel better not only physically but also her mood brightened. When she was dancing she could forget Nick and the dinner date but when she was alone she was still tormented by the experience and undecided what she should do. She was staying in digs near to the theatre while Robert was able to travel back to the flat each day from the theatre where he was directing a new play. They spoke to each other every evening and on one occasion Robert mentioned that Nick had called round. This worried her. She was suspicious and felt certain that he had visited Robert because he knew she was staying in digs. Would he be making sure that the seed he had planted about her being 'very drunk' was growing stronger. It was the only ammunition he had, to nurture this thought in everyone's mind. She pushed this worry to the back of her mind and concentrated on her nightly performance.

The short run of the show ended and Eva was tired, more tired than she could ever remember being after a show but she looked and felt well, even putting on a little weight which Robert said suited her.

One evening Robert walked into the lounge and reminded Eva that it was his mum's 60th birthday soon and she must mark the date in her diary. 'I know Dad is arranging a small party for the weekend before mum's birthday for family and a few friends. You know mum doesn't like a fuss but a milestone birthday can't be ignored.'

'No, of course it can't. I'm sure she will enjoy a small party,' Eva replied. The thought of it made her feel anxious. Once again she felt she didn't want to be in the same room as Nick. She would have to think of an excuse not to go but that

The Dinner Date

would be difficult as she knew the only one that would be accepted would be an illness. She couldn't and wouldn't feign an illness, that would be tempting fate, so with that thought in mind she was resigned to the fact that she would have to attend the party. She would have to make sure she mingled with the guests and stayed as far away as possible from Nick without making it too obvious.

Saturday morning 2 weeks before Jill's 60th birthday party Robert picked up the invitation which had been sent in the old fashioned way through the post. Stephen had already made sure that Nick, Robert and Eva were free on that Saturday night. Robert knew that with the help of Jill's sister Annie, his dad had organised caterers to deliver a buffet and a large cake. The actual date of Jill's birthday was during the week and on that day his dad was taking her for a 'posh' meal.

Robert strolled into the kitchen where Eva was sitting eating her breakfast. 'The invitation is here,' Robert said laughing. 'The old fashion way through the post. I'm really looking forward to it. It will be good to get together with other members of our family I haven't seen for ages. I'm sure our family who you haven't already met will be dying to meet you.'

'Yes it will be nice for you, is Nick bringing Kate?'

'No idea, you know Nick he does his own thing. He may come alone or with Kate. He's known about it long enough to make sure she isn't working. Are you looking forward to it?

'Yes of course,' she said lying, anxiety already forming in the pit of her stomach.

'Any ideas what present we can get mum?'

'Leave it with me and I'll give it some thought.' Later that evening Eva came up with an idea. 'Rob, I think I know what might be a good present for your mum.'

'Great. What is it?'

'How about we pay for your mum and dad to have Afternoon Tea at Fortnum & Masons.'

'That sounds like a brilliant idea. Well done. I knew there was a reason I married you.'

With that comment a cushion was thrown across the room hitting Robert full in the face. 'Wow good shot Eva,' he said laughing.

The next day Eva arranged the Afternoon Tea and now all she had to worry about was attending the party if she couldn't think of an acceptable reason not to. And it turned out she couldn't. Two weeks later Robert and Eva arrived at the party. She hadn't seen Nick's car in the drive so she guessed he hadn't arrived yet. She immediately began to relax. A small marquee had been erected in the garden and Eva noticed, as she walked through the kitchen, clearly labelled boxes of food had been delivered.

'I'm going to find your mum and offer to help.'

'Good idea. Let me know if you need me. In the meantime I will mingle with the few guests that have already arrived,' he said turning to join a small cluster of people engrossed in conversation.

Eva eventually found Jill who seemed very calm, but then again she always did Eva thought. Robert and Eva had phoned Jill on the day of her birthday to wish her happy birthday and Eva had emailed her the invitation to Afternoon Tea at Fortnum and Masons, she had been delighted.

'Can I do anything to help,' Eva asked.

'Yes please. You could start unwrapping the food and putting it out on plates and taking it to the marquee. That would be a great help.'

Eva worked happily in the kitchen unpacking the food and placing it decoratively on plates for other helpers to take to the marquee. She had no idea she was being watched until she turned around and suddenly Nick was in front of her. Their eyes met as he stared at her almost challenging her and his eyes were cold and then his persona changed back into the kind and friendly Nick.

The Dinner Date

'Hi Eva, can I help you.'

She knew she had to act as normal as she could but she was finding it difficult, she had seen the two sides of Nick.

'You can take these plates into the marquee,' she replied trying to stay as calm and relaxed as she could.

'Will do,' he said smiling as if nothing was different between them. She struggled to do the same.

It wasn't long before more guests arrived and the house was buzzing and felt so much smaller crowded with people. Once Eva had finished helping, she set off to find Robert and the many introductions began. Eva wasn't a party goer, it was something she never had been but this party was more of a challenge as she attempted to avoid Nick. Robert proudly introduced her to his Aunt Annie, husband Peter and their grown up children, Giles and Gillian. Jill's two best friends, Sarah and Jean had been invited as had several work colleagues. Their neighbours from both sides had turned up and Eva noticed that Jill appeared to be enjoying herself, just as it should be.

It wasn't long before it was time for the speeches and to cut the cake. Robert called for everyone to gather around and he proceeded to make a lovely speech with Nick interrupting several times with amusing quips before his mum cut the beautifully decorated cake which spelt out the number 60. Eva watched Robert noting he was in his element, he loved making speeches and being the centre of attention. Both boys were on either side of their mum. Nick looked around smiling at the guests but when his eyes rested on Eva his expression changed to a derisive smile intimating that this was his family and they would never believe her.

Jill thanked everyone for coming to the party and celebrating with her and then she thanked Stephen for being a wonderful husband all these years and, arms around both the boys, she finished with saying how lucky and proud she was to have such wonderful sons and a lovely daughter-in-law.

Eva watched the happy family. How could she spoil this by accusing Nick of the heinous crime he may have committed, it would destroy this family. But on the other hand how could she keep this a secret, they needed to know the 'real' Nick and what he may have been capable of doing. Eva knew the one thing that was stopping her was the thought that she may be wrong!

'Are you okay Eva? Tell me when you want to go home, you look tired,' Robert said as he put his arms around her.

'I'm fine. It's a lovely party and your mum looks so happy.' But she was tired, tired of playing an acting game in front of everyone and more than anything she wanted to be somewhere else. She wanted to run away from the effort of hiding this awful secret.

As much as possible she avoided Nick for the rest of the party and was relieved when he left first. As soon as he went she started to relax with the few guests who had remained. Eva had no idea that Jill had been watching both her and Nick and could sense there was an atmosphere between them. That revelation would come later.

When all the guests had left, Robert, Eva and Annie helped clear up the remains of the party before leaving for home.

'That was a good party, I enjoyed it, did you?' Robert asked Eva.

'Yes, it was lovely to see your mum so happy and to meet the rest of your family.' And with that comment they made their way home to a well-earned rest.

28

One week after the party Robert and Eva were on the way to visit Jill and Stephen.

'It will be good to hear what mum and dad's Afternoon Tea was like. I'm sure mum is dying to tell you all about it,' Robert enthused.

'Yes, I've always wondered what it would be like and now I'm about to find out. If it's as good as I think we need to treat ourselves,' Eva replied grinning.

'I'll bear that in mind for your birthday,' Robert replied. He had noted that once Eva had started to re-connect with her fellow dancers her mood had improved. They had had three weeks of their lives being normal and enjoying their work commitments.

'So, what does your dad want to talk to you about,' Eva asked.

'Mum thinks he's looking to buy a new car and wants some advice.' Laughing Robert continued, 'I'm no expert but I think I'm a bit better than dad. Anyway it will be nice to see both of them.'

When they arrived at the house Jill ushered them in. 'Afternoon Tea,' she said laughing. 'Sorry it really is only a cup of tea. I can't wait to tell you all about Fortnum and Masons.' Sitting around the table with mugs of tea she described the Afternoon Tea in great detail making both Robert and Eva increasingly envious. 'I don't know whose idea it was but I can guess and it was one of the best birthday presents I've had. A wonderful experience, thank you both so much.'

'It was our pleasure,' Robert said.

Suddenly they heard footsteps coming round the back of the house. Smiling Stephen said, 'Ah that'll be Nick. He said he was going to pop round and return my camera. No idea what he wanted it for but apparently he's managed to copy the photos he had taken onto his computer. I would have thought he could have used his phone but he claims it's not nearly as good as my camera,' he said emphasising the MY.

Eva's heart sank. She had managed to avoid Nick since the 60th birthday party and had been able to push the dinner date to the back of her mind. It still made her feel sick thinking about the Sunday lunch she had endured. Since then she had rehearsed in her mind many times how to react towards Nick when in the presence of his family but she didn't know if she could carry it off.

Nick burst through the door. 'Saw your car in the drive Robert, is this a family get together?'

Robert laughing replied, 'Mum invited us round and it looks like you invited yourself. Mum and dad have been telling us all about the Afternoon Tea they had enjoyed. It sounds delicious and it's making me hungry.'

'Sit down Nick, would you like a cuppa,' Jill asked.

'No I'm okay thanks mum. Here's your camera dad. It takes wonderful photos, or perhaps it's just because I'm a wonderful photographer,' he said grinning.

'What were you taking photos of? Robert enquired.

'Just wildlife.'

Eva noticed that he briefly glanced over at her before commenting 'So the Afternoon Tea was good was it. Who's idea was it, Eva's I guess,' and then he turned and looked at her. 'How did you come up with the idea?'

She looked directly at him, 'It was something I knew I would enjoy and I trusted my instincts, as I always do, and thought it was something your mum would love. Your mum and I both have the same high standards.' She was surprised at how calm and in control she felt. She was certain Nick would be careful of what he said in front of his family. Of course she knew it would be different if she was alone with

The Dinner Date

him, the last encounter had proved it. It was a side of Nick she had never seen before and it had scared her but perhaps it had shown he was worried about what she might reveal to Robert.

'Am I going to have the pleasure of all my family staying for supper later,' Jill asked.

'Not for us mum, Eva has things she wants to do back at the flat. Dad do you want me to take you to see that car you were talking about and you could possibly test drive it?

'Yes that would be great Robert. I would be happier if you saw the car before I decide to buy it.'

'How about you Nick, can you stay for supper?'

'No sorry mum I need to get back I'm on the late shift at the hospital.'

I've just had a thought if you're not staying for supper Nick, could you drop Eva off at the flat?' Robert asked. Eva froze when she heard Robert's suggestion.

'Yes of course Rob, no problem. It would be my pleasure to be Eva's chauffeur,' he said smiling at her but she noticed his eyes were cold, they displayed the real Nick.

The panic began to rise in her. She didn't want to be alone with Nick in the confined space of his car. She willed herself to keep calm and taking a deep breath she turned towards Robert. 'I don't mind waiting for you while you help your dad,' Eva said hoping she sounded calmer than she felt.

'I don't know how long I will be, these things always take longer than you think. Nick can go past the flat so it makes sense. Decision made!' Robert proclaimed. If she continued to object Eva knew it would make her behaviour appear odd. Before the dinner date she wouldn't have thought twice about sharing a car with Nick but now she could feel her stomach tighten into a knot.

'Are you ready to go now Dad?'

'Yes Robert, I'll just get my coat.'

'I'm going to make a move as well,' Nick said, 'Are you ready Eva?'

She wasn't ready, she would never be ready to take this journey. She could feel everyone's eyes on her waiting for her reply.

Jill stepped forward and hugged her. 'It's been lovely seeing you and thank you once again for suggesting and organising the Afternoon Tea,' Jill said and then continued much quieter, 'when you are next at home on your own I will come round and bring cakes and we can have our own Afternoon Tea.'

As Jill pulled away from Eva she looked straight into her face, into her eyes and what she saw worried her, something wasn't right, Eva looked distressed almost agitated as if she was carrying a huge unpleasant secret.

Eva said, 'That would be lovely.' But Jill felt there was a reticence in Eva's reply almost as if she didn't want it to happen.

Once outside Nick held the car door open for Eva, playing the gentleman! Very reluctantly she climbed in and Nick walked to the driver's side and climbed in beside her. Robert, getting into his own car alongside his dad shouted, 'Take care of my wife Nick. See you later Eva.'

'Of course I will, I always do, don't I Eva?' And with that Nick put his foot down and drove away in silence. Neither spoke until they were well out of sight of the house.

'Well this is nice isn't it Eva. So kind of Robert to suggest that I drive you home,' Nick said briefly taking his eyes off the road to look at her. A horn blared out as Nick only just missed a car pulling out. Eva gripped the side of the car. 'Are you trying to kill me Nick? Would that solve all your problems?' Eva asked.

'Eva I don't have a problem, it's you that has the problem. You have to stop thinking that I did something to you that night, I didn't. If you even think about saying what you imagine happened to Robert, I promise you will regret it. Think about it we both have so much to lose. We need to put any misunderstanding behind us and we can go back to how we used to be, for the sake of Robert.'

'Why are you so worried about me saying something to Robert? If you are so innocent surely you would be able to convince Robert that I am mistaken.'

'God Eva, I'm sorry I ever asked you out on the date. I thought I was being kind and helping my injured sister-in-law but according to you I'm the evil brother-in-law who planned to get you drunk to take advantage of you. You should listen to what you are saying and how ridiculous it is. Just leave it Eva, let's get on with our lives. Shut the door on the date and I promise you I will never ask you out again for dinner. Christ I would be mad to do so.'

Eva turned to him, 'And I would be crazy to accept. Just concentrate on your driving and get me home in one piece.'

Nick pulled up abruptly outside the flat. 'Thanks for the lift Nick. Just to let you know I will do what I have to do.' And with that comment she walked calmly to the safety of her home and as she entered she immediately rushed to the bathroom where she threw up shaking violently and still having no idea exactly what she was going to do.

She sat on the bathroom floor leaning against the bath with her head in her hands. She let out a loud almost animal like scream as she rocked from side to side trying to understand why this had happened to her, to them. Everything was spoilt. The three of them had been such good friends. She had always felt so comfortable with Nick and enjoyed his company. Eva couldn't have asked for a better brother-in-law, but not now, that had all changed. Yes, she had to admit to herself that she was scared of Nick, scared to be alone with him but she had to hide this fear from Robert and from both Jill and Stephen. This awful secret she held was tearing her apart.

When her rapid breathing had steadied she slowly got to her feet and splashed cold water on her face. She hoped she had time to compose herself before Robert came home. He couldn't see her like this, how would she explain it to him! She flushed the toilet and sprayed the bathroom to get rid of the smell of sick. That was the easy bit, she wished it was so easy to get rid of the dinner date from her mind, to pretend it had never happened, to flush that down the toilet. If only she could! She went into the lounge and curled up like a child on the sofa rocking herself to sleep.

After an exhausting trip around several garages Robert eventually dropped his dad back home. 'Was it a successful exercise,' Jill asked.

'I think so,' he said pulling a face. While his dad took the stack of car brochures he had acquired into his study Robert asked his mum, 'Mum do you think there is an atmosphere between Nick and Eva. I get the feeling Eva is uncomfortable when Nick is around. Have you noticed?'

'Yes I have noticed there is not the normal banter between them. Perhaps Eva is embarrassed about being a little drunk on her date with Nick. I'm sure it's nothing to worry about.'

'Yes you're probably right. I will leave you to discuss cars with dad.'

'Oh please don't,' she said laughing.

Two hours after he had left Eva with Nick, Robert finally arrived home. 'Sorry I've been so long,' he shouted as he walked through the door. 'We decided to visit some other garages, just to compare cars. I know we could do all this online but dad wanted to get the feel of the different makes and models of cars. I think it was helpful.' There was no response from Eva so he made his way through to the lounge. She was still lying on the sofa and as he looked at her he asked, 'Are you okay Eva, you look very pale?' She sat up and he wrapped his arms around her.

The Dinner Date

'That feels so good, a hug was just what I needed. I do feel tired. I'm glad that I've got a couple of weeks rest before I go back to work,' she replied.

'You've been through a lot since your accident perhaps you haven't given yourself enough time to recover,' he commented. 'You know you don't have to accept every job offered. It won't be held against you. You've had a tough few months and sometimes your body knows best and tells you when you have to slow down.'

Eva looked at Robert, he had no idea what she had been through. She smiled at him and said, 'You are the last person to tell me to reject potential work. You can be on your knees and you still won't say no.'

He grinned, 'Yes I know. I guess that's just what we creative people are like, always worried that a time will come when we can no longer compete with the youngsters coming into the business. For the moment the most important thing to consider is,' he paused and she waited, holding her breath, anxious that he was going to ask how the car journey home with Nick had been, but he didn't that came later, 'what will I cook for our supper?'

Since her accident and Robert's unexpected cookery lessons he had started to enjoy cooking and often cooked for the two of them with some success, and on this occasion it was a definite success. After the meal she helped to clean up a very messy kitchen. Smiling to herself she could never understand why Robert made so much mess when he cooked. She made coffee which they took into the lounge.

'So, did my big brother look after you on the drive home. He didn't decide to make several stops on the way. I remember when he could drive but I was still too young to drive, he would offer to take me to friend's houses or collect me. He could never drive straight home, he always had to go somewhere else first. He didn't do that to you did he?'

'No we came straight here.'

'And he didn't tease you too much. I noticed you didn't look too pleased when I suggested he drop you off on his way home.'

'Robert, the journey was fine,' and she quickly changed the subject. 'Your mum and dad seemed to enjoy the Afternoon Tea. I'm so pleased I thought of it.'

'So am I, but I'm even more pleased you're my wife. Shall we have an early night?'

That was the last thing Eva wanted but she couldn't say that to Robert.

29

Eva hadn't told Jill she had the next couple weeks off work because she didn't want her visiting when she was on her own. She guessed Jill had noticed that the relationship between her and Nick was strained and she was worried that she would ask her questions she really didn't want to answer. That wasn't actually true, she did want to share her thoughts and feelings with someone but not with Jill, Nick's mother! She could never tell her what she thought had happened, Jill would be devastated.

But it didn't stop Jill and, instead of contacting Eva to make sure she would be at home, she very casually asked the question at the end of a phone call with Robert. 'Do you know if Eva will be home tomorrow afternoon? I'm passing the flat and thought I would drop by and say hello.'

'As far as I know she will be, I don't think she has anything planned. She has been so tired lately and she just wants to rest. I'm worried that she's still suffering from the consequences of the accident, not physically but mentally. I think a visit from you is just what the doctor ordered.'

'Yes, I do order a visit,' she replied laughing. 'If you speak to Nick let me know what he's up to. It was such a brief visit from him the other day.'

'Will do. Enjoy your visit with Eva.'

The following afternoon Eva lay on her bed staring at the ceiling trying hard to focus her mind on something other than Nick. She had tried to concentrate on reading a book, something she rarely had time to do, watching a film and then a comedy programme but to no avail. Her mind kept re-visiting the decision she had to make, to share her suspicions or to keep them to herself locked deep inside her for the rest of her life. She didn't think she could do that but the consequences of any action she took seemed too great to bear. It seemed either way she couldn't win. When she heard the doorbell she did consider ignoring it but whoever it was wouldn't go away. The fear in her began to increase, what if it was Nick. She made sure this time that she checked her phone and the security camera showed it was Jill. She released the door to the block of flats and then opened the door to her flat.

Jill stood smiling. 'I've come for afternoon tea. I've brought the cakes, you just need to make the tea,' she said as she stepped inside. 'How are you Eva? You look at though you need a good chat and some delicious cakes.'

Even though she was anxious when she saw it was Jill, Eva couldn't help but smile. Jill was always so upbeat. 'I'm fine thanks Jill. Have you recovered from your party?' she asked as they walked to the kitchen.

'Yes, it was lovely, I really enjoyed it. Did you?'

'Yes, it was nice to meet your friends and relatives who I hadn't met before,' Eva replied.

Jill watched Eva's reaction trying to assess her true feelings about the party. She was sure there was something bothering Eva but she couldn't think what it might be.

'Did you want tea or coffee,' Eva asked.

'Tea please,' Jill replied as she opened the box of cakes she had brought.

They sat down at the small kitchen table with mugs of hot tea and a selection of delicious small fancy cream cakes.

'Please Eva help yourself to a cake.'

Eva smiled but it felt like she was acting in a play. She didn't want a cake and she didn't want to be sitting here opposite Jill waiting to be asked questions she didn't want to answer. As she took a cake she said, 'These cakes look yummy, thank you this is a lovely treat to share with you.'

'So Eva, how are you feeling. Is it good to be back dancing? As soon as you have time we must take another shopping trip. That was so much fun last time. We did laugh didn't we?'

'Yes we did. That seems such a long time ago although I know it wasn't,' Eva said with a sigh which registered with Jill. Eva continued to answer Jill's question, 'It is good to be back dancing but I must admit I've never felt so exhausted after each performance and it seems to take me ages to get my energy back. At one time it would only be an hour after the end of the show when I would be ready to do it all again but not now. I think I'm getting old,' she said laughing.

Jill smiled thoughtfully. 'Stress can strip you of energy when something is constantly on your mind and you can't walk away from it. You do seem to have something that is worrying you. Would it help to tell me?'

Here it was the question that Eva had been dreading and she had no idea how she was going to answer it. She didn't want to lie and say there was nothing wrong but also she didn't want to share with Jill her thoughts on what happened on the night of the date. Would Jill even believe her – she doubted it. Eva was sure Jill would defend Nick, any mother would and it could also make her hate Eva for even suggesting it. And if that was the case it could split the family apart and Robert would have to know the reason why.

Jill reached out to touch Eva's hand. 'You know the cliché "a trouble shared is a trouble halved". You can tell me anything.' Jill smiled, 'As a doctor I've probably heard it all before.'

Eva doubted that and gently moved her hand and looked at Jill. She couldn't hurt this kind, caring woman. It would break her heart and even worse if Eva was wrong and accuses her son of something he didn't do she could never face Jill again. So many lives could be ruined. Perhaps she should just walk away from her suspicions and convince herself it never happened. Would that be the best thing to do? It would be for Nick and for his family but could she do that she questioned herself. She could walk away but she knew she could never convince herself that Nick was innocent.

'Oh Jill you are so kind and I'm lucky to have you as my mother-in-law.' Tears began to well up in Eva's eyes and Jill noticed. She immediately got up and went to Eva, putting her arms around her.

'Don't worry Eva whatever is bothering you I'm sure we can sort it out.'

Eva wished more than anything it could be that easy.

'I have noticed that the relationship between you and Nick is strained. Has Nick done something to upset you? Has he said something to offend you? Nick can be insensitive sometimes. From the age of 10 until his late teens he went through a difficult stage emotionally and he could be very cruel at times. Stephen and I noticed at the time that he displayed some sort of grudge against Robert. We thought it may have been because we told him too late that he had been adopted, but then we came to the conclusion it was just Nick growing into an adult. If he has upset you I apologise for my son. Nick is a good person and a wonderful doctor.'

Eva didn't know how to answer Jill. She was surprised and shocked by Jill acknowledging the tension between her and Nick. Jill was so near to the truth. Eva was struggling to suppress the desire to confess that she suspected Nick had raped her. It was on the tip of her tongue to let go of this awful secret but she just couldn't bring herself to do it. To hurt Jill.

'Okay Eva, wipe your tears. I understand if you don't want to share your problem with me today but remember I'm always ready to listen when you want to talk. Call or text me anytime. Really it doesn't matter what the problem is, even if it involves Nick we can sort it out, I promise you. Let's move on to something else. Have you and Robert got any time off work organised. A stay in a posh hotel being totally spoilt is

The Dinner Date

just what you both need. Suggest it to Robert and if you don't I will,' Jill said with a look of concern on her face.

Eva managed to compose herself and thanked Jill for her kindness and understanding. Jill made sure that she would leave Eva smiling by reminding her of the awful dress she had tried on when they went shopping. The clear vision Eva had in her mind did make her smile.

When Jill was standing at the door about to leave she surprised Eva by saying, 'You're not pregnant by any chance are you?'

Eva was totally taken aback by this question. 'No of course not, Robert and I don't want children just yet and I'm on the pill.'

'Have you accidentally missed taking it, perhaps when you had your accident.'

'No, I definitely took it.'

Eva looked at Jill confused. Why was Jill, a doctor, asking her this question.

'What made you ask me if I could be pregnant.'

Jill smiled. 'Don't look so worried. The fact that you are feeling so tired and that you appear to have put on weight made me wonder. If you were pregnant it wouldn't be the end of the world would it. Have you still had your periods?'

'Yes,' but then when Eva thought about it she had bled but it wasn't like her normal monthly period. Still, she thought, she couldn't be pregnant she was on the pill.

'Have you had a course of antibiotics recently? This can affect the success of the pill in preventing pregnancy. Have you felt sick at all?'

'No I haven't.' And then she thought about how many times recently she had been sick. She had thought it was stress causing it. What would Robert say, would he be pleased or upset at an unplanned pregnancy.

Jill leaned across to kiss Eva before she stepped outside the flat. 'Don't worry you probably aren't but it might be as well to do a pregnancy test just to make sure and if you are we will all be delighted, including Robert I'm sure.' As she turned to walk away she said, 'And don't forget whenever you need to talk I'm always here for you.'

Eva stood and watched as Jill made her way to her car. She really couldn't be pregnant could she? For the rest of the day she tried to put the thought out of her mind but kept looking down at her belly wondering if there was a tiny baby growing inside. She knew she had been prescribed antibiotics for a slight throat infection but she couldn't remember exactly when she had taken them. She seemed to think it was shortly after her accident. As soon as she had time she would get a pregnancy test kit, but until she was certain of the results of the test she wasn't going to share Jill's suspicions with Robert.

When Robert came home and after giving her a huge hug which she needed so much, he said, 'How did your Afternoon Tea go with mum?'

'How did you know?'

'Mum asked me if you would be at home, she wanted to surprise you.'

'It was good. Your mum is very good company.'

'More importantly are there any cakes left?'

'Of course, we left you some for after your dinner.'

Snuggled up on the sofa Eva wondered whether she should broach the subject of children. It was something they hadn't discussed for a while but she decided not to. If it was a false alarm, which she hoped it was, Robert need never know. When they had talked about having a family Eva had made it clear that she wanted to keep dancing for a few more years before starting a family. When that happened they had decided she would retire from dancing until the child or children were past toddler age and then she would start a career teaching dancing. She hoped that plan wasn't going to be spoilt.

The Dinner Date

After the weekend and on the Monday morning when Robert had gone back to work, Eva went and bought a pregnancy test. Her hands were shaking as she read the instructions and then peed on the stick. Tears started to fall as she waited for the results. She began to question whether she should have told Robert that she might be pregnant. Too late now she had done the test and now she just had to wait for the result. When the time was up the test clearly showed positive. She was pregnant. She burst into uncontrollable sobbing. Robert should have been here with her, sharing the news. She sat on the bathroom floor, head in her hands wondering how many weeks she was pregnant and when did she conceive this child. She was sure a doctor would be able to tell roughly when conception had taken place. She was scared very scared. She knew she would have to confide in Jill not only as her mother-in-law but as a doctor that she was pregnant but would she share with her the fear that Robert may not be the father!

30

For the next few days Eva found it difficult to concentrate. Her mind was working all the time trying to make a decision on what to do next. She was due to start rehearsals at the start of the following week and her free time would be limited so with trepidation she made a doctor's appointment. She wanted to know roughly the date of conception. As she sat in the waiting room she grew more and more anxious. What if the date was around the day of the dinner date with Nick. She couldn't bear to even think that would be the case. If it wasn't she could relax and share the news she was pregnant with Robert without any fear that the baby wasn't his.

She hated doctors waiting rooms at the best of times but today it felt even worse. She watched as names were called and slowly the waiting room started to empty. When her name was eventually called she reluctantly went to learn her fate.

Eva left the doctors surgery in a daze. She didn't want to go straight home, she couldn't bear the idea of being alone with her thoughts in the confines of the flat, she needed to be outside. She went to the nearest small park and walked around the lake until she found an empty bench. Although it was a pleasant day there were only a few people in the park.

Dr Sarah Jones had been lovely, confirming the pregnancy and reassuring Eva that her general health was good. She was also able to give a date of conception which she said was not a 100% accurate but an indication of the date. Eva tried to pretend she was thrilled to be pregnant but it had been difficult. Now she sat on a bench in an almost deserted park wondering what she should do. With thoughts swirling around in her mind she watched a young mother with a small child. The little girl was enthusiastically throwing bread to

The Dinner Date

the ducks on the pond and displaying screams of delight. Eva noticed the mother's face was a picture of contentment. Would that be her one day with her child?

As Eva had found out that it was likely the baby was conceived around the time of the dinner date she knew that if Nick had raped her he could be the father but there was also a chance it could be Robert's child. The most awful thought came into her mind – she really wanted to miscarry then this problem would go away naturally or should she think about having an abortion. It was a terrible thought one which she couldn't believe she was thinking – to wish this tiny baby inside her would die – what a terrible mother she was, because that's what she was a mother to this tiny embryo, this new human being that she would bring into this world and, after all, Robert could be the father. She was already beginning to feel a bond with this child and this shocked her but made her feel stronger and protective. Whatever happened this child would be loved.

Eva knew she would have to share the news with Robert very soon but not today. She had to come to terms with carrying a child that could be Nick's. And, of course, she realised that Jill would be contacting her to make sure she had been to see the doctor. Eva knew Jill would be so excited that she was about to become a grandmother not knowing that either of her sons could be the father. What a mess Eva thought and once again wished she could turn the clock back and the dinner date had never happened.

A few days later Jill texted Eva asking how she was and if she had any news? Eva didn't reply. She kept looking at the text not knowing what to say. If she admitted she was pregnant Jill would be delighted and want to share the news. Eva hadn't even told Robert. Every minute when she was talking to him she wanted to tell him, she knew he would be delighted to know he was to become a father but she was scared she couldn't hide her fear that the baby may not be his.

She knew she would have to tell Robert this weekend and also decide how far into her pregnancy she wanted to carry on dancing. The show was to be a short run of 4 weeks which meant that if the pregnancy went as planned she could continue with her performance until the end of the show but of course that would be only if the producer was in agreement. It might be that they would have to slightly change her role to accommodate her changed physical situation. She would have to tell Ken, the producer as soon as she started rehearsals.

On the Friday afternoon Eva still hadn't replied to Jill's text, so Jill did the only thing she could and went round to confront Eva. Deep down she had a feeling that something serious was wrong. When Eva came to the door Jill thought she didn't look at all well.

'Hi Eva, I was just passing and thought I would call in and see if you had any news,' she said smiling but decided not to mention the text as she felt certain Eva had, for some reason, ignored it.

'Hi Jill, come in,' Eva said as she led the way to the lounge. 'Please sit down.' Eva knew this was the moment she had to take the decision to ignore the fact the Nick might be the father or tell Jill everything. She was so tired of thinking about it and at this moment she felt very alone and scared of what might be about to happen. Whatever she said could change all their lives.

Jill looked at Eva eagerly awaiting the news. 'Well are you pregnant, am I to become a grandmother. That makes me feel old,' she said laughing.

'Yes you are.'

'Oh that's brilliant, congratulations. I bet Robert is so excited,' Jill said as she went over and gave Eva a huge hug.

'Robert doesn't know.'

Jill looked puzzled. 'Why haven't you told him? Eva what aren't you telling me. Something is not right here. You

The Dinner Date

should be so excited that you are to become a mum. Is it because you will have to give up your career for a while? Once you've had the baby you can resume your dancing. We can solve any problems that might arise. It's great news.'

'Yes it is good news,' Eva said without conviction.

'What's the matter Eva? Why aren't you excited by the thought of becoming a mum? Please tell me.'

Eva slowly looked up at Jill and their eyes met. She paused. How was she going to answer. Whatever she said now could never be taken back.

Stuttering Eva said, 'I'm sorry Jill I can't share this with you or anyone.'

At first Jill had appeared compassionate but now Eva could hear annoyance and anger in her voice and she surprised Eva by saying, 'Is Robert not the father? Have you been with someone else, had an affair?'

Eva stood up, anger flaring up inside her. 'Of course not. How dare you even suggest I would cheat on Robert.'

'I'm sorry Eva. I don't know what to say. Just tell me what the problem is, please. Let me help.'

Eva sat down. She was exhausted. She couldn't continue to carry this burden alone. Without looking at Jill she said, 'If I share something with you and I'm wrong with what I believe happened you will be devastated and never forgive me and carrying this child makes it even harder for me. But I will tell you because I can no longer keep it a secret.'

Jill didn't respond but waited for Eva to continue.

'I don't remember a huge part of the night of the dinner date with Nick. I can remember going back to his flat and taking a sip of wine he had given me but I don't remember anything else until I woke up the next morning alone in his bed wearing just my underwear. I felt sore inside and my arms were bruised. I felt groggy and very frightened.'

'What are you telling me Eva, didn't Nick take you home that night?'

'No he didn't, he took me back to his flat. Robert thinks Nick took me straight home after the meal but that didn't happen. I remember going back to his flat and Nick insisted I tasted some wine which I think his friend had produced but I don't know what happened after that. I have no memory of Nick carrying me to his bed and undressing me.'

Are you saying that you think Nick did something to you, perhaps something sexual. Are you suggesting Nick raped you?'

'Jill I don't know. I just don't know what happened, all I do know for certain is that I woke up the next morning in Nick's bed in my bra and pants. I felt very sore and with bruises on my arms as if I had been restrained. My head was very groggy almost as if I had taken some sort of drug but I know I didn't, well not willingly.'

Jill sat in silence taking in the devastating information Eva had just shared with her.

Eva broke down, the weeks of keeping this secret had taken its toll.

Shaking her head Jill said, 'I can't believe Nick would do something like that. What does Nick say happened?'

'He just keeps saying that I was very drunk, but I wasn't and even if I had been a little drunk I would still have had some memory of what happened. He's also threatened me that if I say anything no one will believe me. This baby changes everything. It could be Nick's.'

Taking a huge sigh Jill said, 'Eva, I do believe you think Nick raped you but I'm not convinced he did. I'm not saying Nick is perfect, far from it. There is a part of Nick that both Stephen and I have struggled to get to know. He holds back on a lot of his feelings. I need to speak to Nick and see what he has to say.'

'He will only deny what I'm saying,' Eva said.

'I know that. He is hardly going to put his hands up and admit to raping you but believe me I will know if he is lying.

The Dinner Date

He won't be able to hide it from me. We also have to be mindful that you may be wrong and what he is saying that you were very drunk is true. I am concerned about the memory loss but until I speak to Nick I don't want to say any more. I don't want Stephen or Robert involved. We need to keep this between the three of us. The most important thing is that you and the baby are okay. I'm going to go back home and arrange a time to meet Nick. The sooner I hear his version of events the better. You get some rest. As soon as I can, I will get back to you on a decision about what we should do, if anything. And don't worry Eva, what's done is done and can't be undone. Trust me I will always be here to support you and my grandchild. Look after yourself and the baby.' And with that comment Jill once again put her arms around Eva, hugged her and left the flat.

Eva didn't know whether she felt relief that she had shared her thoughts or terrified that Nick would convince his mum he was innocent. Jill would never forgive her for falsely accusing Nick but she was beginning to feel even more certain he was guilty.

31

After her visit with Eva, Jill returned home her head spinning full of thoughts, trying to come to terms with the accusation Eva had made about Nick. Could he have done it, raped Eva. To Jill it seemed impossible but would she ever find out the truth she wondered.

She was glad Stephen was out, she wanted to sit and think about the relationship her boys had with each other or rather Nick had with Robert when they were children. Had she missed something when they were growing up, signs that all was not well with Nick?

Jill smiled when she remembered Robert had been the very annoying little brother. As soon as he could walk he followed Nick everywhere. Everything Nick did Robert copied as little brothers tend to do but Nick seemed so proud to have a little brother he didn't appear to mind, well sometimes he did! She can only recall Nick being very patient with his brother. Even when Robert took his very first teetering steps they were towards his big brother. It had been a bit of a competition between her, Stephen and Nick. The three of them had encouraged Robert to walk towards them and, much to Nick's delight, he had been chosen. Little Robert walked three steps before he fell into the arms of his brother. She recalls how delighted they had been that the boys got on so well.

Jill recollects that once Robert started to walk there was no stopping him and he would race around looking for Nick. One of the first words Robert said was Nick. Quite an easy word for a baby to say, and once he got the hang of saying it, he never stopped. Calling out all the time for 'Nick'. She knew it did become slightly irritating for Nick, however he

The Dinner Date

never lost his temper and even though he was still so young himself he always gave Robert his time.

Jill sat nursing her cup of tea and staring into space. She had always thought that there had been a subtle change in the way Nick reacted to Robert after they revealed to him that he was adopted. She sat shaking her head. She had discussed it with Stephen many times after Robert was born trying to decide when would be the best time to tell Nick but no time seemed the right time. She realised now that they had been avoiding telling him. They had their perfect family, two healthy boys who played together and were the best of friends. They didn't want to rock the boat and as time went on they found it harder to reveal the truth until one day, after she had been talking to a work colleague she knew she had to explain to Nick that he had been adopted. At that time he was 10 years old and would soon be entering into the 'teenage' years. Her colleague explained to her that the age a child was told they were adopted was very important. The earlier the better and preferably as soon as the child was old enough to understand what adoption meant. At the time they told Nick she recalls he was at first both confused and then upset by the news. Then the anger came fuelled by his distress. If she remembers correctly it had taken a while for the tears to subside but then when she gently explained how he was a very special little boy and that they had chosen him he seemed to accept the news. Had they got it wrong? From the moment he had been told the news had he always been carrying deep inside him a grudge, or jealousy towards Robert? He never showed it. But now she wondered!

Looking back, she realised that the family shied away from discussing with Nick how he felt about his adoption. As Nick became an adult she always wondered if he had any desire to find his birth mother and possibly his half siblings but she never had the courage to ask him. Something always stopped her at the last moment and she knew what that was, she was scared that if this was a path he wanted to take it would mean she had failed as a mother. He had never suggested that it was something he longed to do and for this she was grateful.

She did once ask Robert if he had ever discussed the adoption with his brother and he said no, if Nick wanted to discuss it with him that was fine but he was never going to bring up the subject. Nick was his brother and that was all that mattered.

Jill brought herself back to the present and the problem she faced and made the decision to speak to Nick that evening and arrange a visit as soon as possible.

32

Jill phoned Nick that evening. 'Hi mum.'
'Hi Nick. Are you around tomorrow? I've got something for you.'
'Ooh lovely, what is it?'
'It's a surprise.'
'I can come and collect if you like?'
'No, I will come to your flat. When is a good time?' she asked trying to sound casual as if it was something she often did instead of a rare occasion.
'I'm in tomorrow morning. I don't start work until after lunch.'
'Great, I will see you about 10, have the kettle on.'
'Okay will do.' And Jill hung up leaving Nick to think it was a very odd call, his mum rarely came round to his flat.
The next morning Jill went and bought an Air Fryer for Nick. She knew he had wanted one for a while but had never got around to buying one. Arriving at his door, box in hand, she began to feel anxious but was determined not to show it.
As Nick answered the door he said, 'Hi mum, is this my surprise?'
'Yes Nick. Can you take it from me it's heavy.'
'An Air Fryer, thanks mum. I'm part of the modern world now,' he said grinning.
'Nick, don't unpack it now, I want to talk to you.'
'That sounds serious. What's up.'
'First make some coffee and then I need to ask you some questions.'
'Okay, go and sit in the lounge,' he said with concern in his voice.

Jill went through to the lounge and as she sat waiting for Nick she thought about the consequences of the next few minutes and felt the tension rise in her. She had to stay calm.

Nick brought in the coffee and handed a mug to his mum and then sat down opposite to her. 'Go on then ask me these questions, I'm curious,' he said grinning and sipping his coffee. 'You're not going to give me a lecture on how to safely use the Air Fryer are you?'

'No Nick it's nothing to do with the Air Fryer.' She paused looking down at her coffee giving herself time to consider how to phrase the question and then she continued, 'I just wanted to know why there is a bit of an atmosphere between you and Eva. You used to get on so well together. I always thought you were like brother and sister, but that seems to have changed since you took her out for a meal.'

Jill noticed he hesitated before giving his reply as though carefully thinking about what he should say. 'I wasn't aware there was a problem, there certainly isn't with me. Has Eva said something?' As Jill looked at her son she noticed a worried frown had appeared on his face.

'Yes she has. What do you think that might be Nick?'

'I've no idea. We had a lovely meal together. Eva is good company and very funny when she is drunk,' he said smiling but Jill noticed it was a forced nervous smile.

'So, tell me about that evening when you came back here. Why did you bring Eva here, was it to give her more wine to get her drunk, thinking it would be funny? Does Robert know you brought Eva back to your flat?'

'Mum, what's this all about. What has Eva been saying? I haven't thought to mention to Robert that we came back here, I don't know if Eva has.'

'She told me about the evening or as much as she can remember. Any idea what she might have told me?'

'Mum, I have no idea what she has said to you but all I did was bring her back here to give her a present, a good luck pendant and let her taste some excellent wine and share her opinion with me. But she fell asleep and I put her to bed. And really mum that is all that happened and if Eva is telling you something different I need to know.'

Jill had noticed that Nick had started to fidget and tap his foot – something he always did as a child when he was lying. 'That's exactly what Eva said you told her had happened but what she can't understand is that she has no memory after drinking the wine. The next thing she remembers is waking up in the morning half naked in your bed feeling sore with deep bruises on her arms. Nick why do you think she would have suffered memory loss. You and I are both doctors and that would usually happen as a result of taking a drug for medical reasons to make the patient unaware of a procedure that was to take place.'

'What are you inferring that I drugged Eva!'

'That's my next question Nick. Did you drug Eva and why?'

'How can you ask that. No I didn't drug Eva. Why would I do that.' Nick stood up and started pacing the floor before shouting, 'I can't believe you're suggesting I did.'

Jill watched her son as his anger began to develop. He was beginning to look like a trapped animal who couldn't find an escape route.

'Nick, calm down. I'm not suggesting anything, I'm simply asking you a question.'

'Calm down – how can I calm down. What exactly are you accusing me of doing?'

'I'm not accusing you of anything, I'm asking you if you gave Eva something to make her sleep, perhaps to ease the pain of her injury?'

'I only gave her a glass of wine and nothing else. She didn't complain about being in pain. I don't understand what she is saying?'

'Nick, Eva is confused and upset that she can't remember most of that evening including you undressing her and putting her to bed.'

Still pacing up and down his anger mounting Nick replied, 'I took her outer garments off so they wouldn't crease as she lay in bed. God I wish I hadn't bothered – it was a struggle. If I'd known it was going to cause some 'questions' I would have left her on the sofa. I can't believe she is suggesting something happened that evening.'

Jill watched as he paced up and down noticing that he avoided looking directly at her – again something he did as a child when he got caught doing something he had been told not to do.

'Nick, please sit down and we can talk about this calmly. Eva is worried about what happened during the hours she can't remember. I'm sure you want to put her mind at rest.'

Jill carefully watched his body language. He was so agitated. 'Mum I tried the next morning to put her mind at rest but she wouldn't listen to me. She doesn't believe me. I can't make her believe me. I swear NOTHING HAPPENED,' he shouted. 'If you want to know Eva flirted with me and in her drunken stupor came on to me. I fended her off.' And then under his breath he murmured. 'She was gagging for it.'

Jill got up and walked over to her son reaching out and holding his shoulders while turning him to face her. He wouldn't make eye contact and this made her think he could be guilty of raping Eva, but why would he do it. Was it something to do with his feelings towards Robert, only Nick could answer that. Without Nick confessing they had no proof and he would never confess.

'Nick, I'm going to leave you now. Think about what I've said. This conversation must stay between you and me. Robert and your dad must never know about it, do you understand?'

He didn't answer and she left the flat with a sinking heart contemplating the awful mess.

33

That evening Jill left Stephen busy with his photography while she sat in the lounge returning over and over again to both the conversations with Nick and Eva. The more she remembered Nick's response the more she thought this was not the reaction of an innocent man. She couldn't see a way forward. She needed time to think. The one thing she was certain of was that no-one else should know what Eva suspected. It must stay a secret between Nick, Eva and herself. Of course Eva may not want that. It would have to be her decision. If she wanted to, she could report Nick to the police but Jill was sure that wasn't what Eva would want to do – it would be devastating for all the family but especially Robert.

Jill needed to talk to Eva again and as soon as possible. She texted her and asked could they meet up either here or once again at her flat. Jill was lucky she worked part time as a GP and enjoyed flexible hours going in mainly when they were short staffed, she could work around what free time Eva had. Eva texted back immediately and said it would have to be this coming Monday, after that she would be in rehearsals. Jill replied *Okay see you at 10.*

When Robert arrived home on Friday evening Eva noticed how tired he looked 'You look as if you've had a hard week,' she said.

'It hasn't been the best, how's your week been. Your last week of freedom before you start rehearsals.'

Eva looked at Robert and she felt so sad, she wanted to share her news with him, he would be so excited but she couldn't. She would have to wait until after seeing Jill on Monday. It was a promise she had made to her and Monday couldn't come soon enough.

The Dinner Date

'It's been okay but I'm glad your home. I need a hug.'

'Well I can certainly oblige,' and with that he wrapped his arms around her and she gave a huge sigh of relief.

They didn't do much at the weekend just spent time with each other and soon the weekend was over and Robert was on his way back to his digs. Eva spent an anxious evening wondering what had happened at the meeting between Jill and Nick.

Jill hadn't heard anything from Nick over the weekend and on Monday morning at 10 am she stood at the door of Eva's flat. When Eva opened the door she immediately hugged her and Eva responded by embracing the hug. They walked together side by side, arms around each other as they made their way to the lounge. Two women sharing a terrible secret.

Eva asked Jill, 'Do you want a coffee?'

'Not at the moment. Perhaps later.'

'How did it go with Nick? What did he say?' Eva asked.

'He said what we thought he would say that nothing happened that night.'

Eva sighed in the silence that ensued. 'And did you believe him?'

'Eva I really don't understand what happened that night. I find it hard to believe that Nick, my son, would ever abuse any woman let alone his sister-in-law.'

'Does that mean you think Nick is innocent. Perhaps you think I'm lying,' Eva replied, her normal gentle voice rising.

'Calm down Eva. No I don't think you are lying but you don't know for sure anything did happen. We have no proof. Please believe me I'm not saying Nick is innocent almost the opposite. I think by the way he reacted to my questioning he could be guilty. Truth is Eva I don't want to think the worst of Nick. He is my son and I do love him but if he has done something to you I can never forgive him.'

They sat in silence, Eva with her head bent deep in thought and then she looked up at Jill, 'I don't want Nick to be guilty. Since I became part of your family he has been the best brother-in-law I could have wished for. But on the other hand if he is guilty he may have done this before and he may do it again to someone else. I don't want that do you?'

'No of course not. But I doubt that's the case. As I said we have no proof or do we!'

'What do you mean. What proof have we got,' Eva asked.

'We don't yet! But you said the doctor said the date of conception was around the time of the dinner date.'

'Yes, what are you saying?'

'I'm just suggesting that when the baby is born you could have a DNA test done. It could be matched with my DNA without Robert knowing. You have to remember that Nick is not biologically related to us. If the baby's DNA matched my DNA then there would be no doubt Robert is the father. If you decide not to have a DNA test done you will soon see as the child grows whether there is a resemblance towards either of our families or if the child has similar features to Nick. If that happens Robert will not only be surprised but he may become more and more suspicious.'

Eva sat listening to Jill and then the tears started to roll down her face. Jill went to her to comfort her.

'I can't win,' she said with her head in her hands. 'If I have a DNA test done when the child is born and find out it doesn't match your DNA then we would know that Nick is the father but what do I do then. How will I explain it to Robert or do we just keep it a secret, our secret. What is the point of knowing. If I tell him Nick raped me, will he believe me nine months after it happened. Wouldn't he question why I didn't say something sooner. He might even think I was a willing participant. How could I convince him otherwise. Robert would be devastated if he found out he wasn't the father. It would ruin our marriage and the innocent child, my child would be brought up in a broken home. And what do I do about Nick? Would he want to claim the child as his own? He will never admit to what he did, he will say I consented and I can't prove otherwise.'

'Eva, calm down. You don't have to have a DNA test done.'

'I know Jill, but as you said what if as the child grows up it strongly resembles Nick and not Robert. How would I explain that?'

'I don't know Eva. I don't have the answers.'

They sat in silence for a while and then Jill made a comment she later regretted. 'If the DNA test shows Robert is the father perhaps you were mistaken about Nick.'

Eva turned and looked at Jill. 'I know it must be hard for you and you don't want to believe your son could do such a thing but I knew when I woke up the next morning that something bad had happened to me. I wasn't dreaming, it was reality. I feel sorry for me and sorry for you.'

They sat in silence for a while both consumed by their own thoughts and then Jill said, 'Only you can make the choice of what your next step will be. I don't know what else I can say Eva, this is such a terrible decision you have to make. What I do know is that you will have to tell Robert very soon that you are expecting, you are beginning to show. I'm surprised Robert hasn't noticed.'

Eva couldn't help smiling with that comment. 'He thinks I've just put on weight after being inactive for a while.' She sighed and looked at Jill. 'If I tell Robert this weekend I'm pregnant I will text you.' She reaches for Jill's hand. 'This must be so difficult for you. I know how much you adore Nick but please believe me I never led him on. Robert is the only one for me and it breaks my heart to think this child may not be his. If a DNA test shows Robert is the father it doesn't prove that Nick didn't rape me, it just shows that Nick isn't the father of my child. It would allow me to make the decision to bury the secret deep inside me and not reveal it to anyone else.'

'You look worn out Eva. I'm going to leave you to get some rest. I hope you make the right decision,' and with that comment Jill left Eva to spend the next hour struggling with her thoughts. She was so tired of thinking about it. She couldn't change what had happened and it was then she made her decision.

34

Eva started her rehearsals the next day and the first thing she did was to inform Ken, the theatre producer, that she was pregnant. Although Robert didn't even know yet she felt, out of courtesy, she should tell Ken and give him time to replace her if that was what he wanted to do. But that was not the case. He was surprised and she explained to him that it hadn't been planned. Ken was an older gentleman with a grown up family and he kindly said, 'Well, accidents do happen.' He would never know how much he had touched a nerve with that remark she thought. He stated that if she wanted to continue he was happy for her to do so although he did need written confirmation from her doctor that she was fit and healthy to continue. He explained it wasn't the first time this had happened during a show and on that occasion everything had worked out fine and he was sure it would this time.

Each day, for the short run of the show, she would be taking the train to a small theatre on the outskirts of London. She welcomed this journey it would give her time to think. Time to make sure the decision she would make was the right one for her.

It was Saturday morning and the four days of intensive rehearsals had been exhausting and Eva was ready for a relaxing weekend. The cast and crew had all worked on this show before so the rehearsal time would be shorter than usual with only one week left to iron out any problems, after that the show would open the following Monday. That would leave Eva two weekends free before the run of the show started.

Robert had slept peacefully through the night next to Eva as she lay waiting for the dawn to break. In the early hours she carefully slid out of bed and went and sat in the lounge with a cup of coffee. Shortly before 8 am Robert got up and joined her.

'You look tired Eva, have the rehearsals this week worn you out? he asked.'

'No, I just couldn't sleep. Come and sit down I have something to tell you.'

'That sounds very serious. You're not ill are you?'

'No', she replied smiling, 'I'm not ill but I am pregnant.' There was silence in the room as Robert stared at her. 'Are you pleased?' she asked.

'Pleased, I'm delighted Eva, we're going to be parents. But are you happy? I know you didn't want to start a family yet.'

'Yes I think so, although it was a shock.'

'It's a lovely shock,' he said grinning. 'The best news in the world. I can't wait to tell mum and dad and Nick. Nick will be so excited, he's always wanted to be an uncle.' Laughing Robert continued, 'Nick always said he would rather be an uncle than a parent - much less responsibility and more fun being a favourite uncle who could spoil his nephew or niece. Can we tell them this weekend? Does your mum know yet?'

'Calm down Robert. It's early days yet, I'm only a few weeks pregnant and no I haven't told my mum, I wouldn't tell her before I told you. Why don't we keep the news to ourselves this weekend. Perhaps next weekend we can call in and see your mum and dad and share the news.'

'Okay if that's what you want. Eva you don't seem very happy. There's nothing wrong is there?'

'No, the doctor has said I am healthy and everything seems okay with the pregnancy. I think we should just take some time to absorb the fact that we will be parents. It's a big thing and something we were thinking about in the future but not yet.'

The Dinner Date

'I know,' he said as his smile spread across his face, 'but it's happened and it's great news. How did it happen, did you forget to take the pill?'

'No, the doctor said it could have been the antibiotics I had taken for the throat infection which may have stopped the pill being as effective.'

'Well I'm thrilled you took antibiotics. We have to celebrate this weekend. I will book a table at the pub Nick took you to, it can be our dinner date!'

Eva couldn't believe what she had just heard Robert say and it made her stomach tighten. There is no way she could go back to that pub. She would have to think of a good reason not to go there and quickly.

'That's a nice thought but I would rather stay in and perhaps get a take-away. I'm tired after my first week rehearsing. We can perhaps celebrate next weekend and try a different pub.'

'Okay I agree it will be nice just the two of us this evening. What about your dancing?'

'I should be okay to carry on. It's only a short 4 week run but after that I will have to stop until after the baby is born.' She paused and then continued, 'It seems so strange that in a few months' time we will have a little person in our lives to look after. It's exciting but scary.'

'It is so exciting. I don't know how I will keep this a secret until next weekend. I want to tell everyone,' Robert said. Unlike Eva who didn't want to share this news with anyone especially with Nick. She wondered if it would even cross his mind that the baby might be his, probably not.

The weekend passed with Eva trying to join in with Robert's excitement pushing the feeling of despair at the terrible secret she carried with her to the back of her mind. But she couldn't help but laugh at him. He was so excited he couldn't keep still. She looked at him and wondered what sort of father he would be but there was no doubt in her mind he would be a doting one and spoil his son or daughter. Eva also felt guilty because she still couldn't help thinking that a miscarriage would solve the dilemma she was in. This thought troubled her and she kept pushing it away and thinking only of the tiny human being growing inside her.

The following week she was fully occupied with rehearsals and, as always, her dancing calmed her but on the train back home the following Friday her thoughts were very much on the weekend ahead. She had promised Robert that they could visit his parents and Nick to share the news, something she wasn't looking forward to. Of course Jill already knew she was pregnant and would have to feign surprise.

Once Eva returned home she sat in the lounge with her hands tightly clutching a cup of tea feeling the tension build as she waited for Robert. She knew this was going to be a difficult weekend for her and she wasn't looking forward to it, unlike Robert who she knew couldn't wait to share the news. Eva heard the key in the door as Robert arrived home. She had to smile when he walked into the lounge, he was still so excited and had begun to treat Eva as though she was made of porcelain. Last weekend he had waited on her, barely letting her lift a finger and she let him. She would milk this attentiveness for as long as she could – she knew it wouldn't last but while it did she would enjoy being spoilt.

'How has your week been? I hope they haven't worked you too hard.' Robert asked as he took her in his arms.

'It's been good. The completion of the rehearsals went well. I have told Ken, and he is happy for me to continue and to tell the rest of the cast when I'm ready.'

'Can we share the news with mum, dad and Nick this weekend? Have you told your mum yet.'

'Yes, I phoned her during the week. Her comment was – it made her feel very old and she didn't want to be called 'granny'.' But I think she was pleased.'

The Dinner Date

'My mum will be thrilled I know she will,' Robert said beaming.

Later that evening when Robert phoned his mum to arrange a time to visit, Eva could hear he was fighting a losing battle not to sound excited. 'Mum said to come round about 3pm. Nick is supposed to be bringing a book on photography that he has picked up for dad so we can tell them all together. Is that okay with you?'

Eva looked at her husband, she loved him so much. He was the kindest most generous person she had ever met. He would be devastated if he knew this baby might not be his child. 'Yes that's fine,' she replied but of course it wasn't. She couldn't bear the thought of being in the same room as Nick when they shared their news but she had no choice. She had to start the process of believing this child was Robert's and put to the back of her mind the chance it could be Nick's. The next few months she knew were going to be very difficult for her.

On Saturday morning Robert asked Eva, 'Do you fancy going into town? We could have a look around the shops, there are few bits and pieces I need and then we could go to a café for a sandwich and then on to mum and dad's. What do you think?'

She really didn't want to but she could see that Robert was restless and would be until he had told his parents the good news. 'Okay, that's a good idea.'

Eva knew she had never been good at hiding her feelings, she always wore them on her sleeve so hiding the worst secret she could ever imagine was draining her. Once the knowledge of her pregnancy was out in the open perhaps she could concentrate on the child growing inside her and not on who the father might be.

She noticed as they walked around some of the bigger department stores Robert would linger a little bit longer as they passed the baby section. It should be her doing this she thought but all she wanted to do was to run the other way and pretend this was all a dream or in her case a nightmare. They stopped at a café and ordered two toasted cheese sandwiches. Robert eating his with enthusiasm but Eva barely touching hers. 'Are you not hungry? he asked. 'You need to eat, our baby needs feeding.'

'No I'm not really hungry, perhaps it's a type of morning sickness,' she replied knowing full well that her stomach was churning in anticipation of Nick hearing she was pregnant.

'We have two doctors in the family so any questions you have about the pregnancy you will be able to get instant answers,' Robert said and continued, 'Come on let's go I can't wait any longer to spread the news.'

When they arrived at Jill and Stephen's house Eva noticed that Nick's car wasn't in the drive which was such a relief. The tension she felt eased. When Jill answered the door she hesitated briefly as her eyes met Eva's. She smiled hoping this would help relax her. 'Come on in. How was your week at work Eva. Did the rehearsals go well?'

'We had a few issues at the beginning of the week,' she replied smiling and then continued, 'but all sorted and the rest of the week went well. It was good to concentrate solely on my dancing, but I am tired now.'

'Come and sit down and I'll make some tea. Robert, your dad's in the conservatory with his camera,' Jill said raising her eyebrows. 'Can you go and ask him to join us. I've got some homemade chocolate cake. He won't want to miss that.' Robert returned to the kitchen with Stephen and as they sat round the large kitchen table Robert asked, 'Is Nick joining us?'

'I thought he was,' Jill answered, 'but perhaps he was called into work unexpectedly.'

Robert looked at Eva, 'Can I tell them?'

'Yes of course.'

'You are going to be grandparents. Eva's pregnant.'

The Dinner Date

Jill caught Eva's eye, 'Oh Robert that's wonderful news, congratulations,' she said and stood up first hugging Robert and then as she went to Eva she smiled and mouthed 'well done.'

Stephen followed closely behind beaming with delight. Jill stood back and looked at Eva, her lovely daughter-in-law, she should be buzzing with excitement instead there is such sadness and fear in her eyes and it could all be for nothing.

Jill knew that if Eva decided to have a DNA test and Robert was the father although it wouldn't prove Nick was innocent Robert need never know about her suspicions of what happened that night. Eva had said she couldn't remember what happened but with the right result could she move on without accusing Nick. And of course if Nick is innocent it would be impossible for him to prove it – it would always be her word against his. Who is telling the truth Jill thought – she just didn't know.

While Robert spent time with his dad, Jill and Eva sat in the kitchen waiting for Nick to arrive. However much they tried the conversation between them was strained. They had to make small talk avoiding the secret only they knew. Jill asked Eva to tell her about the new show she was in – that seemed like safe ground. Eva tried her best watching the door all the time, waiting, just waiting for Nick to appear and then he was there, in the doorway.

'Hi mum, Eva,' he said eyeing up the crumbs of chocolate cake on the plates. 'Any left for me?'

'Of course there is,' Jill said, 'Do you want a coffee.'

'Yes please mum. How is my favourite sister-in-law? I hear you are in a new show.'

Eva found she couldn't look at him directly when she answered, 'Yes I have just finished rehearsals. The show starts on Monday and is only for 4 weeks, which is enough.'

'Oh dear are you getting tired of dancing?'

'No Nick, that will never happen.'

'Nick, here's your cake and coffee, I will go and get dad and Robert.'

When Jill left the room Nick said, 'Why is mum going to get dad and Robert. Eva what have you said? What's going on?'

Eva didn't have time to answer before they all came back into the kitchen.

'Robert do you want to share your good news with your brother,' Jill asked.

'Don't tell me, let me guess. You've been awarded a knighthood for your contribution to the World of Theatre and Art,' Nick said laughing.

'No Nick something much better than that. I'm going to be a dad and you are going to be an uncle.'

'Wow that's great news. Congratulations.'

'I wonder what sort of uncle you will make, a very annoying one I'm sure,' Robert said laughing.

Eva didn't speak, she couldn't. She just watched Nick's reaction. Was he really pleased for them?

'I will be a great uncle. When's the baby due?' Nick asked looking at Eva.

Bravely she met his eyes. 'Not sure of the exact dates yet but I know the baby was conceived shortly after I had my accident.'

She noticed there was a slight hesitation before Nick continued, 'This is such great news. I know you can't wait to be a grandma,' he said turning to Jill.

'Yes I'm thrilled but it does make me feel a bit old!'

'Mum you will never be old,' Nick said hugging her. 'Where is the alcohol, we should be raising a glass to the soon to be borne baby. But of course Eva can't have any alcohol because she is pregnant and we know it doesn't agree with her anyway,' Nick said fixing his eyes on her.

The Dinner Date

She stared him out while Jill carefully watched Nick's reaction. He showed no outward signs of concern, but Jill knew that Nick had fine-tuned his skill to mask his emotions.

'Oh well if there's no alcohol on offer I think I will go. Hope you enjoy the book dad. Well done Robert,' Nick said as he patted his brother on the back. 'And Eva, you will make a great mum,' he said as he wrapped his arms around her squeezing her tightly. She felt herself go rigid. 'I'm off,' he said starting to walk out of the door.

'Aren't you going to stay a bit longer Nick,' Jill asked.

'No mum, I've things I must do. See you all later.' And he was gone.

'Well, that was short and sweet. I think Nick is jealous, he needs to find himself a nice young lady and start a family, don't you think Jill,' Stephen said.

Jill looked at Stephen and said, 'Yes you're probably right.' If only it was that easy she thought.

On the way home in the car Robert commented on Nick's quick exit. 'I think dad was right, Nick is jealous. I've got a wonderful wife and a baby on the way, I am so lucky.'

That night Eva couldn't sleep. She lay awake listening to Robert gently snoring. She had no idea what to do. She had months ahead of her carrying this child, her child. She already felt protective towards her son or daughter but somehow she couldn't think of this child as being Robert's offspring, how could she when she didn't know who the father was.

35

A couple of months after the baby announcement Nick dropped in on his mum and dad very unexpectedly. Jill was in the kitchen finishing off one of her famous chocolate cakes when Stephen walked in followed by Nick. 'What a lovely surprise Nick. We haven't seen you for a while and guessed you must have been very busy at the hospital. Sit down. Do you want some tea and a piece of chocolate cake?'

'Tea and cake would be lovely mum.'

'I expect you want a piece of cake too, don't you Stephen.'

'Have I ever refused your chocolate cake,' he replied with a laugh.

Sitting round the table Nick said, 'This cake is lovely mum. I better make the most of it.'

'Don't be silly Nick you know you can always come round for a piece of cake,' Jill said looking at him and then asking, 'Nick, I know you, is there something you came to tell us?'

'Yes you do know me, well I hope you know me!' he said his eyes narrowed looking directly at his mum. 'I have accepted a post in a hospital in Cornwall.'

Stephen showing no surprise and still enthusiastically savouring his cake said, 'I suppose it's a good career move for you is it?'

Jill just stared at her son and he quickly looked away. 'Yes dad, it is a career move. It was about time I moved on and experienced work at a different hospital.'

'Yes, of course it's a career move,' Jill said with an air of doubt in her tone, noticing how Nick avoided looking at her. 'And what about your flat and Kate. Is she going with you?'

The Dinner Date

'Kate and I parted a while ago, it was never serious. The tenancy agreement for the flat was coming to an end so it works out well. I have found a nice ex-holiday cottage to rent near to the hospital and I'm really looking forward to the change and a new challenge.'

'Seems like a good move, doesn't it Jill,' his dad said oblivious to the slight tension in the air.

Jill looked at Stephen, he would be heartbroken if he knew the real reason. She was sure, very sure that Nick was running away but she would keep it to herself and never say her thoughts out loud. 'If that's what you feel you have to do Nick we wish you well. It's a shame you won't see much of your new niece or nephew.' Nick didn't comment.

'Have you told Robert?' Jill asked.

'Not yet, I thought I would tell you and dad first. I'll give him a call tomorrow.'

Why don't you go round and you can tell both Robert and Eva,' Jill suggested knowing full well why he wouldn't do that.

'Yes I could do that,' he agreed with no conviction in his voice.

'When will you be moving?' Jill enquired.

'In 2 weeks.'

'So you have known for a while but haven't shared this life changing move with your family. Why Nick?' Jill asked.

'That's not the case mum. Everything has happened very quickly and I didn't want to miss this opportunity.'

'Of course,' said Stephen, 'take every opportunity in life that comes your way. Your mum and I both wish you well but we will miss you.'

'Thanks dad.'

With a heavy heart Jill looked at her son and sensed this move was almost a confession of guilt. Perhaps it was for the best if he moved away she thought with such a feeling of sadness in her heart.

Eva wasn't at all surprised when Robert told her Nick had called him and explained he had a new job and was moving very soon. It saddened her that she felt such relief that she wouldn't come in contact with Nick very often and thought the move could be a sign of guilt. It was different for Robert and he had been shocked by his brother's sudden decision. Although Nick had explained to his mum, dad and Robert that it would be a good career move Robert was unsure that was the real reason, his dad believed him, his mum did not.

36

As time and her pregnancy progressed Eva learned to live with her secret, made easier by the fact that Nick had moved away and she rarely saw him. One day nearer her due date Jill visited her bringing with her Eva's latest food craving, chocolate brownies. Jill had carefully chosen the mini version hoping they would satisfy the craving without raising Eva's blood sugar levels. As always Eva was pleased to see Jill. They sat drinking mugs of tea, another craving of Eva's.
'How are you Eva? Everything okay?' she asked.
'Yes I feel fine. I can't wait to welcome this little one into the world,' she said looking down at her ever increasing belly.
Jill sat talking to Eva knowing she had come for a reason. She had to know the answer. Jill had never been one to shy away from difficult situations but this was different. This involved her much loved daughter-in-law and her eldest son and she felt nervous about asking Eva.
'Eva, I have to ask you have you made a decision about doing a DNA test soon after the baby is born?'
Eva looked at Jill. She couldn't wish for a better mother-in-law and knew how difficult these past few months must have been for her. Jill had never raised the subject again but Eva realised that inside she must be struggling with her feelings unsure if her eldest son had committed one of the worst crimes a man can do to a woman, and not any woman but his sister-in-law.
'I haven't Jill. One minute I've decided definitely I want to know if Robert is the father and then I think how would I keep the secret if it turns out Nick is the father. I could never tell Robert or Stephen and I would never want Nick to know. If he did know he might at some stage think he has some

claim to the child but he doesn't. If I do decide to have the test done Robert must never find out. There must never be a doubt in his mind that this child is his son or daughter. If I do find out the child is Robert's it wouldn't change the fact Nick did something to me that night. I wasn't mistaken but I have no proof. If I did accuse Nick, I know he would say I had consented to sex but I didn't Jill. I still have no memory of what happened. Whatever I decide I can't win.'

'Eva, I am so sorry you are going through this. I can't make this decision for you but whatever you decide I will stand by you. I will always be here for you. I'm still struggling to comprehend that Nick would do such a thing to you but I am sure you wouldn't have led him on.'

'No Jill, why would I! Robert is my husband and I don't want anyone else. I have never understood how men and women can cheat on their partners. I couldn't and wouldn't want to.'

'Yes I can understand how you feel, I have never looked at another man since I have been married to Stephen, even though he drives me mad sometimes,' she replied smiling and continued, 'Eva, if Nick ever admits to what he has done I will stand by him because if what you suspect is true then what he did is not normal and he needs help.'

She stood up and went to Eva. 'I'm going to head home now,' and giving Eva a hug she said, 'You are so precious to me and so is this baby. Either way one of my sons is the father. Don't get up Eva I will see myself out.'

37

After a long hard labour Eva welcomed her perfect son into the world. Robert had struggled with watching his wife in so much pain but once the child was safely born he relaxed holding his son.

Cradling his son he looked at Eva, 'Thank you for giving me a beautiful son. I'm so proud of you.'

Eva was tired, she was so very tired. She watched Robert as he looked at his son and the delight and relief she had felt with successfully giving birth to a healthy baby slowly turned to sadness. What if this baby is Nick's. She knew she had to make a decision but not yet.

Robert stroked the soft dark brown hair of his son. 'He takes after his father, dark brown hair,' he commented.

Eva knew that could change. Lots of babies were born with dark hair which changed during the first few months, it certainly wasn't any proof that Robert was the father. Robert handed Eva their son and encouraged by the midwife she put the child to her breast. To her delight he suckled enthusiastically. A contented sight, mother, father and son.

After a short while Robert said, 'I'm just going to stretch my legs and make some important phone calls. I know mum and dad will be eagerly waiting by the phone for news.'

'Okay,' she said briefly lifting her eyes before quickly returning them to gaze at her beautiful son. Alone with her boy, she tenderly stroked his face taking in every minute detail. His eyes were closed but as she stroked his face she could see the eyelids flicker slightly. She let her fingers move down to touch his tiny button nose and then his perfectly formed cupid lips. She could see a slight twitch of his lips as if he was thinking about smiling and then he opened his eyes and stared at her. Her smile widened as she said to her new born 'I promise I will always look after you and protect you. I will never let anything happen to you.' She knew that however hard she tried that wouldn't always be possible. He had to make his own way in life but his mum and dad would always be there for him. The love she felt for him was almost overwhelming.

She thought about the last few months since the dinner date. She had been through so much but she had survived. She now believed in herself and what she was capable of. She thinks back to the person she had once been, anxious and nervous of so many silly things. One in particular stood out – how scared she was of the photo shoot. How trivial that now seemed after all she had been through. She was a different person, much stronger. Her inner strength had pulled her through. Carrying this child had helped her, she had focused all her attention on him. She was so absorbed in her thoughts and her son that she didn't hear the nurse quietly enter the room. 'I think it's about time you had a well-earned rest,' she said as she lifted the tiny bundle and put him in his cot. 'I'll be back to check on both of you shortly but for now this little boy looks very content,' and with that final comment she left the room and Eva fell into a contented sleep.

Eva was discharged from hospital the next day. Robert proudly carried the tiny baby to the car, firmly clutching the baby car seat terrified he would drop his son. When they arrived home Eva found the flat filled with cards and flowers. Their first visitors were Jill and Stephen who cooed and gushed over their grandson. Stephen commenting, 'He's definitely got the look of you Robert.' Jill and Eva looked at each other, perhaps he was right!

As Jill held the baby she asked, 'Have you decided on a name?'

Robert answered, 'Yes Daniel, for no other reason than we liked the name but his middle name will be Stephen.'

Stephen beamed with pride and said a simple, 'thank you.' They didn't stay too long and Jill reluctantly handed Daniel back to his mum.

Nick phoned Robert and congratulated him on becoming a dad. 'When are you coming to meet your nephew,' Robert asked.

'I will let you know but probably within the next 2 weeks. I've got a weekend off so I will come and stay with mum and dad. What's it like being a dad?'

'Exhausting,' Robert said laughing,' but saying that I can recommend it. There's nothing beats looking down at the face of your own flesh and blood. You should try it someday.'

'Yes, perhaps. See you in a couple of weeks.'

Friday evening two weeks later Nick arrived on his mum and dad's doorstep. Sitting in the conservatory, Nick and his dad drinking a beer with his mum enjoying a glass of white wine, Jill asked, 'Are you enjoying your new job. Is it all you expected it to be?'

'Yes it's good, there's lots of things happening at the moment,' but Jill noticed he didn't want to elaborate and changed the subject. 'I've told Robert I will visit tomorrow, he suggested the afternoon. Apparently their mornings are a bit chaotic and they are struggling to achieve a proper routine.'

'Yes I remember that feeling, albeit a long time ago. Are you looking forward to seeing your nephew,' Jill asked.

'Yes of course.'

The next day, never missing an opportunity to be with her grandson, Jill accompanied Nick on his visit to see Daniel. Nick expected to see Robert at home but Eva explained he had been called into work, some problem no one else but Robert could solve. Eva grinned, 'I'm not sure that's exactly the case. I suspect Robert wants some time away from a very vocal little boy, he's got a good set of lungs,' she said smiling. Jill noticed how tired Eva looked.

Nick stood awkwardly in the room with two people who didn't believe his version of the events of the night of the date.

'Well come on Nick, meet Daniel,' Jill said. Eva picked up Daniel and held him out to Nick. 'Here Nick, hold your nephew,' and carefully put Daniel into Nick's arms.

Eva and Jill watched as Nick looked down at the baby.

'Who do you think Daniel takes after,' Jill asked Nick, 'Robert is convinced he takes after him.'

She looked at Nick, at first there was no comment, he just stared at Daniel. And then he said, 'Yes I agree with Robert, Daniel looks just like Robert did as a baby, red faced and angry,' Nick said laughing as the baby started to cry. He continued, 'I have this effect on babies,' and quickly handed Daniel back to his mum.

It wasn't long before Daniel was content and had fallen asleep. Jill stood up and said to Nick, 'Come on Nick let's go home Eva needs to take a nap while Daniel is sleeping.' Nick was relieved.

Eva stood at the door, Daniel in her arms, and watched as they started to walk back to Nick's car. Nick looked back and for the first time she detected a hint of sadness on his face.

On the way home Jill commented on how lovely Daniel was and Nick agreed although he did think the baby looked just like any other baby. But then out of the blue he felt he had to say, 'Mum, you know nothing did happen that night. I can't make you or Eva believe me, but I am innocent.' Jill didn't comment, what could she say. Nick was the only one who truly knew what happened and would he ever admit his possible crime she just didn't know.

***

It was now a month since Daniel's birth. And in that time Jill had been a doting grandmother and a great help to Eva. Eva sat feeding her son with Jill watching. A peaceful, calm picture. 'Have you made a decision yet,' she asked Eva.

Eva never took her eyes away from her son. Smiling she said, 'Yes I have. I adore this little boy and so does Robert. We are a family and I don't want that to change. As far as I'm concerned Robert is Daniel's dad and I don't want to know otherwise. If, in the future, the resemblance to Nick is striking and questions are asked I will have to think again but until then I'm going to enjoy being a mum and hope the events of that night continue to fade with time.'

Jill looked at her brave daughter-in-law. She knew she could never feel the same. She wanted to know the truth and one day she felt sure Nick would tell her. Until then she didn't want to believe Nick could have raped Eva, that wasn't the son she knew.

38

Once Daniel had been born Eva and Robert decided that the flat was too small and with the help of Jill and Stephen they looked around for a house with a small garden. After viewing several properties and beginning to despair at finding the 'perfect' house Robert spent one Sunday afternoon trawling the internet for houses for sale in their preferred area. He came across a small three bedroom detached house which looked promising and he shouted to Eva to come and have a look.

'What do you think? Is it worth booking a viewing?'

'Definitely,' Eva replied with enthusiasm. 'It's quite near to your mum and dad, isn't it.'

'Yes, I know where it is and it is among a lovely small collection of houses. It's only just come on the market so we need to be quick to view. I'll give the Estate Agent a call tomorrow.'

The next morning Robert rang the Estate Agent and organised a viewing for the following morning. Eva phoned Jill and explained they had a viewing booked and asked if she was available to look after Daniel and, as always, she was delighted to be of help.

As the morning arrived Eva began to feel optimistically excited and as they travelled to the house her excitement continued to grow. She somehow felt positive that this house would be the one and as they stood in the spacious driveway surveying the front of the property they looked at each other smiling. It was the first house Eva thought that felt right.

They were met by the Estate Agent. 'Hello, you must be Mr and Mrs Brown,' he said extending his hand to Robert and then Eva. 'I'm John Partridge. I'll show you around first

The Dinner Date

and then let you have a wander around on your own, if that's okay.'

'Yes that sounds good,' Robert replied.

The house was situated in a small well established cul-de-sac and John explained it was built in the late 1950s. As they entered the bright hallway he informed them that the house had been modernised and the wall between the two downstairs rooms had been removed to give a spacious large lounge. He opened the door to the lounge and stepped aside to let Robert and Eva view the room before they went inside to look around.

'Oh, the size of this room is lovely,' Eva said with enthusiasm. The double fronted aspect allowed plenty of light to flood the room showing off the plain walls with just the faintest hint of a subtle rose colour.

Looking around Robert pointed at the fireplace 'There's a wood burner. I've always wanted one. This room must be so cosy in the winter,' he commented.

'I love the wallpaper,' Eva enthused stepping towards the wallpaper around the fireplace and gently touching the slightly raised silver birds of paradise perched on silver branches adorned with silver flowers.

Moving on to the kitchen Eva's delight increased when she saw it had been substantially extended to include a dining area. 'I love the Shaker Style kitchen,' Eva said looking around at the very light grey units with a darker grey marble effect work surface. She grabbed Robert's hand and squeezed it. So far this house looked a definite contender she thought.

'As you can see,' John went on to explain, 'the present owners have extended the kitchen and installed doors which lead out to the patio and south facing garden.' He took them through the kitchen and out into the garden. 'There is also a detached garage which has been converted into a garden room, perfect as an office or playroom for children. Let's go upstairs and then I will give you some time to look around on your own.'

The upstairs had one large bedroom with an ensuite bathroom and two smaller bedrooms but still good sizes. The family bathroom, much to Eva's delight, still had a bath. Many of the houses they had viewed had bathrooms converted into wet rooms. 'I'll leave you to walk around on your own. Come and find me when you are ready, I will be in the garden enjoying the sunshine,' John said.'

When John had departed Robert asked Eva, 'Well what do you think?'

'It's perfect. I love it,' excitement rising in her voice.

'Yes, so do I. It's by far the best we've seen.'

They spent a bit more time wandering around with Eva already imagining their furniture in place and Daniel's toys scattered around. When they had finished they joined John in the garden where he was sitting on a bench with his face held up to catch the morning rays of sunshine. It was so peaceful. 'Well what do you think?' he asked, 'are you interested in putting in an offer?'

Trying not to give too much away Robert said, 'Yes we are very interested and will consider making an offer by the end of the day.'

'Just to warn you,' John continued, 'we have two other people interested so don't delay. I would hate you to lose this house if you really want it.'

Robert smiled. Was this Estate Agent talk or was it true? It didn't matter this house was perfect for them and he would make an offer that afternoon and if he had to it could be the asking price.

That afternoon, after discussing it with Eva, Robert contacted the Estate Agent and offered the asking price knowing they didn't want to lose the purchase of this property. The Estate Agent explained that the seller was not always easy to contact and not too worry if they didn't hear

The Dinner Date

back from him immediately. To both Robert and Eva the wait seemed endless, with both of them secretly clock watching as they kept Daniel occupied until finally, out of mental exhaustion, they busied themselves around the flat while Daniel sat watching his favourite cartoon. And that was when the call came and their offer had been accepted. Eva jumped up and down with excitement as the huge smile on Robert's face conveyed the successful news. Daniel also jumped up and down with excitement loving this new game.

Later on that evening Eva was reading Daniel a bedtime story watching his eyelids as they began to droop. She stopped reading aloud and waited until his breathing became shallow as he fell into a relaxed sleep. She loved sitting and watching her son sleep, his eyelids gently twitching and she wondered what he was dreaming of. As she sat beside him she began to feel that this house would start a fresh chapter in her life. She would be away from the flat and she could distance herself from the painful memories that still haunted her. With this move she felt she could do that. As she reflected on the dinner date she could never forget what she suspected had happened but she began to feel, as she could not change the events of that night, she had to accept them and move on.

Robert would often ring Nick but Nick rarely rang Robert. When Robert would sometimes end a call with Nick he would comment on how Nick had changed and that they seemed to have drifted apart. Eva's muscles would tighten with tension. She was relieved Nick had moved away and rarely visited but she also felt such sadness that the fun and friendship the three of them had enjoyed appeared to have been a smoke screen for Nick. A lie.

When the day of moving arrived Jill offered to look after Daniel while Robert supervised the removal men at the flat and Eva waited at the new house eager to start making the house look like a home. By the end of the day they were both exhausted after having shifted boxes from room to room.

'I never realised just how much stuff we have,' Eva said with slight despair in her voice looking around at the many boxes.

Robert collapsed onto the sofa. 'Yes, it does seem a lot but I'm sure once we start unpacking it won't seem so bad,' he said with little conviction. Let's find the kettle and make some tea and then I suggest we start with sorting out the bedrooms.'

'Good idea,' Eva agreed and immediately started rummaging in boxes for the kettle and some mugs. After a reviving cup of tea they made their way up to the bedrooms where the boxes, which had been clearly labelled bedroom 1 and bedroom 2, had been placed in the correct rooms with Robert's guidance. The 3rd smaller bedroom was left empty. They stood in bedroom 2 which was to be Daniel's room and agreed it definitely had the most boxes but Robert suggested they leave this room as Daniel was having a sleepover with his adoring grandparents.

They sat on the bed in the main bedroom, their bedroom and looked around. 'Where do we start?' Eva asked in despair.

As Robert looked around the room his eyes stopped at the box marked clearly in bold writing EVA'S PERSONAL STUFF. 'I think we should start with this box,' he said pulling it towards him and placing it in front of them. He turned and looked at Eva, their eyes met. 'I've always wondered what was in this box. We shouldn't have any secrets,' he said.

Eva felt the sadness creep into her body. That box held no secret as big as the one she carried in her heart every day. The secret she never wanted to keep from Robert but she knew she had to, she had no choice. With a deep breath and smiling she said, 'Okay I don't mind if you open it. I'll leave you to look through the contents on your own. I'm going to start sorting the kitchen out.' And to his surprise she stood up and walked out of the room and his curiosity about the box grew.

Sitting down on the floor with the box in front of him he carefully undid the tape, which appeared to have sealed the box for many years and looked inside. The box revealed a collection of small childish keepsakes which included a tiny teddy bear on a key ring and a lucky charm on a neck chain. There was also some handmade beaded jewellery which he thought Eva had probably made herself and, as often found in boxes, an assortment of small coins.

Alongside these items was another slightly smaller box which had been carefully decorated to look like a trinket box and once again written on by Eva clearly stating, 'Private Do Not Open'. He picked up the box and examined it. It was beautifully decorated, so typical of his wife he thought. Robert undid the bright pink ribbon that was keeping it closed and lifted the lid. The box held a row of neatly stacked small journals. Each carefully dated and labelled Eva Thomas – Strictly Private. Very carefully he picked out the first journal. It was in immaculate condition and showed how much she always valued every one of her possessions even as a child. The date on it suggested that Eva would have been about 6 years old. He felt nervous opening it, almost as if he was prying into Eva's life as a child but he had her permission so he opened the first page. Her handwriting for a 6-year-old was very neat and legible. Each section was headed by the day and date and then a sentence written describing what she had done that day. To begin with she wrote something every day but of course that didn't last long. He could see she had continued to occasionally write in her journal over the next few years.

Although Eva had been so young when she had first started writing them, he noticed that as the years went by her maturity began to show. This had been a place where she could write down her secret thoughts and it gave him an insight into what a very lonely and insecure young child she had been. He was sure her parents had been unaware of her insecurities.

At the very start of her journals she described her mum making her go to dancing lessons. She wrote down in large letters coloured in bright red, I don't want to go!! Each entry would make reference to hating all the other girls watching her. She wrote down everything she felt and how scared she was. It seemed she spent her first few terms at dancing class desperately trying to fit in. Her words summed it up – *nobody likes me, nobody wants to be my friend, they all have friends and don't want me.* Robert could see how her thoughts changed as the dancing classes continued. The journals showed the change from isolation and misery to a small child being accepted by her peers. Dancing had brought about the change. Without dancing and the encouragement which she had received, her life would have been so different. As he read on through the years, he could see her confidence had grown.

Eva had written in her journal on the day of her very first competition describing how terrified she felt. But she had won! Robert could see that after that success she had to write something in her journal before each competition. It almost seemed like a compulsion she had to do to bring good luck, if she didn't she wouldn't win. Even at an early age she was superstitious he thought smiling to himself.

He heard footsteps coming up the stairs and as he turned he saw Eva standing in the doorway holding a cup of coffee.

'I thought you might like a coffee,' she said looking at him trying to assess his reaction to the journals.

'Why don't you get your coffee and come and join me,' Robert suggested.

'No, I've lots to do in the kitchen,' she said smiling but that wasn't the real reason. She was allowing him to share the inner thoughts she had had as a child but she wanted him to do this alone.

He sat for the next half hour reading through each journal. Her last entry was short and abrupt. It merely said that the house had been sold and that they were moving. Nothing more was ever written. It was almost as though the move from the family home indicated closure of one part of her life and the start of the next phase. He wondered if she felt the same about this move to their new house. When Robert had finished reading the journals, he put them back in the 'trinket' box and placed it once again in the larger box.

Searching through the cases he found the bedding and made up the bed and then unpacked some of his clothes placing them in the fitted wardrobes. He stepped back and looked at the room and he was pleased with what he saw. He was looking forward to this evening here in this room, where they would have some welcome time on their own to physically enjoy each other. He would open a bottle of wine and they would enjoy a date night and indulge in passionate sex, he hoped!

He went downstairs and stood in the doorway of the kitchen. Eva had her back to him as she carefully unpacked one of the many boxes marked 'Kitchen'. Robert could now picture her as a child and understand some of her surprising personality traits. The anxieties and lack of confidence she sometimes had when at other times she portrayed full belief that she could do anything. He had noticed the anxieties had grown over the past year or so which he thought was a normal part of being a parent although with Eva this had started well before they had become parents. It seemed to begin very soon after she had her accident. She was never quite the same. In fact he often thought she appeared to change after Nick had taken her out for dinner. He wondered if her anxieties were somehow linked to Nick but he couldn't imagine what that could be. Eva had always been very reluctant to talk about the dinner date and he had learned not to ask too many questions. If she wanted to tell him she would. Nick and Eva seemed okay with each other but he had noticed there wasn't the usual banter between them. They used to act like brother and sister but that had changed. They now appeared to have a very stinted relationship almost as if they were putting on an act for the benefit of others. Oh well, he thought, he was sure it wasn't a problem and as Eva turned around sensing she was being watched Robert walked over and put his arms around her as if wrapping her in a secure blanket. He didn't comment about her journals but just said, 'I always want to protect you and Daniel.' Eva smiled knowing that wouldn't always be possible.

They continued sorting through boxes until lunch time. Eva had been very organised and knew exactly which box the bread, butter and sandwich fillings were in and quickly made them a sandwich. They sat eating their lunch in the lounge on the sofa which had been placed in the middle of the room. Looking around they discussed how they would arrange the furniture and after a short break continued the mammoth task of making the house look like a home. It was getting late when exhausted, but also pleased with the progress they had made, Robert suggested, 'Why don't we order a take-away, open a bottle of wine and have an early night. Might as well take advantage of Mum and Dad having Daniel. We can christen our new bedroom,' he said with a glint in his eye. Laughing Eva agreed, 'That sounds like a good idea.'

After eating the Chinese take-away and consuming a bottle of wine they made their way upstairs like newlyweds. 'It seems strange not to have Daniel in the house,' Eva commented. 'Yes, strange but nice. Some grown up time on our own,' Robert replied.

Eva entered the bedroom first and stood looking around the room and smiling. She noticed Robert had carefully made the bed and unpacked some of their belongings including the

The Dinner Date

lovely photo Stephen had taken only a month ago of the three of them. It showed 5 month old Daniel sitting on her knee giggling as Robert tickled him. It captured the perfect family and Stephen had paid for it to be framed for them. She loved this room, it already felt like home.

    She turned around to face Robert who had been watching her and smiling. He stepped forward and gently kissed her before he slowly started to undress her. His eyes never strayed from hers as he removed her outer garments. She started to become aroused as he stroked her neck before bringing his lips to hers and kissing her softly before the urgency took over and the kiss became more intense and deeper. He scooped her up in his arms and laid her on the bed. She watched as he finished undressing her and then swiftly removed his clothes throwing them on the floor. As Robert caressed her she felt any tension she had fade away and the wonderful feeling of the start of an orgasm. She felt so relaxed. Everything about their bedroom in the flat had reminded her of the morning she came back to the flat and the horrific realisation of what she was sure Nick had done to her. Now this new room made her feel safe. She could start afresh with the man she loved so much. He began to touch all the parts he knew turned her on and her orgasm started to grow and she was ready for him to enter her. He thrust deep inside her with urgency and they climaxed together.

    As they lay sated in each other's arms Robert stroked her hair and said, 'That was so good Eva, just like it used to be when we first got together before,' he paused, 'I don't know something changed long before Daniel was born. You were never relaxed when we made love. I could always feel how you would tense when I entered you. But tonight was different, I could feel how much you enjoyed it, just like you used. Perhaps it's the move or having the house to ourselves. We need mum and dad to have Daniel more often,' he said with a grin.

Eva didn't speak for a while she just lay in Robert's arms stroking the tiny hairs on his chest. It was something she had always enjoyed after sex at the start of their relationship. She knew this was a turning point for her. This moment in time. She could now move on with her life and put the past into a part of her brain she never wanted to visit again.

They both fell into a contented sleep and when Eva woke up after the most relaxed sleep she had enjoyed for a very long time with no nightmares, Robert was standing in front of her with a tray of tea and toast. She sat up and he placed the tray on her lap and then climbed back into bed. 'Do you remember we used to have breakfast in bed as often as we could before Daniel came along. I thought after such a busy day yesterday unpacking boxes and ending the day with some wonderful sex we deserved breakfast in bed this morning.'

'Yes it's a wonderful idea, just what we needed before we start another exhausting day. We need to get Daniel's room sorted out and then go and pick him up.'

'It's okay mum is happy to have him all day so it gives us more time. We can have a slow start and perhaps resume where we left off last night. I'm sure I can persuade you.' And he did.

Daniel had been sleeping in his own bedroom for the past couple of months which, in the flat was situated alongside Eva and Robert's bedroom. They always left the doors open so they could hear Daniel if he cried or the reassuring gentle snuffling sound he made when he slept. Eva loved this sound and as a new mum found it very comforting. Now, with the move to a new house and a new bedroom which was also alongside their room, they knew it was very important to try and make his room familiar and inviting. They spent ages arranging his favourite toys around the room and, of course, introducing some new ones to make his bedroom extra special. Daniel had his favourite teddy with him at Jill and

The Dinner Date

Stephen's house. Eva had called the small brown bear Cuddles because Daniel liked to sleep hugging him tightly.

'We must make sure Daniel doesn't forget to bring Cuddles back with him, it will be a nightmare if the bear is left behind and Daniel finds he is in a new and unfamiliar bedroom without his toy,' Eva commented. Robert smiled agreeing and remembering the one time Daniel had left Cuddles at Nana's, they had experienced a very disturbed and stressful night with him. He didn't want that again.

They continued to work hard emptying even more boxes before stopping for a quick lunch and then mid-afternoon they walked round to collect 6 month old Daniel from his doting grandparents. Very conveniently their new house was just a short walk away from Jill and Stephen. They both knew how lucky they were that Jill and Stephen were always on hand to help out when needed. Both had now retired although Jill returned to the GP practice if and when she was needed.

They arrived at the house relaxed after a leisurely walk. Jill opened the door. 'Hi mum. How did the sleepover go?'

'It was absolutely fine. More importantly how did the move go?

She's lying thought Eva. Daniel has been a little monkey as he so often could be when it was bedtime. Jill looked tired but Eva knew she would never confess that she had struggled to settle Daniel. To Jill, Eva knew it would seem a failure and she didn't like to fail. She was a strong lady and she had instilled in her boys that failure was not an option. To Eva it had seemed hard but to Jill's credit both her boys had succeeded in their careers but that didn't extend for both boys as far as contentment in their personal life.

'The move went well and Daniel's new bedroom is all ready for him. We just hope he likes his room and the few new toys we have scattered around. Hopefully it will be a gentle persuasion that this new bedroom is much better than his old one. Fingers crossed it works!' Robert said.

They went into the conservatory where Stephen was reading Daniel a story. Eva and Robert smiled at each other. They could see that both granddad and grandson were on the verge of falling asleep.

'Stephen, Robert and Eva are here to collect Daniel,' Jill said.

Both Stephen and Daniel jumped at her voice. Daniel started to cry until he saw his mum and both arms went out to her. Eva went across and picked up her son. It felt so good to hold him and drink in his baby smell. 'Have you been a good boy,' she asked. He nuzzled into her resting his head on her shoulder while clutching Cuddles tightly in his chubby hands. 'Come on, let's get you home.'

'Do you want something to drink before you go,' Jill asked.

'No it's okay mum we'll leave you to get some rest. Daniel needs his afternoon nap, a bit like dad. Thanks for looking after Daniel, it was a huge help,' he said grinning remembering the previous evening he had very much enjoyed with Eva.

Eva noticed that Daniel had already fallen asleep in her arms. She carefully placed him inside his buggy without waking him up, strapped him in and walked out of the conservatory. Robert invited his parents round for coffee the next day before following Eva on the walk back to their new home.

When they entered the house Eva decided to leave Daniel sleeping in his buggy. She knew if she woke him up he would be extremely grumpy, and in this case probably frightened in unfamiliar surroundings. She sat with him until he woke up naturally and he immediately reached his arms out to her. She shouted to Robert and when he joined her together they introduced Daniel to his new home and his new bedroom. She put him down in the middle of his toys, new and old and his face lit up. He was content. Eva and Robert took turns to stay with him while he played in his room hoping that by bedtime the room would have become familiar to Daniel, and it worked. Although Eva checked on Daniel several times during the night, he slept right through until morning. Smiling to herself she thought this was Daniel's seal of approval and she knew this move had been the best thing for her and her family. She could now move on.

39

Life was good now, Eva was content and it was to get even better. After 11 months at home with Daniel, she was approached out of the blue with the chance to audition for a new show. She wouldn't be the lead female dancer but she would be one of the main dancers.

Although she hadn't danced professionally for over a year, Eva had kept up a dance routine for the past few months in the garden room which was now known as the 'studio'. It had been Robert's suggestion to change this room into a dance studio. It worked perfectly for Eva allowing her to watch over her son whilst dancing. They had a routine, her and Daniel, and once he had eaten his lunch he would usually sit in his playpen watching his mum and listening to the music. The music would successfully send him to sleep for his afternoon nap.

So when the chance to audition for a part came she grabbed it knowing that she was still in good shape and not too rusty. She had never intended to resume her dancing career so soon after having a child but then again Daniel was never planned and she was still young. Daniel and Robert would always come first but her dancing came a close second. This audition would be a test to see if she was deemed good enough to be in a show and it proved she was.

Although Robert was delighted for her he was naturally concerned about what would happen with Daniel. Who would look after him? Eva knew just the person to help them and, one afternoon soon after she had been successful with her audition, she took Daniel to see Nana. Jill had refused to be called grandma and was horrified at the thought of being called granny – both conjured up little old ladies with white hair in a bun, very much not Jill. So Nana it was. Daniel

The Dinner Date

loved Nana and Jill was besotted with her grandson. Both Jill and Stephen had time on their hands so, according to Eva, she had the perfect solution but would Jill see it that way?

Jill greeted Eva and her grandson with delight as Daniel reached out for his hug from Nana. 'This is an unexpected but lovely surprise. I'll put the kettle on and we can take our cups of tea and Daniel's toys outside. What will Daniel have to drink?'

'He's fine Jill. He's not long had a drink.'

Jill spread a large blanket on the lawn under a eucalyptus tree to give some shade and tipped Daniel's box of toys onto it. He was delighted. His chubby little arms waving frantically with excitement. Jill and Eva sat at the patio table watching Daniel carefully examining each toy and then throwing it as far as he could, laughing loudly. They watched as he crawled around the garden picking up each toy, examining it and then throwing it away before going on to the next toy. 'He's so inquisitive now he's crawling and he's into everything. You have to watch him all the time,' Eva said immediately wishing it was a comment she hadn't made knowing she was just going to ask Jill such a big favour.

'He's getting up some speed with his crawling. He'll soon be walking,' Jill said smiling and sitting back in the chair continued, 'This is a nice surprise,' and then her face darkened. 'There's nothing wrong is there?'

Eva sighed, 'No there's nothing wrong.'

Jill smiled at Eva, 'Sorry Eva, I always fear the worst and that you have found conclusive evidence of what happened that night and I wouldn't like it!'

'I know Jill,' Eva commented, 'but I promise you it's not something awful, although on the other hand you may think it is,' she said laughing and then continued, 'I have come to ask a favour, it's a huge favour and I won't be offended if you say no.'

Jill's eyes widened as she waited for Eva to continue.

'Recently, out of the blue, I had the opportunity to audition for a part in a show and I was successful.'

'That's great news but I thought you didn't want to go back to work while Daniel was still so young.'

'I didn't think I did but dancing relaxes me so much. I've missed it. It's good for my body and more importantly my mind. I still sometimes have nightmares about that night.'

Jill thought as much and was always concerned that Eva was still very much traumatised by what might have happened although she hid it well.

'How can I help?' Jill enquired knowing full well what she was about to be asked. She had butterflies in her stomach at the thought of spending so much more time with Daniel. She adored him. She had made a supreme effort not to be an interfering mother-in-law and usually congratulated herself at getting the balance right, but now, if her thought was correct, she could be more 'hands on' with Daniel.

'I wondered if, and please feel free to say no, you would consider looking after Daniel while I'm in this show. We could combine it with Daniel going to a nursery. I know it would be a huge commitment for you.'

Jill, with a straight face, paused while considering the question, teasing Eva. And then a huge grin spread across her face. 'I would be delighted to look after Daniel and I know so would Stephen. When do you start?'

'That's great Jill, thank you so much,' Eva said feigning relief but always knowing the answer would be yes. 'We start rehearsals in two weeks. Would that be too soon for you to get organised?'

'There's nothing to organise and I think I know of a nursery just around the corner from here. If you are interested I could find out more about it.'

'That would be amazing, thank you.' She turned to her son, 'Daniel do you want to be with Nana every day?'

The Dinner Date

Daniel enthusiastically started laughing and nodding his head repeating the word Nana. They laughed knowing full well that he had no idea what his mum had just asked him. When Eva and Daniel finished their afternoon with Jill they returned home and later that evening she was able to share the news with Robert that his mum would be thrilled to look after Daniel.

'Are you sure,' he asked. 'It's a long time since she has had a baby to look after full time and they are hard work.'

Eva laughed and thought Robert had no idea what hard work babies and, in particular, curious toddlers were. 'Yes I'm sure. She's very excited about it.'

'Okay we'll see how it goes,' he replied not seeming at all enthusiastic about the arrangement.

He needn't have worried. Jill and Stephen loved looking after Daniel and Jill informed Eva it kept them 'young'. Once the show had ended Eva was offered another role and, although she was reluctant to ask Jill once again for help, when she did Jill was adamant that she should accept the part and was more than delighted to continue looking after her grandson. Robert was not so pleased and felt that Eva should spend more time with their son.

Watching Daniel grow from a tiny baby to a toddler brought back memories for Jill. One afternoon after she had collected Daniel from Nursery she sat in the garden watching him play with his toys and thinking back to the first time she held Nick. At just two days old Nick had been handed to her wrapped up in a soft powder blue blanket. He was fast asleep and looked so tiny and content. They had been on the waiting list to adopt a baby for a couple of years and were delighted to be told that their waiting was over. They watched their beautiful boy develop and then Robert came along. Two very different little boys not only in appearance but also temperament. And now she could see how Daniel was changing.

As he grew into a toddler she watched his features slowly alter and his personality develop. He was a gentle little boy with a caring nature who was fascinated by insects and spiders in particular and was happy to pick up any spider in the house and carefully place it outside. A trait Jill found amusing and was so similar to what Robert used to do. At each stage of his life so far she would compare photographs of Daniel with photographs of Robert at that age and eagerly show them to both Eva and Robert. Eva understood why but Robert would often comment to Eva saying he was becoming a bit tired of the constant comparisons his mum was making.

But at each new stage the likeness became stronger and there was no doubt in her mind that Robert was Daniel's father and, although they never discussed it, she sensed Eva felt the same. Smiling to herself as she watched Daniel she recalled Stephen looking bemused on one occasion when she yet again commented on the likeness. He had looked at her and said, 'Of course he looks like Robert, Robert's his father.' Thankfully Stephen had never suspected anything happened that fateful night.

After Eva's second stint of returning to work Robert got his way when she fell pregnant and her return to dancing was once again put on hold. When Daniel was nearly 3 years old his baby brother Oliver was born. Daniel's caring nature continued and he adored his baby brother. As they grew the resemblance between them was striking. They were carbon copies of each other, both with dark hair and brown eyes just like Robert. There was no question the boys were brothers! It brought some relief to Jill and Eva, although they both knew that the question about the events of that night would never be answered but at least they could be certain that Robert was Daniel's father. Eva believed and would always believe that Nick had raped her. For Robert's sake she would never reveal her thoughts. And Jill, if she was honest with herself, she too

The Dinner Date

believed Nick could have raped Eva and that Eva was telling the truth. It was a thought that always lay heavy in her heart.

    Time and their busy lives meant that the details of that night began to fade for Eva. When she saw Nick at family occasions she continued to do her best to act as normal as possible but it always remained difficult for her. Not so for Nick he showed no signs of guilt or even regret and she did still sometimes wonder had she got it wrong but that thought would quickly evaporate. Even after all this time she would get the occasional flashbacks and she would remember the morning after the dinner date and then she knew in her heart what had happened.

40

And as for Nick, he did occasionally visit Robert and Eva knowing it would appear very odd if he didn't see his nephews and, if he was honest, he did enjoy the time he spent with them. On these occasions Eva still tried to make sure she was never alone with him. The tension between them had eased a little over time for Robert and the children's sake but she could never feel comfortable in his company. Robert did comment on how the strong bond between the three of them had been broken and put it down to the distance between them and work commitments. The closeness the brothers had once enjoyed had disappeared and, to some extent, they had now drifted apart but only Nick knew the real reason why!

It took time but eventually Nick settled into his new job in Cornwall. The small cottage was rented out fully furnished and it suited his needs. He had easily become popular at the hospital and enjoyed the company of his colleagues. One of his colleagues, Pete, a keen surfer persuaded Nick that he should try the sport. Pete was originally from Australia and surfing was very much in his blood. He had married an English girl and moved to Penzance 4 years previously. Unfortunately the marriage had broken down but he had decided to stay in the UK for the time being. Learning to surf was a challenge that Nick took on board and enjoyed.

As he sat in the cottage on a cold miserable day he knew it was time he took on another challenge and that was when he made his decision, today was the day he would start his search. He needed to know where he had come from and he still desperately wanted to meet a blood relative who could give him more information about his birth family and especially his birth mother. He had all the information from a DNA testing company spread out in front of him. He had to take a simple saliva swab and then send it away to be added to a database. Of course he realised that there might be no match with this company and if that was the case he could always try again with another company but this one claimed to have the largest DNA database. It was a start and if one of his half siblings felt the need to find him they might already be on the database. He hoped that would be the case and it turned out it was.

A few weeks later he received a message from a 42-year-old woman called Sarah indicating that she thought he might be her half-brother. He was excited and intrigued and quickly replied asking for more details. The information she gave him matched the few details he had about his birth mother and the reasons why she had to give him up for adoption. Sarah surprised Nick by telling him she now lived with her husband and two children just outside Sidney, Australia having emigrated from the UK 6 months ago.

Nick was eager to learn more about their mother but he felt he didn't want to rush Sarah and hoped she would initiate the conversation. He felt he would then be able to ask all the questions that had laid heavy in his heart since he found out he had been adopted, but until then the messages were just about getting to know each other. After a few more messages Nick decided it would be good to see what Sarah looked like and arranged to FaceTime her. He felt a nervous excitement waiting for her to answer. And then she was there, in front of him, his half-sister, his blood relative. She was beaming and he matched her smile noticing the similarities in their features. He could see they shared the same nose and mouth but her face was more rounded and her eyes a warm dark brown. Her blonde hair, he wondered if she was a natural blonde, was cut into a short straight bob. She was laughing as she said, 'Great to see you brother.'

That was the first of many FaceTime and Skype contacts they enjoyed. They both acknowledged there was a family resemblance albeit not strong. Sarah shared with him the news that his mother, Cathleen, had died two years previously. It shocked and saddened him that he had left it too late to meet her but he couldn't change that. He had his sister.

She also explained, during one of their Skype calls, 'Mum told me and Luke, our brother, that the baby had died shortly after it was born and it had been a little boy.' Nick grinned when he knew that he had a half-brother. Sarah continued, 'That all changed once we reached adulthood and our father had left the family home to live with another woman. Mum and dad had always argued a lot, it was never a happy marriage. Mum confessed to us that you hadn't died but had been adopted and it had been something that dad had forced her to do. He had told her that if she kept the baby he would leave and take me and Luke with him. He wasn't prepared to bring up another man's child. After that she often talked about you, her son, wondering if you had had a happy life. She went to her grave with the ache of what she had done still in her heart. I know she didn't want to give you away but she felt it was her only choice, for the sake of me and Luke but she never rejected you. She was terrified that dad would take us away from her. You were a tiny baby and could have a life with another family. It would have been much harder for us to lose our mum.'

Nick noticed that Sarah's face changed when she talked about her mother and showed in her eyes the sadness she felt. When Nick asked about his father Sarah explained, 'Mum never mentioned the affair and even as an adult I never questioned her. There were many times when I wanted to but I didn't want to upset her and perhaps cause a rift between us. So I don't know who your father was. Perhaps he will come up as a match on the database,' she said smiling.

Nick knew that for the time being finding Sarah and Luke would be enough but that thought was dashed when Nick

The Dinner Date

asked about Luke and did she think he would be happy to make contact. That was when Sarah shared with him the sad news that Luke had tragically been killed a year ago in a car accident. Luke had been 38 years old. Sarah went on to explain, 'Having lost mum and then Luke I knew I wanted to try and find you, my lost half- brother.'

'I'm glad you did,' Nick said and he really meant it. That something he had been missing all his life he had now found, a blood relative.

During the many conversations they enjoyed Nick found they had the same sense of humour and each time they spoke he saw the friendship and bond between them grow. Nick knew he wanted to meet his sister in person. And so, one evening 4 years after Daniel had been born Nick stood at the door of his parents' house. He needed to speak to them and had decided to surprise them by his visit. As he rang the bell he began to feel nervous. He knew they wouldn't like what he had to tell them.

Jill came to the door surprised but delighted to see her eldest son. 'Nick, what a lovely surprise. Stephen, Nick's here,' she called out. 'What are you doing here and why didn't you let us know you were coming?'

'I need to talk to you both,' he said noticing his mum's reaction. He could see her jaw tense as she began to look worried.

'Okay Nick, nothing's wrong is there, you're not ill are you?'

Nick couldn't help but smile, his mum always thinking the worst.

'No I'm not ill.'

'I will make us some tea, unless we need something stronger,' she said concern showing on her face.

'Tea will be fine. Where's dad?'

'He must be in the conservatory, probably with his headphones on listening to some Jazz music which he's suddenly taken a liking to. We can join him when I've made some tea. You are okay aren't you Nick?'

'Stop fussing mum, I'm okay. I'll go and see dad while you make the tea.'

Five minutes later Jill joined Nick and Stephen with a tray of tea and cake in case her son was hungry. 'What's this all about Nick. You've got me worried,' his mum asked.

'I don't know how to say this,' he said pausing. Jill waited with bated breath, was he going to confess to what he had done to Eva all those years ago she wondered.

'I have decided that I would like to go and work in Australia.' He saw the look of horror on his mum's face. His dad, as always showed no reaction but waited patiently for further information.

'Why Australia? Jill asked.

He explained, 'A colleague at the hospital moved back to his native Australia a few months ago. He taught me how to surf on the Cornish coast and said I'm a natural,' Nick said smiling. 'I think he was joking. I didn't tell you what I was doing because I knew you would only worry that I might drown! We've kept in touch and he has painted a glowing picture of the country so I've decided that I would like to see it for myself. He's told me that with my qualifications I would easily find a position in a hospital and he would be there to help me. I know it will be a shock to you both and to Robert but it will be a great experience for me and it's just something I want to do.'

'Oh Nick, Australia is so far away,' Jill said with anguish.

'I know it is mum but it won't be forever. I just need to do this for me now, it's the right time. Don't worry we can Skype and FaceTime often. You will probably see more of me than you do now,' he said laughing.

Jill got up and went over to hug her son. 'But it won't be the same.' After pausing she said, 'There's no other reason is there Nick?'

The Dinner Date

He moved away from his mum. 'No, why would there be?'

'It just seems strange you've never mentioned that you wanted to work abroad and then suddenly you are thinking about going to the other side of the world.'

Stephen sat watching his son. 'Nick, if that's what you feel you need to do then do it while you have no responsibilities here in the UK.'

They sat in silence for a while. Jill watched her son and noticed how he was reluctant to make eye contact with her. 'Nick is there anything else you want to tell us,' Jill asked as her whole body started to tense.

He looked up at his mum and she held her breath once again wondering if after all these years he was going to tell the truth about that night with Eva.

'Okay there is something else but you may not want to hear this.'

Jill's heart started to pound waiting for his confession.

'I've traced my half-sister,' he said smiling 'or rather she traced me.' Jill immediately let out a sigh of relief. Nick continued, 'We were both on the same DNA Database and we've been in touch for the past year. We regularly FaceTime each other and we do look similar,' he said grinning. 'I've always wanted to know where I came from. I'm sorry I don't want to hurt you or cause you any distress. You have been the most wonderful parents but ever since you told me I was adopted I felt I didn't fit in with you and Robert. I always felt different, almost like an outsider looking in at someone else's family. I needed to find someone that was my blood relative and now I have found that person.'

Jill went over to her son and putting her arms around him said, 'Why did you never tell us how you felt?'

'I couldn't, I just couldn't. You were both such wonderful parents and Robert, well Robert was the perfect son and brother wasn't he. How could I ever match that! That's why I became a doctor, I wanted to show you I was better than Robert but it didn't work I still felt inferior, lost. I was jealous that Robert had his real mum but I didn't. It made me feel the rejection by my own mother even stronger and I could never shake off that feeling.'

'Nick, what has this got to do with you moving to Australia,' Stephen asked puzzled.

'My half-sister lives just outside of Sidney. I thought I could experience Australia and get to know her. As I've said it doesn't have to be forever but it is something I want and need to do right now. Sadly my biological mother died two years ago but my sister is happy to share with me information about our mother and perhaps it will help me to understand how she could have given me away and then I could forgive her.'

Jill looked at her son and she couldn't help but ask, 'Okay Nick if that's what you want to do but you're not running away from something are you?'

Stephen looked surprised, Nick didn't. He turned to face his mum, their eyes locked and he said, 'No mum, I've nothing to hide.' Jill wished she could believe him.

'Didn't your mother have two other children?' Jill asked.

'Yes she did. Sarah had a brother, Luke, my half-brother.'

'Had a brother?' Jill enquired.

'Yes she did but unfortunately Luke died in a car crash just over a year ago. That's why she had decided to try and find me.' Nick couldn't help but smile.

'Have you told Robert and Eva,' Jill asked.

'No, not yet. I'm going home tonight but I will phone Robert and tell him.' He couldn't face Robert and Eva, he knew Robert would be upset and Eva, well he didn't know what she would think!

Later that evening when he told Robert he was understandably surprised. Australia was so far away and he would miss Nick. Eva was saddened but also relieved and

The Dinner Date

regretted with all her heart that she had gone on that dinner date with Nick – it had changed all their lives.

Two months later Nick was back staying the weekend with his mum and dad, it would be the last weekend before he travelled to Australia. Robert came round to say goodbye and wish him well. Eva did not. Her excuse was that Oliver was not well and she would stay home with the children.

Jill and Stephen stood at the door. Jill's heart was breaking as she hugged her eldest son. As she pulled away their eyes met and she knew the answer, she had always known the answer. Nick turned and walked away to start his physical and mental journey in Australia. Would he ever return, he didn't know but he did know that finding his sister and learning about his mother had brought him a strange feeling of contentment. He felt whole, there wasn't a part of him that was still missing. He no longer felt rejected.

About the Author

Louisa Abbott lives in a small, friendly Buckinghamshire village with her super intelligent dog, who has just become a 'teenager' and constantly needs new and interesting things to occupy her – keeping Louisa on her toes at all times.

She also enjoys the company of a very sweet cat who the dog likes to chase whenever possible. Sometimes it can be a pretty chaotic household and other times a very contented one.

*Available worldwide from Amazon
and all good bookstores*

Michael Terence Publishing
www.mtp.agency

www.facebook.com/mtp.agency

@mtp_agency

Printed in Dunstable, United Kingdom